EDGED

KATE HAWTHORNE

TROPHY
DOMS
SOCIAL
CLUB

Edged
Kate Hawthorne

Copyright © 2023 Kate Hawthorne

Edited by:
Jordan Buchanan

Cover Design:
Samantha Santana - Amai Designs

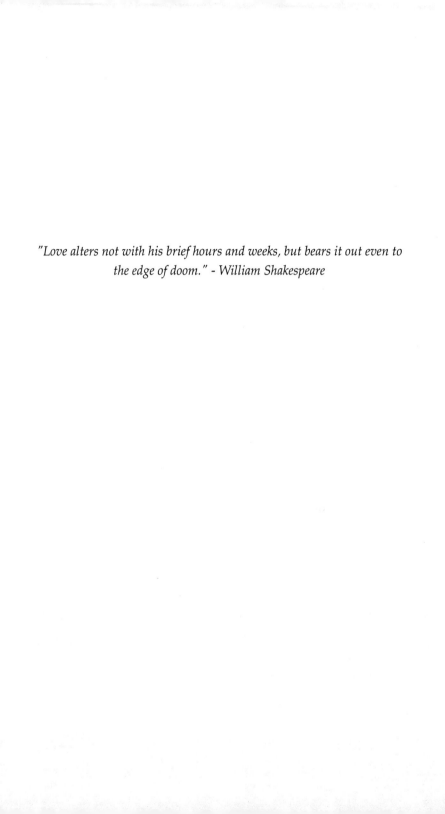

"Love alters not with his brief hours and weeks, but bears it out even to the edge of doom." - William Shakespeare

PROLOGUE

ARCHIE

TWENTY FELT THE SAME AS NINETEEN, FELT THE SAME AS SIXTEEN AND fifteen. But Mandy's square-cut acrylic nails drawing circles up my arm felt different than they had the year before.

Different from the month before.

The night before.

There was a new intent behind her touch, and for as long as I'd been looking forward to the shift, I wasn't sure I wanted it anymore. It felt practiced, pre-meditated and, while I didn't know much about sex, I knew it wasn't supposed to be either of those things.

"You look distracted, Archer," she whispered, letting her hand fall with a focused purpose onto my lap. "You *feel* distracted."

"It was a big day," I managed to answer.

She flexed her fingers against the fly of my jeans, and I closed my eyes, desperately trying to will myself into the right mood for what she had planned.

"It's not every day my boyfriend graduates with his Bachelor's degree at barely twenty."

"It's not every day *anyone* does that," I reminded her.

She laughed, a melodic lilt in my ear.

Mandy pushed her palm harder against my dick, which would have been content to ignore her for the rest of the night if I didn't fight him about it. Ironic, considering for the past three years I'd been borderline desperate for the meal on the table tonight, and now that it *was* on the agenda, I couldn't have wanted anything less.

Three years I'd been with Mandy. Three years of hand jobs and blow jobs, and eating cunt like it was the key to getting on the Dean's list. Three years of coming all over her stomach while we kissed because I was out of my mind with want for the obsidian-haired woman I'd been obsessed with since before my balls had even thought about dropping.

I'd wanted her for as long as I'd known what the words even meant. Mandy was my best friend's older sister, the one person I should have only ever fantasized about and never had. But I'd raced through high school and started college early, running into her on campus on my very first day of classes. Mandy had known me as long as I'd known Owen, but she didn't know about how long I'd wanted her.

So when she offered to show me around campus, it was an immediate yes.

When she asked for help with calculus, I couldn't tell her no.

And when she'd asked me to the movies on winter break of my freshman year, I'd kissed her for the first time while the credits rolled and never looked back. I was seventeen then, and she held off like a saint until the day I turned eighteen, but she hadn't given me everything. Not at first. Not even now.

She'd wanted to wait until I finished school to fuck, and I'd waited and waited, and now...

And now?

"Are you nervous?" She popped open the button on my jeans.

"I'm here," I lied, forcing a smile.

I was distracted.

Distraught.

Mandy took my earlobe into her mouth, swirling her tongue in the way she knew I liked. I sighed, closing my eyes and leaning back against her headboard, willing every drop of blood that existed in my body to head southward because I didn't want to ruin this for her.

Or for me.

"You know I've done this before," she said, voice quiet like she was embarrassed about the fact she was four years older than me and not a virgin.

"I know."

I didn't mind. If anything, it made things easier between us. Less fumbling and confusion. It was practical for at least one of us to have hands-on experience about the whole deal. But if I'd learned anything in college, if I'd learned anything as the youngest person in every single college class I'd taken over the last three years, it was that book learning rarely translated to real-life experience.

Downstairs, a door slammed, and I startled. It was reflex; it was instinct. I managed to turn my head barely, just enough to get a look at Mandy from the corner of my eye. I loved her.

I *loved* her.

I loved her cheeks were flushed, pink as her fingernails. And if I looked down, which I did, pink as her tits too. I loved her tits. She had on a spaghetti strap tank top without a bra, the heaving mounds of her chest rising and falling with every breath, her nipples hard and pressing against the sheer white top, as ready for attention as my cock should have been.

"Don't worry. Owen knows," Mandy whispered, which was the absolute worst thing she could have said in that moment.

I wrapped my fingers around her wrist and pulled her hand away, leaving it on the cold sheets between our thighs. I knew that Owen knew. He was my best friend and there wasn't a single thing about me that he didn't know.

"What did you say to him?" I asked.

Mandy leaned against my shoulder, putting her hand on the top of my thigh. She exhaled against my ear, still wet from her kisses.

"I told him that I wanted to marry you one day," she whispered.

My heart should have bolted into another stratosphere, but instead it sank like a stone. To the bottom of my stomach, through the floor, and down to the basement I knew Owen had just stormed into after his arrival home.

"What did he say to that?"

There had been a time that I wanted to marry Mandy. I'd wanted to marry her when I woke up yesterday. I wanted to marry her in the shower this morning. Wanted to marry her until...

Her smile faltered, lip gloss smeared down onto her chin from when we'd kissed earlier. But, bless her, she held steady.

"He says you're too young for me."

I snorted, scratching at the back of my ear. "Do you think I'm too young?"

"I told him you were your own man."

This morning I had been, but I didn't feel like it anymore.

Music blared up from the basement, nothing that I could hear the lyrics of, but the bass beat was unmistakable. A framed photo of Mandy and me from her sorority formal the year before rattled against the wall.

"Do you think I'm too young?" I asked again.

She snorted. "Do you think I'm too old?"

"I think you're perfect." It was a half-truth, because Mandy had been perfect to me, for me, for so very long. "Wait for me."

"What?"

I climbed off the bed and shook my arms, letting my polo shirt settle back into place.

"I'll be right back," I told her.

At the time, I didn't know it was a lie.

"I just need a second."

"Owen is fine," she protested, like she knew right where I was going. And I imagined she did because, for as much as I loved her, I loved her brother too.

It was just...different.

"I know," I told her, taking her chin into my hand and tilting her head up for a kiss. She tasted like sweat and strawberries, and I let my tongue lick into her mouth until she moaned before pulling away and standing straight. "But he's my best friend and I just..."

"Okay."

"I'll be right back," I lied again.

Leaving Mandy's room was never easy, but I closed the door behind me all the way like that would force me to go through with it. The upstairs of the house was dark, save for the light that bled out from under her door, and the downstairs was only lit with the stove light from the kitchen. Owen and Mandy's parents were out of town; they had been for weeks on a Mediterranean cruise. It was just good timing that they'd be gone over my graduation, gone for the very special de-virginizing Mandy had been planning for me.

The door to the basement was tucked behind the pantry, and it was closed. It was dark. I twisted the knob anyway, knowing the steps and the splintered handrail by heart. I knew the layout of the furniture and I knew where Owen liked to sit, so even without a shred of light to guide my way, I knew where to go. I knew where to find him.

"Is it done?" he asked.

I sat down beside him on the cracked brown leather couch. "No."

Owen was wound tight, like rubber bands coiled around every muscle and bone beneath his skin, ready to crack or implode him without a moment's notice. He stared at the TV across the room, and I wondered if his eyes had adjusted to the dark. The music was still achingly loud, and it was hard to hear him, hard to think.

"Why not?" he asked. "Mandy wants you."

I dragged my tongue across the front of my teeth and sighed. "I know she does."

"And you want her."

The way he said it—the jealousy, the vitriol—it was sharper than any barb or knife he could have physically injured me with.

His words cut like a cleaver right through my chest, like he'd shattered my sternum to get a good look at my heart so he could better understand whose name was etched across the surface.

Mandy's or his.

"It's complicated now," I told him.

"Why, Archie? Why is it complicated *now*?"

He knew the answer. I didn't need to say it, but he was going to make me. Owen always made me. For as long as I'd known him, he'd been the one I'd chased after, the one whose attention I'd wanted. From the playground in elementary school to high school assemblies and summer vacations, there wasn't a single event in my life I hadn't wanted to desperately share with him.

Until I fell in love with his sister.

"I read the letter you wrote me," I told him.

The letter was in my pocket, folded up and crumpled for how many times I'd read it, the ink smeared from his tears and my sweaty hands. I wanted to take it out and show it to him. Wanted to trace my fingertips over the words he'd said that flipped my whole world upside down, but those fingertips had been other places too, and that felt inherently wrong.

It would have been disrespectful to the honesty Owen had offered me, even if it had been meant as a parting gift.

"That's the point of a letter."

"Why didn't you say something before?"

He turned toward me in the dark. The basement had fallen into silence, the song ended even though I hadn't noticed. Owen's breathing was loud as the bass line, my heart more frenetic than the drum beat. Mandy's saliva on my ear, my neck, my mouth, had long since dried and my lips were chapped, drier as Owen's rough exhales landed against them.

"What would I have said, Archer?"

"Don't call me that."

"Because that's what my sister calls you?" he snapped.

"Because it's not what *you* call me."

Everyone had called me Archie until one day I'd woken up and decided that was a child's name and I was no longer a child. It had taken a year of correcting everyone to Archer until they'd gotten it right, but Owen always had a pass. I was always Archie to him; I always would be.

"I've heard her, you know." Owen cleared his throat, still looking at me head on. My eyes had finally adjusted to the dark enough to watch the way his stare darted across my face like he was inspecting me for use.

For lies.

"What do you mean?"

"I've heard her when you make her come." The confession sounded like it pained him, and I'd never felt more fucking lost than I did in that moment with him there.

I grabbed Owen around the back of his neck, pulling our faces together until our foreheads touched. The side of his nose smashed against mine, his eyes still open, breath still hot. "Owen."

"I've heard...you when..."

His eyes closed and I dug my fingers into the back of his neck. He mirrored the pose, sliding one of hands around the back of my neck, using his nails to get a grip against the slickness of my nape. It hurt, it fucking hurt, and the throb between my legs was the first sign of life my cock had shown since I'd read the opening line of Owen's letter hours before commencement.

"When what?" I asked.

He shook his head, settling somehow closer to me, his exhale damp against my lips for how close we were.

Owen was my best friend, my truest friend. He was my lifeline and this was agony. Whatever was happening between us wasn't something I'd planned for and it was nothing that I wanted, but I didn't know how to stop the trajectories of what had become glaringly separate lives.

"I've sat outside her room," Owen whispered, nails gouging harder into the back of my neck.

"What?"

"When you're in there with her." He let out a pathetic laugh and tried to pull away, but I held him still, pulling him closer so he had nowhere to go but back to me. "I've listened to the way you make her come and the things you say."

I was fully hard from his confession, but I didn't have time to piece together what that meant for either of us. "What do I say?"

I knew what I said. He knew what I said. Why had I asked him that? Why did I want to hear my own words in his voice?

"Not yet, sweetheart." Owen's voice was thick with tears. "Don't come yet, not yet."

"Owen."

"You taste so good, Mandy." He sniffled, breath catching on his sister's name. "I know you want it, but not yet. Last a little longer for me. Can you do that?"

"Owen, stop."

My cheeks were wet and I didn't know when I'd started to cry, but Owen's breath lit up the tracks like a goddamn lava flow.

"That's not what you say." He licked his lips and tried to pull away, and I wanted him to go, but I could never let him leave me. Not like that. "You never tell her to stop, so why are you telling me?"

"This is wrong, Owen," I told him.

I knew if I looked down, he'd be as hard as I was. The truth of the thing that we'd been ignoring for years not utterly unavoidable.

When I'd read his confession letter earlier in the day, I'd played our entire life together back through my head. I'd gone back to lazy summer days when we'd spent the whole day swimming and then strip out of our trunks and dry naked together in the sun. Had there ever been a time he'd tried to hold my hand? Or maybe grazed a finger against mine to see how I'd react? And I thought about homecoming our freshman year of high school when he'd only gone with Chrissy Martin because I'd wanted to go with Chrissy's best friend, and I'd had to beg him to go along with it, but he'd spent the whole night with me instead of her.

Had our entire life been a series of near misses that I'd been blind to?

It felt that way now.

"I always leave after," he carried on, unashamed of the admission or his tears. "I go back to my room and I…"

He trailed off, but I'd known him long enough to know what he was going to say. I didn't have to ask, but I wanted to hear it in his voice. I wanted to know for sure.

"Tell me."

"I pretend you were talking to me," he whispered, words trailing into the softest and most delicate groan I'd ever heard.

Not once in my life had I thought about Owen that way, but now that I played back our friendship, it was clear that he'd seen me that way for years and years. And I'd been oblivious or maybe willfully ignorant, then I'd fallen in love with his sister. And I had no idea how he'd stayed my friend, unless he was a glutton for punishment, because I could hear it in his voice that everything about me—about us—was slowly killing him inside.

As for me, it was stirring up a whole new series of feelings that I'd never expected or wanted. Owen and I were so close I could smell the salt of his tears and I wanted to taste them. I wanted to close the mere inches between us and lick them away from his skin. Take him down onto the couch and feel how hot his cock burned against mine. I'd never thought of him that way, but now it was impossible to not.

But Mandy.

His sister, my girlfriend, the woman who wanted to marry me was upstairs in her room, probably with her hand down her shorts just waiting for me to come back and fuck her, but I couldn't.

I couldn't fuck her and I couldn't go back.

"I know that's pathetic," Owen whispered. "I know I've ruined everything."

"You haven't ruined anything."

"But I'm pathetic?" He sniffled, a choked-off laugh in the back of his throat.

I shook my head, readjusting my grip on the back of his neck. The bottom of his hairline tickled against my fingers, and I shifted my hand up to hold him there. Owen gasped, sighed, and leaned into me like he was made of putty.

"You're not pathetic," I assured him.

He closed his eyes, and I counted the tear tracks that slicked down his cheeks and neck. I should have been embarrassed that he'd overheard me and Mandy, that he'd *eavesdropped* on us, but my body reacted quite the opposite. I was turned on, wondering about what it would be like to have shared those moments with him instead of her and even back then, I knew how wrong that was.

I knew it was selfish and unfair. But I knew I couldn't stop it either.

"Even thinking about it makes me hard," he muttered, trying to pull away from me again, but there was no way I was going to let that happen. I didn't know what else had to be said between us, but I knew we weren't done yet. "This is embarrassing."

"Owen." I grabbed his free hand and shoved it between my legs, raising my hips off the couch to push my erection against his palm. "You're not pathetic."

He squeezed his eyes closed, keeping his hand on my cock even after I took mine away.

"I hate you for loving her," he admitted.

"I think I do too. I wish you..." I paused, sucking in a breath to stop myself from saying something that would have hurt either of them. What was there to say, really? Why didn't you tell me before? Why didn't you say something when I could have done something about it? Why didn't you give me a chance to not break all of our damn hearts?

"I wish I had said something too." He finished the sentence for me, because he knew me as well as I knew him. He knew what I was feeling, what I was thinking. He always had. "But I don't know if it would have made a difference."

"It would have made every difference."

"I'm hard," he said again, the syllables desperate and pained. "Archie, this hurts. It hurts."

Fresh tears slicked down the slope of his nose and I brushed one away with my knuckle. His eyes were still closed, so when I licked his tears from my skin, he didn't see. That taste was mine. It would be my secret for the rest of my life.

"I'm sorry."

"Everything hurts right now, Archie." Owen fell into me, one hand still around the back of my neck and the other curled around my cock. He'd gone from touching to gripping, the half-circle of his fist better than anything I'd felt in my life, even through my jeans.

"How can I help you? How can I stop it?"

It was the least I could do, considering everything was my fault.

"I know you don't think of me the way you think of her," he said.

I wanted to correct him. I needed him to know that just because I hadn't in the past didn't mean I wasn't now. Didn't mean that my erection was for anyone besides him and the truth between us.

"But..."

Another knowing silence passed, the connection between us fundamentally ingrained in our marrow. How had I been so ignorant to Owen's feelings for me? Worse, how had I missed mine for him?

He opened his mouth to finish the sentence, to add one more confession to the pile, but I couldn't let him do it. Not because I didn't want to hear it, but because I already knew it so I did the only thing that felt right in that moment.

I kissed my best friend.

With my chapped lips and open mouth, I licked my tongue around the backs of his teeth, doing my best to quiet the moan he offered up in reply. Owen *moaned* into me, he sighed, he groaned, he went weak against me and then he kissed me back, spilling the physicality of his love back onto my tongue for the first time in our lives.

Owen kissed me like he would die if I didn't let him into my mouth, and what an incomparable and heady feeling that was for me to experience for the very first time. I knew it was wrong to compare him and Mandy, but she'd never kissed me the way he kissed me. And more than that, I'd never felt the way Owen's lips and tongue and hands made me feel in that moment. I found myself glad for the fact I'd come to him instead of staying with her because there was no way I could have given her the thing that was so very rightfully *his*.

"Please."

I didn't know if that was Owen or if it was me, but our clothes were off and his cock was thicker and harder than the last time I'd seen it. He moved frantically, all flailing arms and limbs on the couch, the warm crackle of leather beneath us as he made room for me between his legs. My dick poked at his entrance and I cursed under my breath, feeling the resistance from that tight and unpenetrated ring of muscle.

I didn't know anything about being with a man beyond the innate knowing that I *needed* to be with Owen.

"I don't want to hurt you," I said when he reached down between our bodies and tried to push my dry cock into his hole.

"You already have."

My breath caught in my throat, and Owen spit in his hand and returned his palm to my cock, jacking my length until I was on the edge and as wet as he could get it.

"Please."

That time it was his voice, his grip, his hole spreading to accommodate the bare head of my dick breaching his body for the very first time.

"Owen."

"Talk to me," he begged, spreading his legs wider. He spit in his hand again and again, adding as much saliva to the place where our bodies were joined.

Even though my eyes had adjusted to the darkness, I couldn't really see where we came together, but I could feel it. The hot grip of his asshole as he relaxed and flexed and eased his way around me. With every grimace and grunt, another inch of my cock pushed into him until I was fully inserted and our bodies were sweaty and pressed together.

I braced myself with one hand on the arm of the couch so I could leverage myself over him without suffocating him, even though the expression on his face looked like he wished I would.

"I've never..."

"Me neither," I said, even though we both already knew the truth about it.

"How does it feel for you?" Owen swiped at his eyes, keeping them tightly closed.

"I don't think I have words."

The honest-to-God truth because I hadn't ever felt anything as good as being inside of him, but the pain of how I'd hurt him was enough to make me want to dig my lungs out of my chest and never breathe again.

"Find them," he begged. "For me."

There were some things that I'd known about myself from a very young age, and for as well as Owen knew me, I wondered if he was privy to those secrets too. That the way I talked behind closed doors, the way he'd overheard and taken to make his own, those words were as much for me as they'd been for Mandy. And I worried that if I opened my mouth and gave them to him, I'd make more of fool of myself than I already had.

"I'm close already," I warned him, finding a slow enough pace so I didn't spill into him on my next breath.

Between us, he jerked his cock with long and rough twists of his wrist, head falling back off the arm of the couch with a whimper. "I'm close too," he told me.

My lashes fluttered, eyes rolling back. "Not yet," I warned him.

The muscles of his channel convulsed around me and I shuddered, going still.

"Not yet, Owen. Make it last a little longer for me."

"For you?" He snorted, but slowed his hand.

"For you," I corrected. "Don't come yet because I don't want this to end."

"It's already over."

I shifted back onto my heels and pulled him off the couch. It brought us face to face, his hand still moving between us. I answered him with short pumps of my hips, the weight of him against my balls the most delicious thing I'd ever felt in my life.

"No," I corrected him, even though the fear of his meaning had already taken root at the base of my spine. Tangled up with the treat of my orgasm, it was menacing and angry.

"Archie."

"Don't come yet," I repeated, even as my balls churned with their release.

"I can't just stop it." He dropped his forehead against mine. "Can't stop this."

"Go slower, then," I pleaded—I demanded.

"Archie, fuck."

Owen's entire body seized violently, hot spurts of cum splattering against my stomach as he spilled all over his hand. He let out a sob, which he silenced by sinking his teeth into the meat of my shoulder.

I gritted my teeth, bucking up and, with one last snap of my hips, shooting my load right into him. I wrapped my arms around Owen, and he held onto me with the same sort of clinging desperation that had never been ours until then. With his teeth still lodged in my shoulder, I smoothed my hands down his spine until the tremors of his orgasm, and his crying, had stilled.

Still inside of him, my cock pulsed, the beat of my heart battering out against the inside of Owen's body, and what a wild concept. What a sensation. What a...

What had we done?

"Shit." Owen was the first to feel the gravity tear us back down to earth, but I kept my arms around him, wanting to stay half-drunk on whatever had happened between us for as long as I could. I knew once I was out of his body and he wasn't on my lap, we'd have to turn the lights on, we'd have to face what we'd done, but worse than that, I'd have to face his sister.

"I'm sorry," I whispered.

Sorry to him and to her and to me.

To us.

To everyone.

"You have to go," he said, fighting out of my arms, but that time I didn't stop him.

Owen climbed off my lap and got dressed without looking at me, then threw my clothes onto my lap. My cock was still stained with my own cum and his spit, and it had all been a mistake.

"I'm sorry," I said again.

But he was dressed and halfway up the stairs by the time I got turned around on the couch. He stopped, hand on the rail, and I wanted him to turn around and look at me, I wanted him to see how much I *meant* what had just happened between us, but he didn't. I could see the guilt as a tangible thing around us, wrapped around his shoulders and curled tight around my heart.

He didn't turn back, though, because the confession in his letter had said everything there was left to share between us. Or so I'd thought, because the last words Owen said to me that night were new ones, but I believed them as much as I knew the sky to be blue and my heart to be broken on the floor between us.

"I hate you, Archer."

And he left me alone in the basement, no doubt to fix the mess I'd found us in.

But I was twenty and I was stupid. I was still a child then, so I got dressed, walked out their front door and never, ever looked back.

CHAPTER 1
ARCHIE

My bedroom at home was dark, pitch black until I wanted the sun to break through the blackout curtains, until I was ready to face the day.

I'd never been a morning person, something my parents hoped I would someday grow out of, but as I careened toward the start of my thirties, there was no change in sight. It wasn't their problem anymore, as they'd both passed away while I was across the country in grad school, but wholly mine.

Rather, my actual, current problem was that I wasn't in *my* bedroom. It was Sunday morning, it was early, and I was in a guest room in the house of one of my closest friends. Rob and I were thick as thieves, but he had horrible taste in architecture. His home was a modern monstrosity made almost entirely out of willpower and plate glass.

"What kind of prick puts his guest room on an east-facing wall?" My very good friend, and current bedmate, Flynn, groaned, rolling away from me and tugging the blankets so hard he left half of my body uncovered.

We'd gone out the night before and followed Rob home like puppies because, at the time, it had felt like a better option than watching our other friends Dalton and Barclay take turns trying their fuck friend, Val, on like a glove.

"Robert McAvoy, that's who," I answered, scrubbing a hand down my face. "The kind of prick who lets people stay the night even though he doesn't really want them to."

"He wanted us to."

"To fuck that submissive little dominant of his into the floor is what he wanted," I said, thinking briefly of Rob's new boyfriend, Grayson. A man closer to my age whom I imagined myself becoming friends with, if the circumstances allowed. Grayson was quick-witted and smart, rich enough in his own right, though nowhere near my own net worth. Or Rob's, for that matter. And he made Rob work hard for it, which I appreciated.

"I don't blame him." Flynn rolled onto his back, dark eyes blinking open. "Grayson is a good looking kid."

"He's not a kid. He's my age."

"You're a kid," Flynn offered.

I balled the bedding into my hand and stood, tearing the blanket off of him and dropping them onto the floor. He wasn't wrong that I was the youngest of the lot of us, but they'd never treated me any different than each other, which counted for more than they knew.

I wasn't arrogant enough to say I was a genius, but on paper…

I was.

I graduated high school at seventeen. Accepted my Bachelor's degree at twenty. Finished my second Masters before twenty-five. That was when I met Flynn, when I met Rob. When I'd met the rest of Rob's inner circle—Dalton and Barclay—and back then, for the first time in what felt like a lifetime, I knew what it meant to have friends of my own again.

Before them, my self-imposed isolation after sabotaging the only relationship that had ever mattered in my world felt like a life sentence. And I would have been content to carry it out, for all the hurt and harm my actions had caused. But it was impossible to not be swept away by Rob's charisma or Flynn's quiet confidence. Barclay was a clown, Dalton was a saint, and I wasn't sure who I was out of the five, but I felt at home between them.

And that was enough.

"You're a prick," Flynn groaned, rolling onto his stomach and burying his face in the pillow. "I bet you have an east-facing guest room in your house too."

"I also have walls in my house, but this prick is going to go make us some coffee, so be nice."

Flynn grunted something in response that I didn't bother to listen to, and I left him to his complaints.

Rob's house was bright from the sunrise and the lack of drywall, but otherwise quiet. After the racket he and Grayson had created the night before, I didn't expect either of them to be up for a while, so the frightened gasp that fell out of my mouth when I rounded the corner into the kitchen and found Grayson standing in front of the sink was far less than dignified.

He threw a quick glance at me before turning back toward the stove where his weird little coffee pot lived on the back burner. In the glaring sun, it was impossible for me to not notice the thin rope-shaped bruise angling over the sharp line of Grayson's shoulder blade or the mouth-shaped love bite on the slope of his neck.

"Good morning," he said, clearing his throat and keeping his back to me. He wore only a pair of boxer briefs, which led me to believe he hadn't been expecting kitchen company this early either. "Did you want a coffee?"

"You don't have to make me coffee."

"I wasn't going to." He stepped to the side, a mug in each hand and a shit-eating grin on his face. "I'm sure I'll be seeing you around, Archie."

I huffed, my eyes closing as the noise turned into a laugh. Rob was going to have his hands full with Grayson, that was for sure. But if anyone, Rob was up for the challenge. Grayson had changed him, and only for the better. It was nice to see him stepping into a better version of himself. Not that Rob was a bad guy—he wasn't. He was one of my closest and longest-lasting friends, but Grayson had...softened him in a way that I think he needed.

The two of them were a good pair, and it was hard to not be jealous about that.

So I didn't try.

Instead, I let the dark green jealousy bubble and boil in my veins while I waited for the water in the coffee maker to get warm, and then I let it ooze and wrap around my joints while the coffee brewed. By the time the machine beeped it's completion at me, I was damn near ready to crawl out of my skin because I knew exactly how Grayson made Rob feel and it had been years since I'd experienced that for myself.

I was intimately familiar with the way tension and desire, when carefully cultivated *or* dangerously ignored, could turn into something earth-shattering, something life-changing.

Something catastrophic.

That had happened to me once—or twice—depending on how you wanted to count the occurrences, and that was one or two too many times for my liking, so I'd put up safeguards to ensure I didn't stumble into the same trap a second time.

Owen and Mandy had been a lesson for me about what happened when you let people get close without knowing every possible outcome. The night of my graduation had turned into an escape room, except I'd been absolutely blind to any possible exit short of blowing the walls off the place. It was a mistake I wouldn't make again.

If I didn't know every way that something could play out, I didn't want it. I wasn't going to open myself up to that kind of disaster ever again. I'd made sure of it by leaving them both behind, deleting phone numbers and changing my grad school acceptance from a local school to one in California. But half a country wasn't far enough, it seemed.

The memories of them both haunted me more than I'd ever admit.

I hadn't even told my friends about them because what really was there to say?

"Harvesting the beans yourself?"

Flynn's sleepy voice from behind me was the second jump scare of the day, and I straightened up, schooling my features in the reflection of the window over the sink before turning and rolling my eyes at him.

"You know he has one of these fancy things." I waved my hand dismissively toward Grayson's coffee contraption.

"It's a moka pot."

"What's the point of it?"

I, myself, liked coffee too much to bother with one-cup disasters or boiling it a little bit at a time and whisking it into submission the way Grayson did. I wanted ready access as soon as I'd drank the last drops. So, basically, strike two for Rob's house. But I imagined our nights here were numbered anyway with Rob getting wifed-up by Grayson and all that.

"Are you finished?"

I was, and Flynn took one of the coffees from the counter and shuffled past me and right into the back yard. If I didn't know him better, I'd worry he was going to take a half-asleep header into the jacuzzi, but he managed the steps with relative ease until the entire bottom half of his body disappeared beneath the bubbles.

"You look positively adrift," Grayson said softly from beside me, startling me again. "Unmoored, as it were."

"I would love if you could stop sneaking up on me, you know."

"You were the one who scared yourself the first time," he mused, setting to work making another cup of coffee on the stove.

"I'm not used to people who aren't me spending the night."

Grayson turned the burner on, then rested his ass against the counter, folding his arms over his chest. He had on sleep pants this time, which felt courteous, even though the night before I was fairly certain I'd heard what he sounded like when he came.

"You favor the guest room more than the rest of the trophy doms?"

I snorted, never-endingly amused at the ridiculous nickname he'd come up with for our tight-knit friend group.

"Flynn is here." I pointed toward the hot tub.

"Do you two sleep together?"

"Not in the way you and Rob do."

Grayson smirked and the pot on the stove started to boil, so he poured some into a mug and whisked it quickly with some sugar, then returned it to the flame. "That seems wasteful."

"Are you looking for a little fun on the side, Grayson?" I turned toward him and arched a brow. "We don't all have the same tastes as Rob if you're after something a little more adventurous."

"Rob is plenty for me." He leaned in close and shielded his mouth with the back of his hand, like he was telling me a secret. "Did I pass your test?"

"Not a test."

The coffee cooker *finally* finished brewing Grayson's current dose, which he poured into the mug before setting to work on a second.

"I didn't mean it was wasteful in that I assumed you all wanted to sleep with me, which I wouldn't blame you if you did, but I meant it was wasteful in that I'm sure the lot of you could get up to plenty of trouble if you set your minds to it."

"Taking names and breaking hearts?"

I only had two of those for myself.

"Dalton and Barclay seem to play well together."

"Everyone plays well with Barclay," I murmured. "It's deliberate."

Of all our friends, he was the one who played things the fastest and loosest, sharing and spreading himself around for anyone who wanted a taste. If it had been another time, he would have been a rake. Even more recently, he would have been a slut, but that wasn't a word we were supposed to use anymore.

Not that I thought that about him, because I didn't.

I'd taken my own fair share of people to bed over the course of my life, whether for fucking or for playing. There was no harm in chasing after the high that came with the intimacy from a new partner.

Except I didn't think that was what I was chasing at all.

"I think I like you the most," Grayson said, giving me a fleeting, but honest smile.

"You don't have to make me coffee," I said, a call back to our first encounter that morning.

He had started a third cup, doing the sugar and the mixing and then waiting for the coffee to boil or cook or do whatever it did again.

"I know I don't." Grayson collected the two full mugs and padded back toward the stairs, the pot making a questionable noise as the water boiled faster than the last time.

"Pour that into the mug before it burns," he called over his shoulder.

I flipped the burner off and did as he said, appreciating the rich and decadent smell of coffee made his way compared to the dry smell from the single cup pot Rob had. After a careful sip, I joined Flynn in the back yard. Sitting on the edge of the concrete beside him, I dunked my feet into the hot tub, enjoying the warmth with a groan.

"Do you want to overstay our welcome or go and get drunk on Bloody Marys at the beach?" he asked, eyes closed, coffee already half gone.

If the sun was out and we were awake, might as well face the day.

"The latter," I said, kicking some water back into his face as I climbed up.

He flung himself over the edge and stood, shaking droplets off like a dog and soaking my underwear to my skin.

"You're an asshole," I told him, shoving him toward the door back into the house.

"Soon to be a day-drunk asshole."

I closed the door behind me and locked it, finishing my coffee and rinsing the mug in the sink. Flynn came back dressed, with my clothes bundled up into a wrinkled ball in his arms.

"I hate you," I muttered, looking at the mess he'd made of my underwear and my slacks.

"You'll hate me less after your first drink."

Above us, something—or someone—slammed into a wall. We both looked up, and Flynn chuckled under his breath.

"I sure hope so," I said, shoving my legs into my pants and heading toward the front door with my shirt flung over my forearm. "Now, let's get out of here."

I'd seen enough people in love for one day.

Nothing that a little tomato juice and vodka couldn't erase.

CHAPTER 2
OWEN

THE DESCENT INTO LAX WAS SMOOTH AND EASY, A WELCOME REPRIEVE from the otherwise turbulent five-hour flight. My knees and hips ached, my left foot was asleep, and I was fairly certain the businessman who'd fallen asleep beside me before our wheels had even left the ground had, at some point, drooled on my shoulder.

My cellphone had less than twenty percent battery, but I flipped it off airplane mode to tap out a quick text to my sister to let her know I'd arrived in one piece. I was, after all, in Los Angeles on her bidding.

Me: Landed safe. Phone is dying.
Mandy: Have I told you today how much I love you for this?
Me: When you dropped me off at the airport this morning you told me you hated me.
Mandy: Owen, it was EARLY.
Mandy: I love you for this.
Me: It's the least I can do.

I flipped my phone over so the screen pressed against my thigh, the weight of my last message to her more truth than she would ever really know. In fact, I'd spent the majority of my adult life doing things for my sister. Anything and everything she asked of me I found a way to make happen for her because, while she knew a lot about me, the one thing she didn't know was that the source of her biggest heartbreak had been me.

Well, actually it had been Archer Davidson, but...

The *Fasten Seatbelt* light went off and everybody jumped out of their seats like there was somewhere for them to immediately go. Like we weren't all trapped in the flying death tube until they opened the door and the twenty-some odd rows in front of us struggled with their baggage and made their way out of the plane first. The drooling businessman beside me grumbled his displeasure about me staying seated, but I didn't budge, waiting until the row ahead of us was getting their bags from the overhead bin space before reaching for mine.

The airport was like its own little city and finding a taxi was near impossible, but well over an hour after my flight had landed, I found myself tucked away in the beachfront hotel room my sister's fiancé had been gracious enough to book for me. I'd initially protested about the whole trip and the accommodations because it felt so unnecessary and extravagant. We weren't poor, but we weren't wealthy, and Mandy had been adamant. Mark, on the other hand, was much closer to wealthy than we would ever be, and nothing Mandy wanted for the wedding was too much for him, including my little vacation to L.A.

Mandy managed a daycare that was currently fully enrolled, but had limited staffing, so if she wasn't planning her wedding, she was basically always at work. It was one of her good qualities, but would also be her downfall—her dedication to the causes and people she loved. Like when Archer had left us both, she tabled her own grief when I was around, always concerned about how I was taking the loss of my best friend.

But at night, after our parents had gone to bed, I could sometimes hear her cry through the walls, and the guilt over the whole thing had started to eat at me. That was when I started doing the favors for her. Small things at first, just picking up dinner for her on my way home or getting her flowers on her birthday. I turned into the perfect brother, and eventually things went back to normal.

When Mark proposed to her, he asked me for permission first, and that spoke volumes about how important I was to her. Even if I didn't deserve the ranking. Mark and Mandy were a better couple than she and Archer would have been, even better than he and I would have been, so it was an easy thing to tell him yes. As soon as she got the ring on her finger, she went into full wedding planner mode, and that was how I ended up in California. Los Angeles was Mark's hometown, and a destination style wedding had always been Mandy's dream.

"If I'm thinking of getting married at that hotel, I want to know what the rooms are like," she had said, and from the stern set of her mouth, I knew fighting would have meant a losing battle.

I was just honestly happy that Mandy had a ring on her finger, Archer's betrayal long forgotten. At least, I imagined it was as forgotten as that kind of thing could be. I knew that I hadn't forgotten it at all. But it wasn't just his behavior, the way he ghosted us both without even a shred of regret, that had stuck with me.

It was my own actions. It was the things I'd asked of him. I'd lost sleep over the way I'd begged him, the way I'd forced him to give me something neither of us had a right to offer or to take. We'd been so young and stupid, but there were still some nights when I laid awake, thinking about the way he'd licked my heartbreak off my skin before he came.

I was so helplessly in love with my best friend back then.

And my sister had loved him too.

Thankfully, after Archer, I'd met Frankie, and while things with him had come to a natural—and easy—end, I learned that it wasn't always hard and it didn't always have to hurt. The years I'd spent with Frankie had shown me it was possible to move on and find happiness in things like sharing take-out and watching documentaries until three in the morning.

Everything had not been lost when my best friend turned his back on me.

Frankie had spent the first year with me living in Archer's shadow and he'd done so with more grace than I deserved. He was patient, generous, and kind, and when I finally saw him in his own light, I fell for him. I loved him so much and so hard, for so long, but over time we grew apart. At first, it had felt like a terrible thing and I clung to him with an unexplainable desperation, but we didn't eat take-out anymore and we weren't even interested in the same shows, and much like I'd warmed up to him over time, I cooled over time too.

Frankie was the best life lesson I could have asked for.

To this day, my closest friend.

Me: Jealous?

I sent him a message with the picture of the beach, the ocean fading off into the sky, a single white cloud puffing off toward the corner of the shot.

Frankie: I hate airplanes.
Me: One thing we always had in common
Frankie: Mads is lucky you love her.

My sister was many things, but her relationship with me and what I'd caused in our lives could never be classified as luck.

Me: A free vacation doesn't sound like a real hardship for me, you know.
Frankie: Yeah, don't rub it in. See you this weekend, Winny.

I dropped my phone onto the small wooden table beside me and sighed, happy to listen to the waves crashing against the sand for a little while. The growling of my stomach was quick to overtake the background noise, and with a reluctant groan, I grabbed my phone and headed back into the room. The hotel had a restaurant, which I would be taste-testing the following day, so I decided to venture out onto the boardwalk and find something to eat.

It was admittedly nice, but I liked the quiet bustle of home. After high school, I stayed local for college, finished a Bachelor's degree in finance, which I hadn't used a day in my life. I'd gotten a part-time job at the college my sophomore year, and by the time I graduated, I was making better money part-time than I would have in something entry level, so I never bothered looking for another job.

I rented a duplex unit at the end of a cul-de-sac and my sister and her fiancé lived five miles across town in the same house we'd grown up in, the only change from childhood being the kitchen renovation she'd done five years earlier. My life was steady and predictable, and I found immense levels of comfort in that.

My thoughts of home distracted me, and I'd wandered farther down the boardwalk than I'd meant. But I found myself in front of a cute little cafe that made coffee and sandwiches, so I ordered an iced latte and a turkey club. Both items came out quickly, and I took them to one of the small wire tables on the boardwalk that faced the sand.

It was busy and loud, and I immediately understood how people could get lost in a place like L.A., swept up into the allure of anonymity, but it wasn't for me. I knew who I was, and more than that, I *liked* who I was.

I was accomplished.

I was friendly.

I was decent-looking.

I was single.

Popping a slice of extra-long bacon into my mouth, I fingered through the home screen on my phone until I got to my hook-up app. Then I changed the location to Los Angeles. Almost immediately, my alerts started to go off. Someone at the table beside me looked, eyes full of knowing, and I switched it to silent with a curse under my breath. Apparently, I'd gotten used to the slim enough pickings back home because I really hadn't expected that many people to ping the radius alert.

I was in Los Angeles for three days. Today was a *me* day, which I did try to pay my sister for, but she refused. Tomorrow was a *her* day, as evidenced by the list of locations and venue appointments she'd booked for me to scout on her behalf. The third day was a combination, with one straggling venue that she couldn't fit on the day before, and then I'd be left to my own devices, with an early flight out Sunday morning. The weather was looking impeccable and judging by the near constant vibration of my phone, I'd be able to find myself some company for at least one of the nights.

Frankie said I'd recently entered my slut era, but he'd meant it kindly so I never took offense. He wasn't far from the truth. It had only been within the past handful of months that I'd started being okay with fucking for fun. Up to and after him, I'd really only pursued sex from people I was dating, which was fine and had worked, but I found that I didn't really *want* to date.

I was happy to get off and get going.

Being across the country would make that even easier, so with one quarter of my sandwich left, I opened the app back up and started to scroll through the hits in the area. There were a lot of people who weren't my type, but plenty who were, and I shifted, now faced with the problem of how to narrow it down and choose.

Finishing my sandwich, I carried the empty tray and glass back inside. A corkboard hung above the trash can, spattered with business cards and flyers for local businesses. A small black card in the bottom right corner caught my eye for how *not* flashy it was in comparison to the rest. Sleek and matte black, with a gold edge and an elegant script foiled on the front in a matching metallic, it read *Rapture: A Private Club.*

I flipped it over, but the back was blank. No other information.

Someone came up behind me, clearing their throat. I shoved the business card into my pocket and stepped out of their way with a quick apology. Back on the boardwalk, the card was already forgotten, my brain washed clean with the smell of salt and sunscreen. I walked toward the shore and plopped down onto the sand. It was warm and granules slipped up my shorts, abrading at the backs of my thighs. Nothing a shower couldn't fix later, though.

I sent another picture to Frankie and one to my sister. She answered me back with a crying emoji and a middle finger. Laughing at her, I unlaced my sneakers and set them to the side, digging my toes into the sand and falling onto my back with a huff.

The sky above me was as blue as the ocean, the birds and the laughter playing a nice little soundtrack that was almost enough to lull me to sleep. I would have napped there on the beach were it not for the incessantly vibrating phone in my pocket. A constant—and welcome—reminder that Los Angeles had more than one kind of view to offer, and I was going to see as many of the sights as I could.

CHAPTER 3
ARCHIE

BARCLAY WAS SPEAKING TO ME, BUT I HADN'T HEARD A WORD OUT OF his mouth for at least the past ten minutes. On he went, though, undeterred by my lack of engagement, chattering on about Val this and Val that. With my elbow propped up on the arm of my couch, I blinked slowly, listening to him talk while I tried to stay awake.

A week of insomnia had caught up to me and I was ready to call it a night.

"Perceval, I swear." I rubbed the bridge of my nose, using his legal name to make sure he gave me the attention I'd been denying him.

"What?"

"When are you going to admit you're in love with Val?"

I couldn't remember how long ago he'd met Val, but I'd heard Val's name as much as my own over the past few weeks and it was beginning to slide right toward something far more serious than casual.

"I'm not in love with Val." He rolled his eyes at me, ever the petulant child. "I'm in love with Val's asshole. There's a difference."

"A true romantic."

"It's nothing serious with him, or committed."

"You've repeated with him more than half a dozen times and that's not your usual MO, my friend."

I didn't care one way or the other who Barclay fucked or how often, but I wasn't above calling out when he bucked the trends. Rob had done it with Grayson and Barclay was treacherously close with Val, or Val's asshole, as he claimed.

"We've talked," Barclay assured me. "He likes what I do to him and I like doing it. There's no harm in carrying that through for a while. And, besides, he's fine to share."

"Oh, is he?" I arched a brow. "How long will that last?"

"It will last as long as it lasts, and then when it's done, his time is up."

I snapped my fingers. "Just like that?"

"Just like that," he confirmed, looking down at his phone before tucking the device into the front pocket of his pants. "Were you ready to go? Dalton wants a ride."

"Dalton can call a car."

"I told him we'd pick him up on the way." Barclay jangled his keys and kicked me in the shin. "Get up. Let's get going."

I didn't want to get up or get going, even though that had been the plan the whole time. What I'd hoped to make happen was canceling our plans altogether, but the talk of Val had apparently backfired. Instead of lulling Barclay into a quiet, homebound conversation, he was roaring and ready to go to Rapture like we'd planned all along.

"I might just stay home," I told him, standing up and stretching so far my shoulder popped.

"You can't stay home."

"I can do anything I want," I reminded him.

"You're coming out," he said.

"I don't want to play."

"You can watch."

"Exhibitionist," I accused.

He waggled his eyebrows at me, and I sighed in defeat, knowing there was no way for me to get out of our trip to the club.

I didn't want to play. I didn't want to watch. I didn't even really want to drink. I was tired down to the marrow of my bones, and I had been for the entire week. Work had been grueling, keeping me out longer during the day than I preferred, and even causing me to miss our standing Thursday whiskey night.

There was no real explanation for the shift in my mood, though, other than late nights had pushed me past exhaustion and into a miserable state of consciousness that no one should have ever had to experience. Most nights, I'd been up until the sunrise, barely getting two hours of sleep before having to get going and start the day. Out of the lot of my friends, Rob and Dalton both seemed to pick up on the fact I wasn't my usual self, but neither of them pushed me to talk about it. I'd been going through the motions like a ghost, it felt like sometimes, signing contracts and holding meetings that I had absolutely no recollection of as soon as they passed. Time had blurred into one long and frankly miserable day.

"If you want me to come out tonight, I need to shower first," I said, bartering and trying to buy myself some time.

"You certainly do not. We're already going to be the last ones there."

"Go get Dalton, then come back for me."

"If I leave this house without you, you won't leave." He narrowed his eyes, seeing right through my game.

"I know."

"Go wash your face and grab a snack to kick start your blood sugar." He had the audacity to wave me off *in my own home.* "I'll wait for you in the car, and if I have to wait longer than five minutes, I'm going to come back and drag you out of here kicking and screaming."

"Just save yourself the trip," I muttered, pushing up off the couch and heading toward my bathroom. "I don't even need five minutes."

The light in the bathroom was unfairly harsh, I wagered, so I kept it off while splashing myself down with some cold water. As the youngest of all my friends, it generally did wonders for my ego, but even behind them by decades, I was still right on the brink of thirty and the wrinkles forming around my eyes confirmed it. Leaning over the sink, I smiled, using my fingers to spread the fine lines flat with a quiet curse. The lines were the least of my worries, though. The bags under my eyes a whole monstrosity on their own.

"That's enough water!" Barclay shouted from the couch.

"It's just a couple hours," I promised myself, returning to the living room with a sour look on my face.

"You're going to scare away the men," he groaned, gesturing toward the kitchen. "Go eat."

Much like my sleep schedule, my appetite had gone off kilter too. It wasn't the worst news for my waistline, but I figured it had definitely contributed to the energy issues of the past week. I was on a timetable, though, so with the promise to myself of a salad the next day, I grabbed a can of EZ Cheese from the fridge.

"Not that," Barclay protested as I popped the cap off and turned the can upside down.

I locked eyes with him and pushed down on the nozzle, a slightly hard and definitely cold stream of processed cheese product swirling out onto my waiting tongue.

"That's disgusting," he said, and I smiled at him, finishing off the pile before swallowing it down with a flourish.

"It's a comfort food," I said.

"I wish you were less comfortable."

I recapped the cheese and put the can back into the fridge.

"Alright. Let's go."

"Finally," he grumbled, shaking his keys at me again.

I followed him out of the house, locked up, and obediently climbed into the passenger seat of his Audi. He poked at my attitude the whole drive to Dalton's, but thankfully he'd gotten it out of his system by the time we pulled up to the curb.

"Have you met someone?" he asked me out of nowhere, honking the horn for Dalton at the same time.

I sputtered, the idea preposterous. "What?"

"Have you met someone?"

"What on earth…"

"Rob did this when he was mooning over Grayson and now you're…" He trailed off, frowning at me.

"I'll do my best to frown toward the wall so I don't sour your boyfriend's mood," I assured him.

"He's not my boyfriend and you didn't answer my question."

"What question?" Dalton opened the door and climbed into the back seat in a rush of leather and aftershave.

"I asked Archie if he was seeing anyone."

"He's not," Dalton answered on my behalf. "Are you?"

"I'm not." I let my head fall back against the head rest and my eyes closed while the two of them bantered back and forth about whatever lewd sex acts they intended to perform on Val before the night was through.

We arrived at Rapture before I felt it necessary to throw myself out of the car, and I quietly followed the two of them up the stairs. Rapture was a place I loved, that we all loved. An old church converted into a BDSM club, it was almost like a home away from home. There was dancing if you wanted, private playrooms if that was your style, and plenty of partners to choose from.

When we came out, we spent most of the time in the upstairs play loft, which had recently been renovated again to offer more of a sleek and modern feel. With exposed brick walls, a stained glass rose window high up toward the top of the vaulted ceiling, the loft was never short on entertainment…or pleasure.

I showed the doorman my membership card, and by the time I returned it to my wallet, Dalton and Barclay had already disappeared into the mass of bodies on the main dance floor. The last thing I wanted to do was drink and the first thing I wanted to do was leave, but I knew that there had to be a middle in there somewhere. And the middle probably involved making my way up the stairs in search of Rob, Grayson, and Flynn.

They were easy enough to find, sprawled out on a black leather couch tucked into one of the darkest corners of the space. Flynn's obscenely shiny brown hair was unmistakable, even in the dim lighting, and when he saw me, he slid over to make room on the couch.

"You look miserable," Rob said in greeting.

I gave him the finger and leaned back to get comfortable.

"He's eating canned cheese again," Barclay said, coming up with a drink in hand and Dalton beside him.

"I always eat canned cheese."

"But rarely in front of anyone else," Flynn said.

I pointed at Barclay. "This prick told me to eat before we left so I ate."

"You could literally have cheese flown in from Wisconsin if you felt like it," Grayson chided, smile mischievous and bold as ever. "But canned cheese?"

"It's an old habit," I muttered, waving them all off.

"Are you all right?" Rob asked, leaning across Grayson to get a better look at me. "Do we need to be worried?"

"Just a bit of a slump," I assured them all, pushing back to my feet. "I haven't been sleeping well, but it'll pass."

"You better not be sneaking home already," Barclay warned when I stood.

"I'm going to get a drink."

"Something with a Red Bull chaser," Dalton suggested.

"Thank you, Dad. I'll keep that in mind."

I left them in the loft and went to the main bar, which took me down the stairs and across the whole dance floor. I was trying to buy myself some time, hoping that if I took enough steps I could will myself to get my act together.

Flynn hadn't been wrong about my spray cheese tendencies. Even though it truly was a comfort food, something that I'd eaten my entire life, it was something I leaned more heavily on when I was distressed or distraught. Because the spray cheese had been Owen's thing, and while the taste and the texture of the processed shit spray in my mouth did make me feel better overall, it was definitely always laced with memories of him.

But Owen was a whole lifetime ago, and my friends were upstairs and they were all worried about me, and I needed to get it together before they staged some kind of intervention.

"Just a Red Bull and lime," I told Raf, the bartender. He poured me a glass and added a maraschino cherry for show, which I appreciated.

"You can tell them it's a Seven and 7 if you don't want twenty questions," he said, sliding it toward me.

"Thank you." I raised the glass in toast to him, pushed a five across the bar top, and turned back toward the stairs.

Taking a slow path through the dance floor, I didn't argue when people tried to dance up on me, letting myself get almost swept up in the beat of the music and the desperately horny kind of undercurrent that pulsed through the air. By the time I reached the stairs, I was feeling a little more like myself, and at the top of the landing, I let my feet come to a stop outside of the first play-room door.

It was cracked open, and my first thought went to Barclay, assuming Val had already showed up with a pre-lubed asshole, which was his norm. A low moan fell out of someone's mouth and I knew it wasn't Barclay *or* Val, so I dared a quick glance inside the room.

What I found wasn't anything out of the ordinary for a Friday night at Rapture. Someone with their back pressed against the wall, their attention turned down to the other person on their knees, mouth full of cock. The person getting sucked off had a mop of curls, half dark, half bleached, and their fingers dug hard into the shorter strands of whoever was on the floor.

Listening to the familiar sounds of excess saliva and lack of oxygen that came with a proper throat fucking, I spun my straw toward my mouth to take a small sip. If they'd wanted privacy, the door would have been closed. Those were the rules of the club so my observation didn't require specific consent.

The curly-haired man made another rough grunt and threw his head back in pleasure. I watched as his spine arched, and when his eyes opened, I recognized him before he even saw my face. I almost dropped my glass, because the man currently getting ready to shoot his load down—yeah, that actually was Val's throat—was the one man I never expected to see again. The one man I never *wanted* to see again.

He hadn't changed at all from when we'd been teenagers together in the basement of his parents' house, but he'd also changed in every way at the same time. He was taller maybe, but not much broader. He had tattoos on his hands and one on his chest. A pearl necklace, ironically, around *his* neck, and a silk shirt half-buttoned and spread open.

"Owen?"

His eyes flew open, back bowing as he curled forward over the top of Val's head. I watched light flash in the depths of his irises when he saw me, the unavoidable arousal of his orgasm mixed with the shock and anger at the sight of my face. But it was a house of cards by that point and there was no stopping anything that happened next. He was already right on the brink of it, and the way his mouth went slack as he came was just like it had been the first time I made him come.

He locked his eyes onto mine, and his mouth made the shape of my name while he came into the back of Val's throat.

"Archer."

I took a step backward, blinking like I could vanish him with willpower alone, but to no avail. With his cock still resting on Val's ever waiting tongue, Owen held my stare, stroking his fingers through Val's hair before pulling out.

Val stood and turned, a dazed and happy smile on his face. He saw me almost immediately, wiping a smear of Owen's cum from his mouth.

"Archie." He grinned. "Is Barclay here yet?"

I nodded and pointed toward the couch.

Owen hadn't stopped looking at me. I could feel it, feel him, and I was more awake than I had been in what felt like years. Val slinked out of the room, squeezing past me and heading right for the couch, right for my friends who didn't even know the name of the man who'd just crashed back into my life with no warning and no reason.

"What are you doing here?" I asked.

Owen's lips pulled into a tight line and he tucked his cock, now pierced I noticed, back into his jeans. He buttoned and zipped, adjusted himself and brushed past me toward the stairs like he hadn't seen me at all.

Maybe I was a ghost after all.

CHAPTER 4
OWEN

I'D BARELY GOTTEN MY COCK BACK INTO MY PANTS BEFORE I MADE IT out the front doors of Rapture. The night air was warm, and I sucked in a breath as my cock spasmed through the last pulses of orgasm. Cum smeared against my hand, my underwear. My hands were shaking, the back of my neck dotted with sweat and not from exertion during the blow job either.

"Owen."

Archer's voice saying my name filled my ears again, quickly followed by the slapping of his shoes against the stone steps that led down to the parking lot. I shook my head, feet landing in the gravel as I made a sharp turn right toward the alley. There was one light attached to the middle of the building, casting an umbrella-shaped glow across the space. I went past it, deeper into the dark. Pressing my back against the cool bricks at the end of the alley, I closed my eyes, shoulders sagging when Archer's footsteps continued to approach.

"Owen?"

My name again, but this time a question.

I scrubbed a hand down my face and huffed. My knees were unsteady, but I didn't know if it was from the orgasm or from seeing Archer again after so many years.

"What do you want, Archer?"

He chuckled, like the selfish asshole he always had been.

"To start with, I want to know why you said my name when you came down Val's throat, but I'll start with asking why you're here."

Val.

I hadn't even bothered to ask his name. I hadn't needed to ask, either. Names were a currency I rarely traded in and even though it was my first time at Rapture, I didn't think it was entirely necessary. He'd offered, I'd accepted, we'd agreed.

"I didn't know you were the King of Los Angeles." I leaned against the bricks so I didn't fall over. "Approving entry to everyone who's passing through? Should I have come to pay my respects?"

Archer muttered something under his breath that I didn't catch, then took a couple steps closer. He stopped under the wash of the security light, giving me my first real look at him in ten years. Like the bastard he was, he looked better than I remembered. He'd grown into his shoulders, his height, his face. The t-shirt he wore spread across his chest like it was ready to split down the center, and he had on tight pants that might have been leather but looked soft as silk. With black boots, unlaced and loose around his ankles to complete his look, Archer appeared every inch the threat I knew him to be.

"Did you want to answer the other question?" he asked.

"I don't owe you anything," I spat.

"Do you always think about me when you come?" He took another step closer, stride strong and confident. I was thankful for the wall behind me because if it hadn't been there, I would have taken a step back and I didn't want him to see the nervousness his appearance had caused.

"Do you always watch other men get their dicks sucked?"

"At Rapture?" He glanced up toward the towering facade beside us. "More often than not. But I never expected it would be your dick getting sucked, Owen."

"Stop saying my name."

"Owen."

I pushed off the wall as he closed the space between us, moving quicker than me and walking my shoulders right back against the bricks. Glaring up at him, I balled my hands into fists, working my jaw to stop from grinding my teeth.

"You used to like when I said your name," he whispered.

"I used to like a lot of things."

"Do you still?" Archer dipped his chin down, bringing his nose closer to my neck. The heat of his breath burned like a fire, and I squeezed my eyes closed, no longer sure if I could hold my own against him. I'd never really been able to hold myself against him, at least not in the ways I'd wanted.

When Archer had gotten involved with Mandy, I'd been on board with the idea, but as their relationship developed, so had my jealousy. It wouldn't have taken a rocket scientist to determine that, at some point, I'd fallen in love with my best friend, and it was that love which drove us past the point of no return. With ten years between us and that night, I couldn't help but wonder if Archer's abandonment had been a blessing. If he'd stayed, what would we have done?

It was hard enough for me to face Mandy while I carried the guilt of Archer's and my secret. Would I have been able to survive it with him still in our lives? Would he have stayed with her? Would he have been with me? A thousand questions and could-have-beens raced through my head, clouding what minimal judgement I had left. There was too much blood left in my cock for me to give him the answer he deserved, so I bit my lips to keep them closed.

"Your silence sounds like a yes," Archer murmured.

"Silence is rarely a yes."

"Is it a no, then?" His body went still, and I knew he was asking something more than the four minuscule words let on. "Are you telling me no?"

His lips were warm and wet, grazing over my pulse like butterfly wings.

"No," I rasped.

I hadn't even finished getting my pants up before I'd turned into the alley, and Archer made quick work of my fly. He shoved his hand down my pants and fisted my cock like his fingers were made for my thickness, and when he curled them all the way around me, he smiled against my neck.

"I didn't realize that I missed the way you feel," he whispered.

"Don't say things like that."

"It's true." He stroked his hand toward the still sensitive crown of my dick.

"Yellow, Archer."

Again, his body went still, his grip loosened but didn't go away.

"I said don't say things like that," I repeated.

"Yes, Sir."

He mocked me.

The tease in his voice was louder than the words themselves, and Archer tightened his hand around me again on the down stroke. With his chest pressed against mine, he worked my cock better than I ever had, and what gave him the right? Ten years later, after everything we'd done, after everything *he'd* caused, and he could still touch me better than I could touch myself?

The audacity of this man.

The nerve.

"Don't come again," he warned, and I rolled my eyes, letting my head fall back against the wall.

"I can't control it."

"You could before."

Archer kissed my neck, tongue darting out and swirling over the erratic way my heartbeat pulsed in every touch point of our skin. My body was a traitor, so hard and soft for him after all this time, after no apologies and no warnings.

I didn't know what to say to him, though, because he wasn't wrong.

I swallowed, opening my mouth to get air because my nose wasn't cutting it. Archer against me, in my space, in my pants, it felt like he'd sucked all of the oxygen off the whole damn planet.

"I'm close," I muttered.

"And I told you don't come."

"King of Los Angeles," I grumbled, gritting my teeth in a half-hearted attempt to push off my orgasm. "Does everyone do your fucking bidding, Archer?"

"I think King has a better ring to it, if we're being honest."

"You've never been honest with me."

The pace of his hand faltered. It couldn't have been more of a millisecond of hesitation, but I was so primed and ready for another orgasm my body definitely took notice of it. Archer's hand was hot, his skin smooth against mine, precum smearing down my shaft and around his fingers as he teased me toward the edge and back again. Another orgasm so soon after Val had sucked my balls dry should have been impossible, or at the very least painful, but my body was registering anything but.

"You're not being honest now," he said, tongue sliding out to tease the shell of my ear. "Why are you in Los Angeles?"

I knew he wouldn't like the answer, so I ignored him, focusing instead on the way he touched me like he deserved to have my cock in his hand. More skilled than he'd been when we were teenagers, Archer made quick work of drawing another orgasm out of me. My breath caught in my throat, shoulders straightening and digging into the bricks as it crested over me.

"Not yet, Owen," he whispered, shoving his thigh under my balls and hiking my body farther up the wall. "Don't come yet. Not yet."

"Fuck you, Archer." I forced the curse out as I came, jets of cum spilling over the curl of his fist like a fountain. He didn't stop touching me as the throbbing of my cock subsided. He didn't move away as my balls ached from overuse and my shaft burned from the friction.

"Why are you here?" he asked again.

"A favor."

My eyes rolled back, lashes fluttering. His hand felt good, too good, and I needed him to stop touching me, but I didn't *want* him to. How fucked up was that? With one hand around my cock, he reached behind with the other, fumbling around in his back pocket. For what? I couldn't have cared less because I was too focused on the way my body was priming itself for another go.

"For who?"

"None of your business," I said.

"How long are you here for?"

He squeezed the tip of my cock in his fist, drawing a needy and strained moan from the back of my throat.

"Why does it matter?" I choked the question out, still trying to decide how much of a pushover it would make me to let Archer make me come for a second time. "Worried about running into me if it's *your* cock down someone's throat?"

"I don't care if you get off on watching other men make me come, Owen."

"That's not..." I shook my head, grunting in annoyance.

He was such an asshole.

Such a fucking prick.

"I'm here until Sunday," I told him.

"Good."

"Good because I'll be out of your hair soon?"

I was still hard, still hot in his hand. I didn't think there was much cum left in my body but Archer hadn't fucking stopped touching me since he'd gotten his hand down my pants. He stroked me like it was a leisurely activity and we had all the time in the world to get off, not like we were against a dark wall in a Los Angeles alley, in the back of a BDSM club.

"Just good," he murmured, dragging his nose from my ear toward my mouth. His lips hovered over mine, breath ghosting out across my lips, my cheek, my chin. I angled my face toward the sky to get away from him, to get some air, even though there was none.

Archer was a fucking black hole, sucking up everything that dared to get close. I'd already done it once. There was no way I'd make the same mistake a second time. I couldn't do that to my sister—I *wouldn't* do that to myself.

"Do you have another one in the tank, Owen?" Archer asked, smiling against my mouth, hand still twisting up my shaft with every breath.

"Not for you."

He made an amused sound, then he did the last thing I expected.

He licked me. From my throat to the point of my chin, all of it exposed and on display for him in my attempt to avoid his eyes. It had never been his eyes that were the problem, though. It was always his mouth, the things he did with it, the words he said, the fucking lies he told. Archer nipped my chin between his teeth and groaned, pressing our bodies together and finally stilling his hand.

"No?" he asked.

"No."

Another noise from him, this one sounding more like reluctant concession. After that, he moved efficiently and methodically. Archer's fingers unwound from my traitorously hard cock and he shuffled away. Not far, but enough to put space between us for him to tuck my cock back into my pants where he'd found it. He zipped me up, managed the button on the first try, then reached for my chin, tugging my head down and waiting for me to look at him.

I knew he wouldn't leave until I did, and my legs hadn't stopped shaking since I'd gotten to the club in the first place. I didn't know how much strength—or willpower—I had left in me. So, I squared my shoulders as best I could manage, the attempt at posturing so performative it almost made me laugh at myself, and I let my stare fall toward his face.

Archer looked wild. His eyes were hooded and dark, his lips parted and wet with spit. His stare dragged over my face like fingertips, desperately searching for more consent than I'd verbally offered up. The heavy want in his face barely faltering when recognition dawned he wouldn't get what he was after. The way Archer studied me was familiar, in good ways and bad, in ways that I didn't want to walk away from even though I wanted to walk away from him.

I closed my eyes, dropping the back of my head against the wall.

"Understood, Owen, but one more thing before I go."

It was hardly a question, and in reply I forced myself to focus on him one more time.

He reached for my mouth, with his cum-sticky fingers and tapped the tip of his first finger against my lips, pressing in just enough to curl around my bottom teeth and pull my mouth open. I was ready to bite his finger off when, with his other hand, he placed something between my teeth and I instead closed down around that.

The snap of my teeth drew a growl out of him, and he stepped back a few paces until he was once again under the bright wash of the security light. He smeared my cum across his mouth, holding my stare while he licked himself clean, and then backed up again, again, again, until he reached the parking lot and disappeared into the dark.

I didn't know when I'd stopped breathing, but once he was out of sight, I fell forward, knees digging into the gravel and dirt of the alley before my lungs even had a chance to fill again. Whatever he'd put into my mouth fell out, and I recognized the shape as a business card, which I picked up with shaky hands.

Upon closer inspection, I realized the card was a clean white with his name and phone number centered on the card in crisp black lettering, raised off the page.

Archie Davidson.

Archie.

He used to hate being called Archie. I was the only one he'd allowed to get away with it and now everyone got the courtesy that used to belong only to me? Jealousy rippled up my spine, and I glared at the teeth marks I'd left in the corner of the card.

I crumbled the cardstock in my hand and shoved it into my pocket, pushing up to my feet and getting the hell away from there before I did something I'd regret more than I already had.

CHAPTER 5
ARCHIE

I scrubbed madly at my hand with soap and scalding water, trying to wash away every drop of Owen's cum that my greedy tongue had missed.

What the hell had I been thinking?

Stalking him out into the alley and backing him against a wall. Shoving my hand down his pants and talking to him like I was twenty again? I had no idea what came over me, and when Flynn appeared behind me and turned off the water, I wasn't any closer to an answer.

"What's going on?" he asked.

I shook my head, tearing a paper towel off the roll and drying my hand. My fingers were red as a cherry, no doubt burned to some minor degree from the water and the scrubbing. "Nothing."

"You're a liar," he said.

"It's honestly nothing." I used my hair to dry the rest of my hand, raking my way back and trying to push the strands into place.

"Are we just going to ignore the facts then?"

"What are the facts, asshole?" My hand was trembling, so I folded my arms in front of my chest and tucked it as far away from Flynn's line of sight as I could manage.

"Val said you looked panicked." He held up one finger and

began to count my offenses off. "You disappeared without telling anyone where you were going, which is very unlike you. You have a raging erection that you're ignoring, and I think if you had a hacksaw, you would have already amputated your right hand."

"Are you done?"

He gave me a tired eye roll.

"For one, I'm an adult. I'm allowed to go outside without permission. This surely isn't the first or the last time I'm going to get hard here, and three..." I sucked my tongue across the front of my teeth, my mouth getting too far ahead of my brain because I couldn't speak to the state of my hand.

"It's a good thing you don't carry a pocket knife," he said.

"I'm fine," I assured him, uncrossing my arms and shaking them out at my sides, offering an attempt to appear casual and unaffected when I was anything but. The smell of Owen's soap was still fresh in my nose, the taste of him salty and amazing on my tongue.

Flynn eyed up me up and down, clearly not believing a single thing I said.

"I'm fine," I said again, giving him a shove toward the door. The bathroom was too small for my lies and I needed to get him distracted so he would quit the interrogation. Back on the outskirts of the dance floor, the music was loud enough to drown out whatever he said next, and I gestured at my ear to let him know I couldn't hear.

I *could* hear him, though.

I just didn't want to talk.

I hadn't told any of my friends about Owen yet, and I surely wasn't going to start now. It wasn't that I'd intended to keep that part of my life a secret, but the more removed I found myself from what I'd done, the harder it became to face. Admitting that I'd walked out on my best friend after losing my virginity to him, that I'd been close enough to his older sister to entertain the idea of marriage...it was all marks of the boy I'd been, not the man I'd become.

Going to college in California was the best choice I'd ever made, even if Owen and Mandy were casualties of the decision. Because it was there I'd met Flynn, and there I'd met Rob, and then the rest of them. The trophy doms, as Rob's boyfriend Grayson called us. And it was a joke and it was meant to be biting in the delivery, but it wasn't far from the truth.

Outwardly, at least, I was as eligible as the rest of my friends.

But as much as I was a different man from the boy I'd been, there were still parts of him tucked inside of me. All of those memories laced with longing and regret, but not a desire to go back and change course. The decisions I'd made were the right ones—the execution was what had been wrong.

"Do you want another drink?" Flynn shouted in my ear.

I shook my head. The last thing I needed was more liquor to cloud my already muddled brain.

Owen had done a number on me; that was for sure. As soon as I'd seen him, as soon as I'd watched his mouth whisper my name *while he came*, it was like my brain had flipped to autopilot. There was no stopping anything that happened after that and, in the blink of an eye, he'd reduced me down to the boy I'd been before. Thinking with my cock and my balls instead of my head...or my heart.

Flynn smacked the back of my head, and when I turned to glare at him, he gave me the finger before slinking back onto the dance floor, headed for the bar. My hand still ached from the hot water, and I trudged back up to the loft, not realizing my mistake until I recognized Val's white-blond hair in the crowd on the couch.

"I told you he'd be back." Rob locked eyes with me, a knowing look on his face that I hated.

"I'm fine," I told him.

I told all of them.

"Where did you run off to?" Val asked. "I didn't think you had a problem with watching?"

Barclay collared a possessive hand around the back of Val's

neck and I gave them both a teasing smile. "The only thing I love more than watching you suck cock, Val, is getting my own cock sucked."

"He could if you wanted," Barclay offered.

Val's eyes twinkled, but I shook my head. "I'm good for now, boys. But thank you just the same."

I found room against the wall and pressed my back against the exposed brick, trying to not think about what it had felt like for Owen. With my knee between his legs, rutting against him like a horny kid again.

Fuck.

"Come on." Rob grabbed me by the elbow and hauled me off the wall and down the hallway. I didn't even have time to protest. He shoved me into the private playroom that Val and Owen had occupied earlier and pushed the door closed behind us.

"What's going on?"

"What do you mean?"

"Flynn says you're eating canned cheese again."

I clenched my jaw, narrowing my eyes. "Why are all of you so obsessed with my eating habits?"

"You eat the canned cheese when you think too hard."

"I eat it when I think about all the times I should have thought harder," I muttered.

"You're not yourself," he said.

"Is this turnabout for all the teasing I sent over when you were ass-up over Grayson, because if so—"

He cut me off with a stern look and crossed arms. "This is because we're your friends and we're worried about you."

"We?" I arched a brow and once again leaned against the wall. "Were you elected to come and speak with me about it?"

"I volunteered," Rob responded.

I wasn't a fan of the turned tables because while Rob was the oldest out of the group, he wasn't the most dominant. In fact, when he'd been drowning himself in liquor over the ways Grayson was running him around, I was the only one he'd listen to, so the fact he was trying to play my own game against me was far from appreciated.

But I could tell by the set of his jaw that he wasn't going to let me out of the room without an answer.

"It's better shared over kitchen whiskey," I offered, words as weak as Owen had always made my knees.

"Because it's quieter?"

I nodded.

"Then let's go have some kitchen whiskey." He pulled out his phone and fired off a text, to Flynn or Dalton I assumed, then he looked to me expectantly.

I pulled open the door and stepped into the hallway, putting space between us without looking back. Rob trailed me through the club and into the parking lot where I searched out the ridiculous shine on his Maserati and waited for him to unlock the doors.

Thankfully, he let me sulk in my own misery the whole drive to his house, and he didn't even push me for answers until I was stretched out on a chaise lounge in his back yard with a tumbler of whiskey in my hand. His house was dark, save for the kitchen light, and the yard sparkled a brilliant sapphire blue from the reflections in his pool.

"How's the whiskey?" he finally asked after I'd drank half the glass.

"Unfortunately, it's not enough to erase the shittiest thing I've ever done, but not for lack of trying." I gave the glass a little shake, enjoying the calm way the ice clanked against the edges before resettling in the bottom.

"Do you want to tell me about it?"

I scoffed. "Do I have a choice?"

"Always," Rob answered quickly. He stretched out and kicked my ankle with the toe of his brown oxford.

The night air was quiet and warm, another perk of living as deep in the valley as Rob did. I toed off my boots and finagled my feet out of my socks, trying to find the easiest place to start. The place to start that didn't make me sound like the absolute piece of shit I was.

"Did you want to go in?" he asked, toeing off his shoes and kicking them onto the concrete pool deck.

"In the pool?"

"Sure."

"I don't have a bathing suit," I reminded him.

"Are you wearing underwear?"

Chuckling, I blinked slowly, turning my eyes toward the sky. "Wouldn't you like to know?"

"Honestly, not at all."

"Another time," I told him. "I think if I went in and told you this story, I'd be likely to drown myself."

"I'm sure whatever it is, it isn't that bad," he said, sipping at his drink and staring off toward the tree line on the far edge of his yard.

"When I was in college, I dated this girl. Mandy."

"College when?" Rob asked.

"Bachelor's degree." I cleared my throat, washing away the itchiness with some whiskey. "I was twenty when I graduated."

"Alright. Mandy."

"She was my best friend's older sister."

"How trite," Rob teased.

If only that had been the case.

"The night I graduated, we were supposed to...you know."

"Fuck," he supplied.

"For the first time."

Rob made a knowing sound in the back of his throat and I took another drink of whiskey.

"We were close to it, but she told me Owen, her brother and my friend, was upset about things with me and her. And I think, in hindsight, I'd known that all along. Maybe not at first, but after things had started to get more serious with her, things got weirder between me and him."

I paused, the memories somehow more painful when I gave them voice.

"So, I went to check on him because I didn't want him to be mad. He was…"

"Important," Rob said softly.

The truth of that stuck like a glob of tar in the back of my throat. I nodded, the rest of the night as clear in my mind as if it had just happened.

"Owen had written me a letter earlier that day and he'd come clean. Told me how he was jealous of his sister, how he had feelings for me. And I loved him. Even back then I loved him, but I hadn't thought I loved him like *that*. But I found him in their basement and he was wrecked, like out of his mind with it."

"You don't have to tell me all of this if you don't want to."

"I have to now," I said, and I didn't know why, but it felt true in the moment.

"Let me top you off." Rob took the glass out of my hand and went back inside, filling both of our glasses with more amber liquor. He sat back down in the chair beside me and I took a smaller than fair sip of my drink before continuing.

"Long story short, Owen and I slept together."

Rob choked, whiskey sputtering out all over his shirt and his lap. He sat up straight, coughing, more whiskey sloshing over the edge of the glass and down his hand. I gave him a dubious look, mouth twisted in the corner.

"Not what you were expecting?" I asked.

Rob switched his drink from one hand to the other, shaking the drops of booze off as best he could. "I figured that you were going to say you dumped Mandy and dated Owen, and then it all went wrong when you left for grad school in California."

"I never did either of those things. I slept with Owen and then left both of them without so much as another word. I stopped answering their calls, changed my plans for school, and moved to California without saying goodbye."

"Jesus, Archie."

I shrugged helplessly. "I know."

"And what's brought all this back around to the front of your mind?" he asked.

"Honestly, Rob, there's not a day that goes by that I don't think about Owen in some capacity, but I don't think you could imagine my surprise when I walked upstairs at Rapture tonight and found him with Val's mouth wrapped around his cock."

Rob choked a second time, and I reached over, taking the drink from his hand so he didn't spill the rest of his expensive liquor all over the concrete.

"Archie, come on. Warn a guy."

I took a large swallow of my drink and set it on the small table next to Rob's. "Consider yourself warned, then. Because after that, I followed him into the alley and jacked him off. Made him come for good measure, then ran away from him. Again."

Even in the dark of the back yard, I could see the shock on Rob's face. I didn't know if he thought less of me for the story itself or the actions within the story, but I didn't want to think about it and there was a small and relieved part of me that didn't care. The truth was at least somewhat out in the open now, and there had to be some relief in that for me somewhere.

"You know what? I think I'll take you up on the offer, Rob. Thanks."

I stood up and stripped out of my clothes, the precum stain on my underwear long dry, then I dove headfirst into the pool.

CHAPTER 6
OWEN

THERE WERE FOUR THINGS IN FRONT OF ME.

A leftover plate of hors d'oeuvres from the last venue I visited for Mandy, a bottle of beer, my cell phone, and a crumbled up business card that I'd unfolded and re-crumpled no less than six times since Archer had slid it between my teeth.

"What do you think?" Mandy's voice echoed out from my phone and I glanced at the business card before reaching for the beer.

"They're all good," I told her. "I sent you pics and videos."

"Which has the best food?"

"The hotel I'm staying at has the best food *and* the best view." I picked up the beer, the phone…and the business card, and carried all of it to the patio. Beyond the balcony rail, waves crashed against the sand, a beautiful and loud beat that faded into the background the longer I listened to it.

"Would you want to get married there?"

I scoffed. "I wouldn't want to get married anywhere."

"You say that now," Mandy teased quietly, "but that feeling doesn't last forever. Once you meet the right person."

I didn't want to burst her bubble, but she was wrong. There was no right person for me. There had been once, but…not now. I was so glad Mandy had been able to get over her heartbreak about what Archer had done, but I didn't know if I ever could. The fact that I let him corner me against an alley wall and make me come had no bearing on the way I felt about him.

"Sure, Mandy."

We'd had the same conversation for years and I was tired of it. How my sister hadn't given up on the idea of me finding love and getting married would never cease to amaze me. Then again, it was probably her determination and stubbornness that had gotten her through Archer's abandonment in the first place.

"Will you get me a contract then for the place you like this most?" she asked.

"Are you sure you don't want to come out and see it for yourself? It makes me a little nervous being the deciding factor for you."

"I know you wouldn't let me down, Owen."

I could hear the smile in her voice, and the fresh memories of Archer only served to remind me of just how wrong Mandy was with her assumption.

"Right." I cleared my throat.

"So, what are your plans for the rest of the night? It's early there, isn't it?"

The sun hadn't even set below the horizon and my stomach grumbled for dinner. The business card propped on my knee spoke to a different kind of hunger entirely, though.

"It's early," I confirmed. "I don't know what I'm going to do. There's some leftovers from earlier today I might pick at."

"And you're home tomorrow?"

"Yep." I nodded, even though she couldn't see me. "My flight is pretty early."

"I know. Early for you, not us. I'll pick you up like we planned."

"Alright."

"Don't forget to have them send me a contract," she said.

"Yeah. I won't."

"Love you for this." Mandy blew me a kiss, the sound loud and jarring in my ear.

"Love you too."

I ended the call and dropped the phone into my lap, the business card slid down my knee and landed on top of the screen just as it went dark. My sister's face disappeared from view, leaving Archer's name in glaringly sharp black letters in its place.

Archie.

What a prick.

What had I been thinking? No, what had *he* been thinking. Shoving his hands down my pants and saying those things. He might have been the first to tease rolling orgasms out of me, but up until the night before, he definitely hadn't been the last. I didn't know anything about sex the first time I had it with him, but the way he handled me and the words he used had sparked interests that I'd never even dreamed of before that night.

I wasn't a glutton for punishment, but I was a fan of delayed— and then extended—gratification. Whether it came from someone else's hand or my own, there was a specific kind of pleasure I found in the self-control those kinds of games required. A quick internet search after learning about Rapture the day before had proven the club to be the kind of place where I could probably find what I was after. The man who'd sucked me off before Archer found me didn't drag it out, which I appreciated, even though I'd planned to find someone else for later in the night. He'd taken the edge off, so to speak, so I could climb back on it again later.

After Archer had gotten me off, I left. I took a car straight back to the hotel where I locked myself in the bathroom and took a scalding hot bath, like I could wash the feel of him off of my body, which...I couldn't. Then I'd drank a bottle of wine and watched the goriest movies I could find on pay-per-view. Literally doing anything and everything I could to erase the thought of him again from my mind.

Predictably, I'd failed.

Then I'd spent the whole day at wedding venues for my sister with the very tight grip of Archer's hand burned around my cock. A reminder of what a horrible person—and brother—I was.

Mandy asking my plans for the rest of the night posed a problem because while part of me wanted to go back to Rapture and finish what I'd started the night before, another part of me didn't want to risk it. And there was a third part, smaller, that screamed at me to call Archer.

To what end, I wasn't sure.

Would I let him get me off again? Would we fuck? Would he try to apologize? Would I *let* him? More than all of that, the real question was *could* I do those things?

The answer was yes, whether I liked it or not.

I didn't know if I could live with myself after any of it, but I'd already done it once...

His card had his phone number and his email listed neatly beneath his name, and before I could talk myself out of it, I texted him the name of the hotel and my room number, then I turned off my phone. I left it on the table outside, finished my beer, and went in and ordered myself room service.

The meal came and I ate it.

Still no sign of Archer.

I didn't want to check my phone because whatever was going to happen between us wasn't a negotiation and it wasn't up for debate. He could show up, or not. We could fuck, or not. It wasn't any sweat off my back either way, but as the clock inched on, I found myself growing tense and angry at his absence. A childish reaction, because I didn't know anything about him. He could have had plans, he could have had another girlfriend for all I knew. It wouldn't have been the first time he got tangled up with me while his heart belonged to someone else.

I should have asked, I realized.

I didn't want to be the other man again. I didn't want to be the cause for someone else's heart getting broken the way Mandy's had. The way mine had.

And then there was a knock at the door.

"Fucking idiot," I cursed myself under my breath.

I was still in my clothes from earlier in the day. Tight jeans with a hole in the knee and a black Mayday Parade shirt. I was dressed like a teenager with high hopes and bare feet, a call back to the best and worst night of my life.

Another knock.

It was him.

I knew it was him.

Even through the closed door, I could feel him, hovering, waiting...anticipating.

I flipped the deadbolt latch on the door then pulled it open, breath catching in my throat after seeing him in the light for the first time. I hadn't realized how dark Rapture had been until the smooth curves of Archer's nose and cheeks came into focus. Dark scruff lined his jaw like he hadn't shaved in a couple of days, and his hair sat perfectly gelled and styled on the top of his head. Like he was half put together and half torn apart. He had on the same boots from the night before, with black jeans and a white v-neck t-shirt that looked as soft as the duvet on my bed.

"You texted," he said, like his greeting was an explanation for his presence.

"Stupid of me." I stepped aside and pulled the door wider.

"Do you want me to go?" he asked.

"No."

I let go of the door and headed back toward the patio. If the door closed and locked him out, then so be it. I didn't know if it was luck or not that he caught it, but as I settled into one of the chairs on the balcony, I could feel the heat of him at my back.

"Do you have anything to drink?"

"There's beer in the mini fridge," I told him. "You can get me one too."

I finished off the one I'd been drinking while I talked to Mandy, and quietly accepted the fresh one when Archer sank into the second chair to my left.

"How have you been?"

He asked the question like we were old friends, like it had just been a few weeks since we'd seen each other, not ten years. He asked the question like we were anyone besides who we were.

"Since when, Archer? Since you took my virginity and ghosted me and your girlfriend? Or since last night when you shoved your hand down my pants in an alley behind a BDSM club?"

"Are you finished?"

"Oh, I'm just getting started."

He chuckled like an arrogant piece of shit. I watched the way his throat worked as he swallowed, the way his hands flexed around the bottle, already condensated because the fridge in the hotel room was garbage. He sat in the chair like he owned it, and I bristled, which only earned a deeper laugh out of him.

"Calm down, Owen."

"Fuck you." I shoved the chair back, grunting when it clattered against the glass slider. "I don't even know why I called you."

I stormed back into the hotel room, hands fisted at my sides. Honestly, what had I been thinking? There was a reason for the decade of silence between him and me, and one good hand job wasn't enough to erase the history between us. But much like a man who'd never been told no, Archer followed me inside, closing the slider behind him like we'd agreed to breathe the same air.

"You didn't call," he corrected. "You texted."

"I hate you as much as I did the last time I saw you."

"You didn't hate me at all last night." The corner of his mouth twitched toward a smirk and I wanted to swing at him, put him through the glass, maybe even send him over the balcony entirely. Any of the three would have been satisfying.

"Before that," I reminded him.

"Oh." Archer licked his lips, that sly smirk settling onto his mouth like an expression he'd tailored just for me. "Back when I gave you my virginity?"

"When you *took* mine," I retorted, even though either statement held true.

"You gave it," he said. "If anything, you took *mine*, and we both know that I'm telling the truth here."

"The first and last time you've been honest about anything," I snapped, taking a step toward him out of anger, hands still tight at my sides.

"No."

I turned my back on him, but there was nowhere to go. The room was nice, but it wasn't huge. Besides the balcony, the only places to escape him were the bathroom and the bedroom, neither of which felt like a place where I wanted him to follow.

He closed the space between us, stopping inches away from my back. His body radiated all of the things I simultaneously enjoyed and hated about him. The confidence, the charisma, the attitude. It was all the things that made me fall in love with him when we were in high school, and all the things that made me hate him as an adult.

"I told you then I was sorry," he whispered.

"What exactly were you sorry for?" I was less than a foot away from a framed painting of the Hollywood sign, and I could see myself, and him, in the reflection of the glass. But where my eyes watched him, his were focused on me, the juxtaposition notable and severe.

"Were you sorry for what we did?" I asked, sucking in a breath and watching his reflection, the way his eyes studied the lines of my neck, the way his mouth parted before he spoke.

"I was sorry for hurting your sister, for hurting you." He licked his lips. "I was sorry that I didn't see it all sooner."

"See what?"

When I looked back into the glass, his gaze caught mine and held it.

"That I was in love with you."

I turned quickly, and Archer moved just as fast. He stepped forward and I stepped back, my shoulders hitting the painting and his chest hitting mine. He wedged one leg between my thighs to pin me against the wall but kept his hands at his sides, his eyes on me.

"Don't lie to me," I rasped. "You don't have to lie."

He shook his head, lips wet from his spit and parted just enough so I could see the edges of his teeth.

"I still am," he said it like he was telling me the weather or what time a movie started. Archer said those three words with such confidence and ease, it had me second-guessing why anything in life was hard when being in love could sound so simple.

"Well." My voice was scratchy, the words thick in my throat. "I don't love you. I still fucking hate you."

"That's fine." Archer reached for the button on my jeans, fingers hesitating around the metal. "You don't need to love me to let me fuck you."

"Is that what's happening here?"

He popped the button and dropped his fingers to the zipper, going still. "I don't know, Owen. You tell me."

CHAPTER 7
ARCHIE

OWEN SMELLED LIKE HOPS AND BARLEY, AND A LITTLE BIT LIKE ANGER. When he said he hated me, he meant it, and for some reason that only turned me on more. I had realized, after all, I was a little bit of a masochist and apparently that fetish wasn't limited to physical pain, but emotional as well.

"I'm leaving tomorrow," he said, head dropped against the cheap framed print on the wall behind him. His neck was long and slender, his muscles tight. His hair smelled like rosemary, like hotel shampoo, and his skin like the salt of the ocean mixed with a little sweat. The edges of a tattoo snaked out above his collar, inching toward his neck, and if my hand wasn't glued to his zipper, I would have reached for his shirt to tug it down so I could get a better view.

"Is that supposed to change my mind?" I dragged my nose against the shell of his ear, waiting as patiently for his consent as I could muster. But around Owen, it was always hard to think. If I'd been thinking the night of my graduation, I wouldn't have fucked him and fucked up all of our lives. If I'd been thinking last night, I wouldn't have followed him into the alley, and if I was thinking at all in that moment, I'd have never shown up at his hotel like a dog taking command from its trainer.

That wasn't me.

I didn't *want* that to be me, for Owen or for anyone else.

"I don't think anyone can change your mind about anything." He cleared his throat quietly, rolling his head to bump my face away from his ear. "But what do you want, Archer? Just somewhere to stick your dick?"

"Don't diminish your contributions to my pleasure, Owen. You got me off better than anyone else ever has."

I shouldn't have given him that truth.

After last night, I knew Owen was as much of a sure thing as I was, and there was no reason for us to talk about anything besides consent. No need to drudge up the past to muddy the present.

"You just can't stop, can you?" Owen angled his head toward me, a bleached clump of curls hanging over his forehead.

"Can't stop what?"

My hand was still on his zipper and I thought I'd done a pretty remarkable job of stopping, considering how hard my cock was and how much I wanted to get it inside of him.

"Lying."

I knew there was no trying to convince him that I was anyone besides the man he'd built me up to be in his head. "I'll stop," I promised.

"Use a condom," he said.

I pulled down his zipper the rest of the way. "Always."

"Don't you dare tell me again that you love me."

I pushed his pants down to his knees.

"Alright," I agreed, licking my lower lip with the tip of my tongue.

Owen's stare flickered down toward my mouth and I grinned, waiting for the rest of his rules so I could get him on his back. I didn't even know why it felt as urgent as it did, but getting Owen naked and beneath me felt as necessary as air. I'd gone ten years thinking about him as a specter of my past, like a ghost always out of reach for the rest of my life. The man on the pedestal that no one else would ever compare to, and then here he was. In the present, in the flesh...

In the rock hard, burning hot, and ready-to-come-for-me flesh.

"What else?" I reached down with one hand to open my belt and pop the fly on my jeans. Fingers on my zipper, I waited for Owen's approval to move forward.

I watched the way his jaw worked back and forth while he thought about what to say next, and I couldn't help but wonder how loaded the words on the tip of his tongue had to be. For as much deliberation as he gave before speaking, I worried there was a very real possibility of us both coming in the middle of the room from the tension of the whole encounter.

"The...the way it was before. Then and last night," he whispered.

"You want me to make you work for it, Owen?"

God, I *was* going to come in my pants. Less than a dozen words and Owen had reduced me back to the teenager I used to be.

"Yes."

"Say red if you want me to stop," I told him, hooking my fingers around the waistband of his underwear and pulling him away from the wall. With a quick flip, I gave him a shove toward the bed.

He landed on his back and I grabbed the cuffs of his jeans and pulled them off while he scooted toward the headboard, eyes heavy with want.

"Do you have condoms?" I asked.

He shook his head, like it was a test. Lucky for him, I was a star student.

Reaching into my back pocket, I pulled out my wallet and produced a condom, which earned me half of a smile.

"Lube?" I asked.

He gestured toward the nightstand, a tube right there between the phone and the remote for the TV.

"What a Boy Scout," I murmured, "Now take off your shirt."

"You."

Owen straightened up and reached behind him, rucking up the material before pulling it over his head and tossing it onto the floor. I matched him, tossing my shirt onto the foot of the bed. My pants were undone enough for me to get my cock out, and I crawled up between his legs.

"Red to stop." He repeated my statement from earlier and I confirmed the agreement with a nod. "And no kissing."

"At all?"

"On the mouth."

Owen's lips looked like fucking dessert, but I'd have to entertain myself elsewhere, it seemed.

"Anything else?" I asked.

"This is not the start of a thing, Archer." Owen folded one arm behind his head, half propped and half naked against the white bedding.

He looked like a nightmare that I never wanted to wake up from.

"It's just for right now," I said back to him. "Just for tonight… and last night."

"And ten years ago," he murmured, reaching for my face and stopping himself before his fingers touched my skin. He pulled back quickly as if the proximity to me had burned him, like he'd forgotten who he was and what we'd been.

"You can touch me if you want to."

"I don't," he said quickly, taking the offending hand and tucking it behind his head alongside the other one.

I chuckled and pulled down Owen's tight black briefs, exposing the substantial thickness—and length—of his cock.

"Do you ever top?" I asked softly, tapping my fingertip against his precum-slick slit.

"No."

"That's a shame." I tightened my grip and gave him a slow stroke, the heat of our skin making enough friction for him to wince and throw the bottle of lube at me.

"I don't like when it hurts," he snapped.

"I'm not sure I believe that." I dipped my chin toward my chest and opened the lube, drizzling a small amount into my palm. "I remember the tone of your voice that night."

"Don't start."

"No?" I held up my hand, slippery and cool, then waggled my fingers at him before pressing my fingers down behind his balls.

Owen's asshole was hot and I eased a finger into him, groaning for how tight the hold of his body felt around my knuckle.

"Has anyone ever tried to gag you?" he asked.

"Not successfully."

Twisting my wrist, I pushed another finger into his hole, using my body for leverage to get in deep enough to tag his prostate. His stare locked on me, arousal and anger at war in the depths of his eyes. He was a human hurricane, ready to destroy everything in his wake.

I deserved that.

I grabbed his erection with my other hand and stroked him off, teasing the soft spot inside of him until he looked like he wanted to burn me alive. I was about to remind him this was what he'd wanted, what he'd asked for, when his arm flew out. Owen slapped me against the side of my face, throwing me back.

"What the fuck, asshole?" I wiped my fingers off on the inside of his thigh.

"I was going to come."

"That's the point." I reached up and yanked one of the pillows out from behind his head. I tore the case off and whipped it around on a diagonal and made quick work of using it to tie his wrists together.

He didn't fight and he didn't protest. He just leveled another glare at me like he wanted me dead. He didn't say red; he didn't even tell me to stop.

"You must hate it," I said softly, tearing open the condom wrapper with my teeth.

"What do I hate, Archer?"

If he thought the use of my legal name annoyed me, he was right, but I'd never give him the satisfaction of knowing it.

"That the man you hate the most is the one who makes you come the hardest."

Owen cursed me under his breath, and I lubed my cock and forced my way inside of him. He wasn't ready yet, but he wasn't unprepared, and the look he gave when the thickest part of my shaft stretched him open was enough to almost make *me* come on the spot.

"Touch yourself." I situated myself between his legs, spreading his thighs open to make room for my body. And I liked the control that it gave me, to push his knees out toward the edge of the bed so I could get my cock deeper inside of him.

Grabbing his hands, I spit into his palm and then brought it down, curling his fingers one by one around his dick and showing him how I wanted him to bring himself to the edge. It was hard for him with his wrists tied together, and the eye contact he gave me was top tier. The frustration and hate rolled off him in waves, and that made every little grunt and groan that fell out of his mouth sound even more like heaven.

Owen's body reacted the same way it had before. Little beads of sweat at his temple, the tic in his jaw, and the quickening of his breath.

"Not yet, Owen," I warned, still fucking into him with the same languid swirl of my hips I'd started with.

The mechanics of being with Owen were the same, but I didn't fuck now the way I fucked then, and he definitely didn't take cock the way he used to. Before he was all begging and trembling, and while teasing the outskirts of his orgasm was fun, I wanted more. I wanted all of it, all of him, even though I had no right to any of it.

His lip curled up and his hand slowed down, jaw clenched. I grabbed his thighs and hauled him further down my cock, the heat of him scalding around my length. Even through the condom, his ass was hot and tight, gripping and sucking at me. For as much as his face said *I hate you*, his body told a different story altogether.

"Fuck, your ass is amazing," I rasped, falling forward and

sliding even deeper. The slap of our skin was enough of an aphrodisiac on its own, but the smell of him, the sounds, the feel…

I'd fucked plenty of men in the ten years since I'd given Owen my virginity, but none of them were *him*. None of them made me feel *this*. It was almost a shame he would have hit me with his car given the opportunity, and a good thing for us both that he lived clear across the country.

"Get close again," I said. "When you're on the edge, you clench my cock like a fucking vise grip."

"I hate you." He fisted his cock and jacked himself off again.

The crown of his dick was swollen and red, the skin pulled tight around the flared tip and as angry as he was.

"I know."

I hated me too.

Pulling out, I ripped off the condom and fisted my length, jerking off for less than a minute before spraying cum all over his dick and his hand. His eyes went wide and his mouth fell open, and I pried his fingers loose before he reached his own end.

His hips jerked off the bed, chasing after the friction I'd taken away, precum poured out of his slit like a fountain, and his balls were high and tight against his body. His hole still offered a small gape from where I'd been inside of him and I pushed two of my lube-slick fingers back into his hole.

Intent to put him out of his misery, I took his cock into my other hand and brought him right up to the edge a third time before loosening my grip and pushing harder against his prostate at the same time.

Owen flew off the bed, screaming and cursing, his chest crashing right into mine and taking us both onto the floor. I was still half-dressed, cock out and jeans around my thighs. Owen was naked, covered in my cum and his own sweat, which he smeared all over me as he fought to regain his balance.

He was quick, but I was quicker.

I pushed up and over, shoving him onto the hotel carpet and

digging my knee between his legs so his balls rested on the top of my thigh. He moaned, and he sighed, and he begged.

He *begged* me, "I need to come. Please."

"You're just here for tonight?" I asked, even though I already knew the answer.

"Archer, yes. Please. It hurts. It *hurts.*"

"If tonight is all I get, Owen, then I've got bad news." I circled my finger and thumb around the base of his shaft, admiring the way his erection throbbed and strained for release.

"I need you to make me come," he pleaded, the fight leaving him quicker than my orgasm had just minutes before.

"I will," I promised. "Just...not yet."

CHAPTER 8
OWEN

THERE WAS NO DECISION I'D EVER MADE AROUND ARCHER THAT HAD turned out to be a good one. That was how I found myself covered in sweat, my wrists bound by a pillowcase, on the floor of a hotel room my sister had paid for, with Archer between my legs looking like he wanted to eat me alive.

"You don't need to show off."

I'd meant for the words to come out sounding detached and collected. I'd wanted him to think that even though I was physically affected by him, I wasn't *emotional* about it. But the commentary earned me a treacherously sadistic grin. I barely had time to debate the merits of calling my safeword when Archer folded me in half like a pretzel and buried his face between my cheeks.

I hadn't been far off base with the assertion that he wanted to eat me alive.

Unable to stop the groan that tumbled out of my throat when his tongue speared into my asshole, I flung my arms around his neck, using the restraints to hold him in place. Archer may have been content to play the role of dominant partner, but I was no submissive. Begging and pleading for release didn't give him any power over me, and I hoped he knew that.

I needed him to remember that.

Hell, I needed a reminder too because I'd never been with a

man who ate ass with the focused intensity Archer was currently delivering to my body, and it was only a matter of minutes until the familiar heat had once again begun to pool between my legs.

"You're going to make me come," I warned, using my wrists and the pillowcase to pull him closer to my body.

He made a pleased little humming noise which vibrated up the length of my spine and propelled me closer toward the edge. But he shook his head until I released my hands from around his neck; then he leaned back enough for me to see his face. His eyes were hooded, dark, and the entire lower half of his face shined with spit and lube from how far into my ass he'd been.

Archer rocked back onto his heels and took himself in hand, ready to go again after his orgasm. He didn't need to touch me. The heat and the weight of his stare was enough to feel like a strong hand curled around my achingly hard and cruelly deprived erection. I brought my feet back down to the ground, moving into a less revealing pose.

"Stay longer," Archer whispered.

"What?"

"Stay here longer. Let me get my fill of you." His lashes fluttered, dick shiny with precum.

"My flight is in the morning. I'm leaving tomorrow at five."

Archer looked at his wristwatch and frowned.

"I'm giving you the courtesy of making sure you know that I'm not going to be here when you wake up. We agreed on this. Nothing that matters, just tonight."

"Are you ever going to let me live it down?" He pulled his hand down the length of his cock, letting it slap up against his stomach.

"It doesn't mean anything to me anymore," I lied, and he pulled another condom out of his wallet, expression laced with frustration. "This is the only thing that matters between us now."

Archer grimaced, rolling the condom down his length before returning to his place between my thighs.

"Always like this," he said under his breath, the head of his cock breaching my hole again. The burn and the stretch felt the same, and when the tip of his cock dragged past my prostate, I whimpered, fingers scrabbling at the carpet above my head.

"Like what?"

"It doesn't matter."

Archer bottomed out and went still, throwing his head back in what I assumed was pleasure. I hoped it was pleasure, but I also wanted it to hurt him a little. I'd hurt so much for him, a little denial couldn't have been a bad thing for him to deal with. At least for a little while.

I realized then, in those moments of stillness, Archer was anything but still. His hands around my waist trembled and the vein in his neck pulsed frantically. Was his heart beating that fast? Was he bothered or overcome by the things we were doing together? I didn't want to ask and there were parts of me that didn't want to know. Archer's lower lip quivered, and he rolled his head around, cracking it once before refocusing his attention on my face.

"You still with me?" I whispered.

The corner of his upper lip twitched, and he answered with a rough drag and snap of his hips.

"I wish I could put your cock in a cage," he said. "Tease you so you couldn't get hard, so this thick, gorgeous cock of yours had nowhere to go."

My lashes fluttered and I shifted my arms to my front so I could get a manageable grip on my dick.

"What else?" I asked.

"A thousand things." He shook his head. "It doesn't matter."

"Tell me."

I didn't understand why I said that. I didn't want to know, because every word from Archer's mouth was a lie, a promise of a future that didn't belong to either of us. It wasn't even worth pretending. My mind served me with a flashback I'd never asked for. A memory that I'd buried so deep I was surprised it still existed. A fantasy, the first real one I'd ever had, leaning against

Mandy's bedroom door and listening to him talk to her while he fingered her cunt. The things he said made my cock so hard I could have broken down her door frame with it, and I'd pretended he'd been talking to me.

He knew that now.

The day he graduated college, I'd written him a letter, confessing my feelings for him. It had been cowardly of me to do it in writing instead of face to face, but it had all come to a head for us that night, anyway. When I'd confessed to him my darkest secrets and my truest fantasies.

"You don't want me to tell you," he said, finally setting a pace with his hips that had me thinking I'd be able to get off whether he wanted me to or not. "It doesn't matter. What matters is I'm not done with you yet...with your body."

It sounded like a correction, but...

"Then stop pushing your cock against my prostate," I snapped, frustrated and horny, and very fucking confused about the other feelings circling in my head and in my chest.

"Fine." He pulled out again, shooting a smug glare down at me, and then his fingers were inside me. Easily two fingers, possibly three. And he searched out my prostate like his fingertips were polarized to find it, and within seconds I knew I'd made a mistake.

Archer's fingers inside of me were far more dangerous than his cock, and with one hand inside of me and his other hand loosely circled around my cock, Archer manipulated me toward what felt like the physicality of an orgasm.

"Look at me," he said.

It sounded like a warning, so I searched out his stare.

Earlier where he'd looked lost with arousal was a sharp contrast to the man above me now. I'd never seen a man look like he didn't care about coming, but Archer looked like he'd be content to torture me for the rest of the night and then drop me off at the airport with an unsatisfied cock and throbbing balls.

He said something again under his breath that I couldn't catch, and then cum spurted out of my cock. My body tingled with the tease of an orgasm, and as soon as it had started, it was gone. Archer pulled his hands away from me and grinned down, one eyebrow angled upward as my dick emptied itself like a fountain.

All of the work with none of the reward.

My entire spine arched off the floor and I cried out, thrashing around beneath him like if I could find the right way to move, my body would reward me with the feeling I'd been chasing after, but to no avail.

When my dick finally settled down, Archer dipped his head low and sucked me into his mouth. I cried out again, a pathetic and cracking noise that echoed off the walls of the hotel room. Archer wasn't sucking my cock for either of our pleasure, though. He used his tongue and his mouth to clean me up, make me hard again, and then he let my cock land against my stomach with a wet plop.

"One for you and one for me," he said.

"I'd hardly call those comparable."

"Really?" Archer took me back into his hand and I knew I was going to be quick to regret the statement.

He plucked at the knot on the pillowcase until it unfurled, then he slowly and gingerly took my wrists into his hands. He studied the marks left from the twisted fabric, using his fingertips to knead away at any tension that existed beneath the skin before setting my hands at my sides.

"Get yourself off, then," he said, righting himself onto his knees before standing up. There were two chairs in the corner and he moved like a jaguar toward one, slick and lithe, before turning and settling in the rich velvet upholstery. He looked like a debauched prince, half-dressed and stained with cum, cock on display and hair all mussed. I had no right to look at him the way I was, but it was impossible to look away.

Spitting into my palm, I took my cock into my fist and started to jerk myself toward what I hoped would be a more fulfilling orgasm.

"Touch your balls," Archer said, voice rasping. "Tug on them when you get close, I don't want you to come yet."

"I want to come," I reminded him, cradling my sac in my palm.

"And I want you to last longer." He licked his lips, giving a slow tug up his own length. "You can do that, can't you, Owen? You can wait a little bit longer before you come, can't you?"

Fuck, what was it about this man and that mouth?

I shook my head because I was ready to burst.

"I don't believe you," he murmured, leaning forward and releasing his cock. "I know you can wait a little longer, Owen. I've seen you hold out."

Clenching my jaw, I loosened my grip, hoping it would help me stave off the inevitable for a little longer. I didn't know why I cared or why I bothered. Archer wasn't the boss of me, and I didn't need his permission to come.

But I wanted it just the same.

"Arch—" I couldn't even manage his name, and he hummed, sounding pleased. My dick pulsed like it had done something good when in fact all it had ever done was get me into trouble.

"Not yet." Archer got up from the chair and came back to the floor where I was still sprawled. He laid his body on top of mine, the heat welcome and heavy. I tipped my head back, unable to look him in the eye.

"Please."

It was going to happen, one way or the other, and still I asked for approval of the man who'd broken my heart worse than anyone I'd ever known.

"Almost, Owen." His mouth brushed against my neck, my jaw, my ear. "Not yet, Owen. Can you give me another minute?"

"I don't..."

"One," he whispered, kissing my ear lobe. "Two, three, four..."

Every second he counted off was timed with a stroke up my cock and it was agony, fucking agony. Like pins and needles and velvet and sandpaper all at once, all over me. My spine, my shaft, my fucking heart.

"You're doing so good," Archer whispered. He praised me like his approval mattered. "Fucking hell, Owen, you should see yourself."

"Keep counting," I grit out, the pressure between my legs becoming unbearable.

"Fifty-two, fifty-three, fifty-four." Archer bit my neck, behind my ear and mumbled out the remaining seconds between us. "Sixty."

I came.

With the unspoken permission and the silent command. My body seized and convulsed, and Archer wrapped his arms around me as I flew off the ground. Into the fetal position and into his lap, I shouted, every spasm and sound coming from my body absolutely out of my control.

"Perfect," he murmured, stroking my hair back from my face and kissing sweat from my forehead. "You're such a good listener, Owen. Such a good listener."

Compliment after compliment washed over me, some of them making sense and others feeling undeserved. I was dizzy and mindless, and Archer was careful to bring me to my feet. He stood against me until I had some balance, then he walked me to the bathroom where he set me down on the toilet.

Silently, mind half-blank, I watched him turn on the shower and test the water temperature with his fingertips. Then he helped me under the spray and took a step back toward the door.

"Are you good?" he asked, folding his arms over his chest. His hard cock was still out, glistening under the fluorescent lights.

"Yeah." I was fine, but I was embarrassed. Absolutely taken out by one and a half orgasms felt childish and immature.

"I meant everything I said. You were...that was really good, Owen."

I noticed that he didn't clarify that he'd wanted me to stay, which was good. Because I wasn't going to. No matter how much he asked or begged, which had been nowhere near enough for me to even entertain the idea in the first place.

I cleared my throat and slicked my wet hair off my face, turning to face him.

"I'll go get you some water," he said.

"I'm in the shower, Archer. I'm fine."

"To drink." He let himself out of the bathroom and when he came back, he'd zipped up his pants. Archer passed me one of the small water bottles from the mini fridge and I emptied it in two swallows. I hated he was right, that I'd needed the drink.

"Are you going to stand there and watch?" I asked, maybe a little harsher than was fair, but that was the way of things between us. Our decision-making was once more clouded with sex and then when everything was said and done, when the lights were on, that was when the regret set in.

Archer regarded me carefully, even as the steam of the shower started to fog up the glass and obscure him from my view.

"I'll leave you to it," he said, again slipping out of the bathroom.

The door closed behind him with a soft snick and I busied myself with everything that I was meant to do in a post-sex shower.

And, as expected, when I was finished, Archer was gone.

CHAPTER 9
ARCHIE

Sitting in my car in front of Flynn's house was not how I'd intended to watch the sunrise Sunday morning, but going home seemed like an even worse idea than staying out.

After making Owen shaky with want and then depositing him into the shower, I'd let myself out of the hotel and then driven in a circle of the city, all the while cursing myself and my unbearably impulsive life choices.

Driving up PCH, I reminded myself I was lucky. That I could count the regrettable decisions of my life on one hand. I didn't think many people could say that, but I read them off to myself, out loud, for good measure just the same.

One, sleeping with Owen the night I graduated.

Two, jerking Owen off in an alley behind a BDSM club ten years after that.

Three, going to Owen's hotel and doing it again less than twenty-four hours later.

Yeah, that was pretty much the entirety of my bad decisions.

Sure, I could argue that ghosting him and Mandy after point one was also something that should warrant regret, but they were basically the same thing and three mistakes felt more manageable than four. Three felt like I wasn't a huge fuck-up, even though the sleepless nights I'd experienced in my twenties when I'd been missing my best friend, while also fantasizing far too many times about coming inside of him, often led me to believe otherwise about myself.

The moral of the story was that when it came to Owen Murray, I had no self-control, something I normally prided myself on maintaining. I'd learned my lesson after him, though. I'd come up with rules and expectations, not just for myself but for the people I took to bed. And with the exception of the past weekend, I'd never had an issue sticking to them. Maybe it was better for us both that Owen was going back home the next day.

Or today, as it seemed.

Because if I couldn't trust myself to act in accordance with my own moral and sexual compass, I'd just get us into more trouble.

Again.

A knock on my passenger window startled me, and I jumped, the seatbelt locking around my chest and bolting me to the warm leather seat of my Audi. After I caught my breath, I looked up and found Flynn bent down, two cups of coffee in his hand and reading glasses perched thoughtfully on his nose.

I reached over the center console and pulled the handle to open the door. Flynn climbed into the passenger seat with a groan, then passed me one of the steaming mugs.

"What are you doing here?" he asked, yawning and stretching his legs out as far as the footwell allowed.

"What are *you* doing here?" I countered.

The whole car smelled like coffee already, hopefully enough to mask the smell of salt and sex that no doubt oozed out of my pores.

"I live here." Flynn thumped his head against the headrest and, without looking, sipped at his coffee.

"I meant why did you come out and bring me coffee?" I asked.

"You're welcome, by the way."

I took a careful sip, the hot and bitter brew a welcome taste in my mouth. "Thank you for the coffee," I said.

"Does this have to do with the canned cheese?"

I sighed, grinding my molars together. "Can you just ask Rob about it? I've already told him the gist of it."

"Absolutely not. I've known you longer than him and we're far too old for games of telephone."

Flynn had a fair point, but the thought of having to tell the story about me and Owen three more times sounded about as appealing as nails on a chalkboard.

"Believe it or not, the canned cheese doesn't have anything to do with my visit." I scrubbed a hand down my face, frowning when my stare landed on a dried cum spot on the front of my pants. "I ran into an ex of mine this weekend."

"I didn't think you even had an ex." Flynn made a perplexed sound in the back of this throat that almost sounded like amusement. "I've never seen you date anyone more than twice."

"He's from back home," I said. "Before I came out here for grad school."

"High school sweethearts?" Flynn gave me a teasing smile, like he'd found out some great secret that no one else knew.

"We were friends," I corrected. "I used to date his sister."

Flynn narrowed his eyes, and his jaw worked from side to side while he tried to piece together the information I'd just given him. "You dated siblings?"

I shook my head. "I dated Mandy. I...slept with Owen."

Flynn let loose a low whistle. "You didn't strike me as the type."

"Exactly." I took another swallow of coffee. "I'm not."

"So, what happened then?"

"I ran into him at Rapture, of all places. I gave him my phone number, which was stupid, but he's always just..." I gestured weakly toward the side of my head.

"Redirected your blood flow elsewhere?" Flynn offered.

"Something like that." I scratched the corner of my eye until I accidentally stabbed myself with the sharp edge of my fingernail. "Anyway, I let my cock get the better of me again, but Owen's about to be on a plane back home, so it's over and done."

"Again."

I grunted in agreement, ignoring the implication that we'd already *had* an again.

"I just wonder sometimes…" I stopped myself from finishing the thought, because no good ever came from daydreaming over could-have-beens. Instead, I finished my coffee and then poked Flynn in the bicep with the empty mug. "If you'll let me come inside for a second cup."

He rolled his eyes at me and grabbed the empty mug. "You could have come in to begin with."

"I didn't want to wake you up."

Flynn shouldered open the passenger door and I climbed out of the driver's side, following him up the smooth concrete walk to his front door. He had a nice place on the outskirts of Westwood, all smooth and shiny, with giant paned windows that stretched from floor to ceiling in most of the rooms. The house was dark, save for a small chandelier that hung in the foyer, barely illuminating the entry area. I knew Flynn's house like the back of my hand, though, and I followed him through to the monstrosity of a kitchen at the far end of the house.

Admittedly, it was one of my favorite rooms, sleek and pristine like the rest of the place, with a breakfast nook designed for relaxing with a massive window that overlooked a surprisingly lush and decadent back yard. The greenery just beyond the glass offered a much needed pop of color to the rest of the design, and I was happy to collapse into one of the chairs while Flynn busied himself pouring us fresh coffees.

Flynn made his way toward the table and set both mugs down before dropping his ass onto the cushion with a sigh. He had a hummingbird feeder hanging from the gutter outside and I watched how rapid-fire a hummingbird flapped its wings while coming to take a drink of the bright red sugar water.

The bird was like me with Owen, I realized.

Always coming back for a taste.

"Tell me about this guy," Flynn finally said, after it must have become clear I wasn't going to break the silence.

"What about him?"

He shrugged. "I don't know, Archie. What's important to know? What do you want to tell me?"

"I don't want to tell you anything," I said quietly. The hummingbird was gone. "I don't want to talk about him at all."

"If you hadn't parked your car in front of my house for over an hour, I'd believe that."

I laughed, arching a brow at him. "How do you know how long I was out there for?"

"Cameras." He patted the pocket of his navy blue sleep pants. "Phone alerts. You know."

"I didn't mean to wake you up," I said. "That's why I sat outside instead of knocking."

"Well, you're here now and we're both awake. So, say what you need to say."

"I used to love him." I forced the truth out before I could swallow it down. It wasn't like I felt better about saying it, but Owen deserved my honesty, even if he wasn't around to hear it. "I didn't realize it at the time, but I did. And after we…you know—"

"Fucked."

"I'd hardly call it fucking," I murmured, chasing that confession down with a mouthful of coffee. "But what's done is done, and he and I are done."

"Don't lie."

"Back then, the last thing he said to me, after I…after we gave up our virginities or whatever you want to call it, the last thing he told me was that he hated me."

"What was the last thing he said this time?" Flynn prompted.

"He asked me if I wanted to watch him shower."

I covered my face with my hands and flung my head back, letting out a frustrated, tired, and somehow still horny shout. Beside me, Flynn just laughed and stared out the window at his yard while I struggled to muffle myself and regain my composure.

"And?"

"He didn't mean it in a nice way. He was being short and snappy. As mad at himself about what we'd done as I was, I think."

Replaying the encounter with Owen back in my head, it was easy to see where things had gone right and things had gone wrong. The teasing, the edging, the denial—it was the physical manifestation of what the relationship between us had always been. And just like before, I told him no when it suited me to tell him no. When it pleased me to tell him no. But it pleased him too. He loved it just as he had our very first time.

He said that he'd listened to the way I talked to Mandy, and I didn't think there was any real way to tell if how I clearly got off on denial was what spurned his attraction to the kink or if he'd liked it from the start. That thought left an unwelcome idea in my head, a dream of a life that could have been so different for the two of us. A future that would have seen us together instead of apart.

But that was a pipe dream.

Because there was no world where I could have broken up with Mandy and then moved on to Owen without there being the same number of casualties. No matter how you sliced it, all three of us would have been ruined. At least the way things had gone, I'd given them something to push them out of the heartbreak.

I'd given them anger which, in hindsight, felt like a gift.

Anger was more manageable than sadness, than guilt, even regret.

"Why are you mad about it?" Flynn asked.

I bit the tip of my tongue while I thought about an answer.

"Because it's safer to be mad," I said, the truth of that feeling like a bulletproof vest I could wear. "Because it shouldn't have happened, but it's hard to think right around him."

"Are you mad that he's gone?"

"I'm used to him being gone. I'm mad that he left."

I closed my eyes and pressed my fingertips against my eyelids, groaning at how childish and stupid I felt. I sounded like a lovesick teenager, like someone whose world had gotten thrown into a blender after getting his dick wet for the first time.

"But you knew he was going."

"I asked him not to go." I raised my voice even though I didn't mean to. With a loud exhale, I brought myself back to normal as much as I could manage. "I asked him not to go and he left."

Flynn eyed me over the rim of his coffee mug, eyes a little too bright for how early it was and how early I'd woken him. "Well, did you give him a reason to stay?"

CHAPTER 10
OWEN

IN THE THREE DAYS SINCE I'D GOTTEN HOME, ARCHER HAD CALLED ME on all three of them. I hadn't spoken to him once, making a point of sending his calls to voicemail before they even reached the third ring. But in the four days since I'd gotten home, I'd also jerked off thinking about him *way* more than four times. The number was beyond anything I'd ever imagined possible at twenty-eight years old, but every time I took my dick into my fist, I swore it was going to be the last.

Not the last ever.

Just the last for *him*.

Not that it was even for him.

Just...

I needed it to be enough.

"Do you think gold or silver is better?" Mandy asked, reminding me of exactly how badly it had to be enough. I was in the middle of helping her mood board her wedding, my mind fresh with another replay of Archer's fingers up my asshole.

"For what?" I tried to blink her board into focus, but there were so many pictures and magazine clippings on it, I had no idea what part of it she'd been talking about.

"Silverware, Owen."

"I figured the hotel would handle that?" I gave my sister an awkward shrug and fished my phone out of my pocket. "Sorry, gotta take this."

My phone wasn't ringing, thankfully, but I needed to get out of the house and clear my head.

Once outside, I hopped off Mandy's porch and headed toward the field at the back of our neighborhood. My sister and her fiancé lived in the house Mandy and I had grown up in as kids. Our parents had long ago downsized to an apartment on the edge of town, and that suited them fine. Less money on living, they'd said, more money to enjoy being old. I didn't think either of them was old, but early retirement served them well. They only agreed to let her move in if I signed off, and I had no interest in depriving my sister of anything more than I already had.

Though, it was hard to say whether or not missing out on a life with Archer by her side would have been a loss or not.

It was clear he'd done well for himself, staying in L.A. after college and making more money than I'd ever seen in my life. I didn't know anything about him really, and I couldn't back that up, but his clothes felt nice against my skin and he smelled expensive.

He smelled like everything I'd ever wanted.

But... no.

The field wasn't a great place to go because Archer and I had spent more nights out there than I could count. Back when he was Archie to me, back before things had turned into whatever they'd become. I wondered sometimes, if I'd not written him the letter, if I'd not been so sullen. Would it have ever happened between us? Would he have ever realized I had feelings for him? Or would he have married my sister and tortured me in a completely different way?

I headed the rest of the way through the field and past the tree line. Not terribly far into the woods, but enough to be hidden from view. That was where the fort Archer and I had built still stood to this day. It was worse for wear, the boards weather-stripped and splintered, nails long since rusted. But, the summer before, I'd hauled a lawn chair out into the structure so I didn't have to worry about getting scratched or hurt.

Or worse, spiders.

Throwing myself into the chair, I stretched my legs out and let my head fall back. There were gaps between the beams on the roof now, shrunken from the years of abuse they'd taken from the weather, and the sun peeked through, casting long shadows over my feet and the floor.

It was impossible to be there without thinking about Archer, especially how fresh the memories of him were in my brain and on my skin. I rolled my cell phone around in my hand, knowing the right thing to do was probably the last thing I would.

Archer answered on the fourth ring.

"Owen?" he asked my name like it would be anyone else calling him from my number. Like anyone was as foolish as I was.

"Yeah."

"Hi."

I could picture him shoving his hair out of his face the way he used to do when we were kids and he was nervous. He wasn't nervous that night in the basement and he wasn't nervous at the hotel. Or rather, if he was, he'd leaned into different tells. The only time his hair had shown even a strand out of place was after he'd gotten off. And I hated how good disheveled looked on him.

I'd never tell him that.

"What's up?" he asked, when I didn't say anything back in response to his greeting.

"I don't know, Archer. You're the one who's been calling me."

A butterfly floated in through one of the cracks in the roof, clearly on accident. He flittered around the four walls, not able to find a way back out, and if butterfly wings could feel exasperated, I'm sure his did. His pace across the fort turned frenzied, and I knew how he was feeling. Safe and trapped and exhilarated all at the same time. With a sigh, I stood and used the cup of my hand to urge him toward the door so he could escape.

"I don't like when you call me Archer," he said.

"It's your name," I reminded him.

"You used to call me Archie."

It almost sounded like longing in his voice, but as soon as I'd registered it, it was gone.

"You used to be Archie," I whispered.

"Am I not now?"

"Not to me," I said softly. "Not for a long time."

For years it had been Archie and Owen, Owen and Archie, and then he'd become Archer and me? I was still Owen, just without him.

"Besides." I cleared my throat and settled back into my seat. "Everyone calls you that now. It's not special."

"It was," he countered. "It would be."

"Don't do this," I warned. "That's not why I called."

"Why *did* you call, Owen?"

I didn't have an answer and he knew it.

"To tell you to stop calling me," I lied.

"Are you sure?"

"I'd like to be."

That earned me half of a laugh, which had me closing my eyes and scrubbing a hand down my face in shame. The sensation coursed through my body like some kind of tangled and electrified web that paralyzed me with every inch it crept up my spine. Rooting me in place, forcing me to sit with the way Archer made me feel, the things I wanted from him.

Hell, from anyone.

"If you tell me to stop calling, I will," he said. "If you tell me to get on a plane and come home, I will."

"Your home isn't here."

He answered that with silence.

I sighed, letting all the breath out of my lungs until it felt like my shoulders were going to sink through the chair. "Don't say anything else to me that you don't mean, Archer."

"I've never lied to you."

"Are you sure?" I threw his earlier question back at him, and he chuckled again, a low laugh that almost sounded like an exhalation. "You don't really want the answer to that question."

I did want the answer, but I knew a deflection when I heard one. Whatever Archer thought his truth to be, it was his and he wasn't going to share it. At least, not with me and not on this phone call. Talking to him was agony because my brain battled between wanting to tell him all the horrible things I thought about him while also aching for all the devilish things my body wanted him to do to me.

"What do you want, Archer?"

"I don't think I have a good answer for that," he said after a pause. "But I was serious. I'd get on a plane, Owen."

"You can't come here." I had to be quick to cut that idea off before it turned into something tangible. "Mandy is here and she's getting married soon, and I won't let you ruin her life again."

"How is your sister?"

"Clearly she's fine," I snapped. "She's getting married."

"I know."

"She's fine, Archer." I let my tone soften, because while he deserved my vitriol, he didn't deserve it from me about her. Their past was between them and ours was between us, and even though parts of those lines intersected, they weren't the same. I had to remind myself of that sometimes, because if I focused too much on my sister's heartbreak, it would eclipse my own. My feelings for Archer and what we shared, what he'd done, what he'd caused, were plenty enough for me without hers on top of it.

"I'm glad," he said. "The guy...he..."

"He's good to her."

"Do I know him?" he asked.

"Does it matter?" My neck ached for how tense I was, and I had to will myself to relax against the support of the chair.

"No," Archer said quietly.

"You don't know him," I said, but I didn't want to talk about my sister with him anymore. "What do you do for work now?"

"Do you really care?"

"I fucking asked you, didn't I?"

Archer huffed a breath into the phone. "I'm in corporate real estate."

"I wouldn't have pictured you doing that."

Archer was smart; he always had been. Ahead of his class for so many years that he'd ended up fresh out of college before I'd barely even started. Leaps and bounds ahead of the rest of us, his intellect could run circles around every teacher at our school and they all knew it. He'd never been a problem child, but he was easily bored, attention span fickle.

Except when it came to me.

"Well, my degrees are in marketing and finance. Real estate was a fluke that's paid the bills and then some," he explained.

"Are you rich?"

He laughed again, like the question was part of an inside joke I didn't know about. "Yeah, Owen. You could say that."

"Well, if you want to see me again then you can afford to put me on a plane, right?" As soon as the question left my mouth, I regretted it. Even as my dick pulsed at the promise of Archer's mouth or hand, I knew I shouldn't have let the words out. "That was a dumb question. Never—"

Archer cut me off, "I could put you on a goddamn private jet if you said the words."

"That's ridiculous."

"With the exception of last weekend, Owen, it's been a very long time since you and I have seen each other. You don't know anything about me besides what you remember, and the man I am now scarcely resembles the boy I was back then." Archer's tone dipped down a register, the tease and threat of promise ripe with every word. "I have more money than I'll ever know what to do with and if you won't let me get on a plane and come meet you face to face, then don't for one second think that I won't do the opposite and bring you here to me."

"You won't bring me anywhere, Archer. I'm not a thing for you to shuttle across the country when you want to get off."

"What's ridiculous is you thinking that I need to bring you here in order to get either of us off," he countered. "I can get you off over the phone if I wanted."

"You're such an arrogant piece of shit."

I flipped the phone onto speaker and set it on the floor between my feet. My hands were sweaty and shaking, the adrenaline from the conversation nearly unbearable. Between my legs, my cock pushed a little too forcefully at the fly of my jeans and I had half a mind to rip it off myself for being such a traitor.

But this is what I'd wanted, wasn't it?

This is what I knew would happen if I called him back.

Archer didn't want to stay in touch to talk about paychecks and the weather, and if life had proved anything, it was that he sure as shit didn't care about Mandy. There was no love lost between us. The days of our friendship were far in the past. The only thing between Archer and me was chemistry.

Scorching and all-consuming chemistry.

"You're right." Archer's voice was softer then, like he'd realized we were both getting too riled up at the direction of the conversation. "I am arrogant, but I would send a plane for you, Owen, and I could get you off over the phone."

I barked out a laugh that reverberated off the ancient wood beams that he and I had spent that one summer constructing. My laugh turned into our laugh, a daydream of what life with him used to be like before we crashed together in my basement and ruined it all.

"Tell me that you'll come," he whispered.

"I'm not having phone sex with you," I said, the fight long gone.

"You know that's not what I meant."

I swallowed, shaking my head even though he couldn't see me.

"Goodbye, Archer."

I leaned over and scooped my phone off the floor, poking the disconnect button before setting the device down on my lap. My heart was so loud I could hear it in my ears and my fingers drummed a staccato beat against my thigh, even though I wasn't trying to move. My breathing hadn't even returned to normal when my phone pinged with a text message.

I knew without looking what it was, but I checked the screen just the same to confirm.

The text from Archer was short and to the point, and attached to it was an itinerary with a flight that left Brixton tomorrow afternoon, non-stop to Los Angeles.

CHAPTER 11
ARCHIE

JUST BECAUSE I COULD CHARTER A JET DIDN'T MEAN THAT I OFTEN chartered jets. And I realized, buckled into an oversized and dangerously comfortable leather seat, that the offer to Owen might have come off sounding a little ostentatious. Maybe it had been, but I wanted him to know I was serious about the invitation, that the things I said to him when we were together were honest and true.

My past with Owen wasn't a good one, but having him back in my present narrowed everything down to a new perspective. Like our lives were a snow globe that his arrival in California had shaken up, and only then, thirty-seven thousand feet above the ground, had the flakes began to settle and fall.

"I'm still in love with him," I'd finally admitted to Flynn, who pursed his lips and swallowed thickly, looking at me like I'd sprouted another head or five.

The confession felt like the truest words that had ever left my mouth, and I'd said *a lot* of things in my life that I'd meant in the moment. I'd told men they were the best fuck I'd ever had, and maybe when I was balls deep inside of them my brain had tricked me into thinking that, but I knew now it hadn't been true.

Time had dulled the memory of how good it felt to bury myself in the tight heat of Owen's body, and I was thankful for that. If my body and heart had remembered for even a millisecond how perfect and good and whole it had felt to be with him, I would've had to join the clergy because there'd have been no point in fucking anyone else for the whole of time if he wouldn't have me.

Fortunately for me, the other thing time had done was show me the importance of being goal-oriented and focused. That was how I'd made my money, how I'd met my friends, and that was also how I was going to convince Owen to give me a second chance.

I hadn't told Owen I was coming, just that I would send a plane for him, and I wasn't sure how my presence would be received, but if he was coming to California to see me, to *be* with me, even if temporarily, then it really couldn't be a bad thing. At least, that's what I hoped as the plane made a smooth landing on the runway and taxied over to the private hangar.

After the engines were powered off, I unbuckled and waited for the steward to open the door. Fresh air was always welcome, even if it was the humid East Coast air I'd fled from a decade before. The hangar was air conditioned, and I was getting ready to take a lap and check my messages when the messy tuft of Owen's bleached hair caught my eye.

Tucked against the far wall of the hangar sat a cluster of black leather couches, and he sat on the edge of one, alone and nervous. His shoulders hunched, his lips were pulled into a tight line that looked like it wanted to be a frown even if it wasn't sure how to make it the rest of the way down. But when my shoes hit the polished concrete floor and echoed around the empty space, his head snapped up and his posture and expression completely changed.

He didn't want me to know he was uncomfortable, and that was fair because I wasn't ready to show my hand either. I wanted Owen to think I had things under control, that I wasn't drowning in my feelings for him after all this time. That would have been very uncool and not-put-together of me.

I watched him slowly, coolly, try to give off the air that *he* was put together. He stood, shoulders and back straight, even with a bag slung over one shoulder. He shoved his hair out of his face, even though the blond curls fell right back toward his eye. The roots were a few inches long, dark like mine.

Dark like I remembered.

"You didn't need to come and collect me," Owen said in lieu of a hello. "I would have come on my own."

"I prefer you coming *with* me," I said under my breath.

He rolled his eyes and brushed past me, up the steps and onto the plane. I heard him mutter a curse and drop his bag on one of the seats.

I turned on my heel and climbed the stairs, the plane feeling noticeably smaller with both of us on board.

Owen looked around, counting the seats and the couches and the wood-grained surfaces with a pinched expression.

"If you can afford this, you have too much money," he said.

"I don't own it, Owen."

"You *rent* it?"

I plucked the button of my blazer open before easing back down into one of the seats and stretching out my legs.

"I reserve it when I need it," I said.

"And you needed it?" Owen practically threw himself into the seat across from me, his sneakers rubbing against the edges of my oxfords while he settled.

"Do you really want me to answer that?"

I would have told him the truth. I didn't need the plane, but I needed him. But he didn't ask. He just studied me with that steely gaze he'd adopted since he saw me in the hangar.

"When do we take off?" he asked.

I checked my watch. "We have twenty minutes."

He was up faster than I could blink, halfway down the stairs before I even got my ass out of my seat. My first instinct was to chase after him and drag him back, but he'd left his bag so I knew he wasn't going far or for long. Instead, I pulled my phone out of my pocket and set to checking my messages like I'd planned to do before I set my eyes on him again. A flurry had come through as soon as we'd landed, and I wasn't sure who was so concerned about me, but a quick look confirmed it was less worry and more entertainment.

Flynn: This calls for a group text.

Flynn added you to the group.
Flynn added Rob to the group.
Flynn added Dalton to the group.
Flynn added Perceval to the group.

Barclay: Am I really in your phone as Perceval? You're the hugest piece of shit, Flynn.
Flynn: It's your name, isn't it?
Barclay: What's the point of this conversation?
Me: fwiw you're still Barclay in mine.

Rob renamed the group Trophy Doms Social Club

Rob: Archie is on a plane right now, flying after his man.
Barclay: His what?
Dalton: You know if you took your cock out of Val's mouth for two seconds, you'd know what was going on.
Flynn: Archie's high school <3 LOVER <3 is back on the scene.
Rob: And Archie went back home to collect him.

I licked my lips and squinted, pinching the bridge of my nose until some of the pressure abated.

Me: I landed, for anyone who cared about the flight.
Rob: It's a Challenger 300, your flight was fine.
Me: Last time I use your secretary to book anything
Rob: Good.
Flynn: How's your man????

Me: He's not my man.
Flynn: Yet.
Barclay: Can I leave this chat?
Dalton: No
Rob: No
Flynn: ABSOLUTELY NOT
Me: If I'm stuck here, you're stuck here.
Rob: Was he happy to see you?
Me: That wasn't the word I would use, but he didn't hit me in the mouth.
Dalton: A win is a win.
Me: We're wheels up in 20.
Rob: I want to meet him.
Me: Absolutely not.
Flynn: You'll be home in time for Thursday drinks.
Me: NO

The plane shook as Owen returned, climbing the stairs like each of his legs weighed a thousand pounds. The phone kept vibrating in my hand, so I flipped it to airplane mode so it would be easier to ignore.

"Do you feel better about things?" I asked.

He looked defeated as he shrugged.

"I don't want to force you into this," I said.

Owen stood beside me, smelling a bit like lemons and leather, looking every inch the man who wanted to crawl out of his skin and evaporate into thin air.

"I want you to come back to L.A. because I want to spend time with you, and I want to spend time with you naked and in bed."

"Just in bed?" He cut me off with a weak laugh.

"Anywhere you'll let me have you," I admitted, the confession schooling his features. Owen shifted his weight from one foot to the other, hands fisted at his sides. "But make no mistake, I don't want any of that if you don't want it too."

"I don't even like you."

"You don't even *know* me," I corrected, standing up to meet him face to face.

I was taller than him, I always had been, and while my intent wasn't to overshadow him or make him feel small, I needed him to know there were still things in my life that I controlled and I would be happy for him to be one of them.

"Basically you're saying you're flying me out to California to sleep with you," he muttered. "Like a prostitute."

I rolled my eyes at the comparison.

"And maybe between that," I corrected, "we can get to know each other again."

"That's the plot of *Pretty Woman.*"

"I'm no knight in shining armor, Owen. I can't erase the past between us, and I can't erase how much I haven't been able to stop thinking about you either." I briefly gnawed on the inside of my cheek to filter myself from pouring out the whole truth. "I'm just trying to be honest about who I am and what I want."

"You want to fuck."

"You."

He chuffed out a laugh as the steward popped his head out from the back of the plane. "If you gentlemen want to buckle in, we have clearance to taxi out."

"Right." I nodded at the steward, giving him a professional and cordial smile. "Thank you."

I turned to Owen and dipped my chin toward my chest. He leaned in closer to listen and it took every ounce of strength in my body to not lick him from his jaw to his temple.

"So, you either want that or you don't," I whispered. "I'm not promising you anything more."

Even though I wanted to.

Even though it was all on the tip of my tongue.

Owen scoffed and straightened up. "You never have."

He studied me with such a focused intensity that it very nearly took my breath away. The attention from his stare had me wanting to look away because I knew he didn't see me for who I was, but only who he remembered. A twenty year-old who didn't know up from down and wouldn't have known love if it punched him in the face—which Owen very well should have done. His first new impressions had been of a prick who backed him against a wall in an alley and made him come, then showed up at his hotel room and did it all over again, that time with a side of rug burn. Now, I'd chartered a private plane to go get him and bring him back to me like he was a thing to be bartered or sold.

"Let's sit down," I said, forcing my knees to bend and lowering myself back into the seat.

"This is ridiculous," he mumbled, doing the same.

"I hope you can survive it."

The steward made an appearance, closing the door and locking us in, then bringing us each a crystal tumbler of whiskey for take-off.

Owen gave me an annoyed look, but I could tell it was all bark and no bite. He could pretend to be as put-off as he wanted by the whole thing, but there was no one who didn't like flying on a private plane. There was no one who didn't enjoy—at least some-times—being treated maybe a little better than they thought they deserved.

He could bluster and bristle and try to convince me he disap-proved of me and my show of wealth, but I knew better because I watched the way his hands spread across and stroked the leather seat as he got ready to go. The way his tanned skin and tattoos clashed with the supple white color of the leather. The way his jeans were a little dirty around the knees and the way his belt looked like it was the same one he'd worn for our entire lives, all worn down and soft, and *loved*.

Like him.

Even if he didn't know it.

CHAPTER 12
OWEN

ARCHER LOOKED AT ME LIKE HE WAS IN LOVE WITH ME. AND I KNEW the look because it wasn't a new one. He'd worn it that night in my basement when we were together for the first time. He tried to hide it, just like he had back then, but I could see the softness in the lines around his eyes when he didn't think I was looking. All of that washed away once the plane reached cruising altitude. He unclasped his seatbelt and stood, bringing his belt to my eye level. There was a noticeable bulge behind his zipper, the material of his slacks looking soft as silk.

"How long can you stay in L.A. for?" he asked, striding toward the couches tucked closer to the rear of the plane.

I unlatched my seatbelt and stretched my legs into the aisle, watching him go. "Not long."

The travel itinerary he'd sent didn't have a return date, but it hadn't worried me. I knew Archer wouldn't kidnap me or keep me against my will. If I said the word, he would send me back home, even if he did so reluctantly.

The real problem with the trip wasn't how long I had off work, though. It was how long I could be gone without Mandy and Frankie getting suspicious about my absence. I'd told a little bit of a lie, that I hadn't been feeling well, that I must have caught a cold on the plane. They'd both offered to come and take care of me, but

I'd pushed them off under the guise of not wanting them to get sick. I figured I had at least two days, maybe three, before one of them came knocking with chicken soup and nose spray.

"What's your definition of not long?" Archer sat down on one of the couches, right in the middle, legs spread like he owned the place, even though he swore he didn't.

"Monday."

Archer worked his jaw, the tension clearly telegraphing that Monday wasn't enough time for him, but also understanding he couldn't ask for more.

At thirty-seven thousand feet in the air, barreling back toward Los Angeles, I had no idea what I'd been thinking by saying yes to his ridiculous proposal to come in the first place. There were enough people back home for me to fuck if that's what I needed. There was absolutely no reason for me to come at Archer's beck and call. It shouldn't have mattered that I hadn't found another man who fucked the way he did or who made me feel the way he did. Sex was sex and orgasms were orgasms, and my fist was as good as his.

"On or before?"

I sucked my tongue across the front of my teeth before taking a swallow of whiskey. "On."

"Four days, then?"

I nodded.

Archer's mouth split in a wide grin, halfing his age and offering me a stark reminder of the history—and the years—between us. He finished the whiskey in his glass, set it aside, and then crooked a finger, beckoning me closer.

I wanted to fight him, wanted to resist, but what was the point?

We both knew, we'd both *agreed* about the whole reason I was on this plane with him. He said he wanted me to get to know him again, but I didn't care if his favorite color was still green or if he still hated canned cheese. The only thing I needed to care about was the way he grabbed my cock and dangled me over the edge of sanity with it, pushing us both to the very boundaries of pleasure.

Exhaling loudly, because if I could express my feigned unhappiness, at least he would know he didn't have a chance with me beyond something physical, I stood. With every step I took down the aisle toward him, his expression darkened. Not from danger, but from arousal, from gratification.

"Do you like when people do the things you tell them to?" I asked, coming to stand in front of him.

"I find most people like doing what I tell them to."

"That wasn't what I asked."

"I like it very much, Owen." Archer licked his lips from left to right, slow and sinful, before pulling his lower lip between his teeth and biting down hard enough to discolor the soft skin. "Now take off your shirt."

I threw a glance toward the rear of the plane where the steward has disappeared to after getting us drinks after takeoff.

"He won't come out unless I call for him," he said, stare raking over my body and sending shivers up my spine.

"Seems like bad service," I murmured.

"Seems like he's doing what he's told."

My breath hitched in my throat, and I reached behind me to grab my shirt and ruck up the material. I pulled the shirt over and off my head, tossing it onto Archer's lap.

"Are we allowed to do this?" I asked.

I knew that I should be ashamed the steward knew what was about to happen between Archer and me, but I couldn't find that emotion anywhere inside of me. I was too focused on him, on the heat building at the base of my spine and in my pulsing cock. Something about the idea of maybe being seen, probably being heard, sent an entirely unexpected and new flare of excitement over me.

Archer noticed it, of course, letting out a quiet laugh before crooking his finger for me again.

"It's not a big plane, Owen," he said softly. I shuffled toward him and he hooked his finger around the leather of my belt, pulling it and letting the ends fall open. "He's definitely going to hear you."

"I'll be quiet," I countered.

He grinned, taking my statement as a challenge, then he popped open the button and slid down my zipper. My cock was hard, almost full mast, pressing eagerly against the cotton of my boxers and leaving a noticeable wet spot on the front if the fabric.

"No, you won't," he said. "But I get the feeling that you aren't worried about being heard."

"Of course I am."

"You got your cock sucked in a play room with the door cracked open." Archer raised a brow at me, holding up one finger, then another and another. "You let me jerk you off in an alley, and now here you are on a very small airplane with your cock waving around in the breeze. Owen, we both know that I'm the liar here and you're just the exhibitionist."

Embarrassment flooded my throat, my cheeks, and reflexively, I took a step back. My first thought was always to defend myself, protect myself, and I hated the way Archer saw right through me. Even after all these years and all this time, he still *knew* me, and I fucking hated him for that.

"I hate you," I whispered.

He bit the tip of his tongue and nodded, pulling his belt open with one hand in a practiced move that had me shifting my weight to better balance myself on my feet.

"I know." Archer pulled his cock out and fisted it around the base, his impressive length hard and pink, pointing toward the roof. "Why don't you get on your knees now and show me just how much?"

I mirrored the position of his hand, taking my own dick into my fist and giving my erection a rough pull. Covering my crown with my palm, I slid my hand back, giving long and leisurely over-handed strokes as I went to my knees. His cock was inches from my face, smelling like soap and sweat, and I closed my eyes so he wouldn't see them roll back.

He pushed his cock against my lips, smearing precum across my mouth and my chin, up my cheek, until I finally opened and stuck out the flat of my tongue. Archer groaned, sliding his tip toward the back of my throat, pulling back before even getting close to making me gag.

"Put your hands on my thighs, Owen," he instructed, and I gave another pull down the length of my cock. Groaning, I opened my eyes and blinked up at him, finding his face flushed and his eyes hooded. He pressed his tip back in again, never going far enough for me to really feel it.

"Owen," he said again, voice strained. "Do as you're told."

I wanted to protest, but I could taste the trail of him on my tongue, and my jaw ached for how long I'd been holding it open, but there was no suction, no spit, just the agonizing tease of a blow job. It had to be hell for us both, and I had no idea how he did it because I was near ready to clamp my lips down around the base of his dick and suck his goddamn soul right out of his body.

I'd brought myself close to my own end and he must have known it, hence the command. With as much reluctance as I could muster, I placed my palms on his thighs. There was precum slicked across my palm and I took great pleasure at rubbing it into the no doubt expensive wool blend of his pants. Let him pay to get them dry cleaned for all I cared.

"Good," Archer whispered, letting his head fall back. "Good boy."

I grunted in protest, and he withdrew his cock from my mouth entirely, smacking it against my cheek and raising his face to once again stare down at me.

"Does it hurt yet?" he asked, shifting below me to nudge the swollen head of my cock with the tip of his shoe.

"Yes."

It always hurts with you.

He made a pleased sound and settled his cock back onto the flat of my tongue.

"Don't come, Owen," he warned, easing himself toward the

back of my throat, further than the other times. He moved his weight forward, straightening his spine and scooting toward the edge of the couch so he could get all the way into my throat.

I gagged and he went still, one hand coming to rest on the top of my head. He wasn't holding me down or forcing me, he was steadying me. Archer's touch was soft and reassuring as I adjusted to the stretch in my jaw, and when the convulsions in my throat settled, he pushed another inch deeper into my mouth. Tears freely fell down my face, sliding down my cheeks and off my face. Onto my throbbing erection and undoubtedly onto Archer's shoes as well.

I flexed my hands, digging my fingers into the meat of his thighs, and he pressed another inch of his cock into my mouth, making his way toward my throat. I gagged again, finding it impossible to not. Breathing was hard, thinking was hard, not touching myself was *agony*.

"You can dig in," he said, as if sensing my battle. "I can take it."

I gouged his legs with the sharp half-moons of my nails, the bite of pain only making Archer's cock pulse and leak into the back of my throat. He groaned, snapping his hips and burying the rest of his length in my mouth. I sputtered, and his hand in my hair finally tightened, holding me in place while I struggled to find room for him.

"There you go," he whispered, lashes fluttering.

The top of his shaft burned against the roof of my mouth, and I moved my hands higher up his legs until I reached his waist. I tore his shirt out from behind his waistband until my fingers found his skin and I grabbed him again. I relished the way my blood sang when his skin touched mine, and I once again dug my nails into him, wanting him to really feel it.

The pain only served to spur him on, though, another hot burst of wetness landing against the back of my tongue. I was fairly certain snot was bubbling out of my nose, I knew I was drooling and crying, and between my legs against the side of his shoe, my cock leaked a copious puddle of precum.

"Fucking hell, Owen. Your mouth." Archer made a pleased sound and kicked his foot inward, teasing my balls with his foot. I groaned, gyrating against his shoe and closer to coming than I realized. "Your mouth is what my dreams are made of."

How did he fucking do that?

Why did my body respond to his torment like it was pleasure?

But worse, why did I like it? What was it about the things Archer said or the way he said them that brought me off better, harder, and faster than anyone else after him?

"Are you close?" He nudged me again with the tip of his shoe and I managed a nod.

He hummed, tugging my head just barely to the side, somehow making more room for his swollen erection to fill my mouth.

"Me too. I can't wait to come right into your stomach, Owen."

I groaned, raising off my knees and trying to rub my cock against the couch, his shoe, the floor, anything that would give me friction.

Archer made a tutting sound with his tongue against the roof of his mouth, drawing his hips back just enough for air to flood my throat and my lungs. I choked and gagged, the response purely reflexive after having my airflow constricted for so long.

"Does your dick ache?" he asked, fucking my mouth with short and shallow thrusts.

I curled my fingers around the waistband of his pants and grunted confirmation.

"Not like that," he said. "Put your hands back on me."

I narrowed my eyes, managing to get my fingers half around his waist before digging my nails back into his skin. Archer groaned, lifting off the seat, the steady thrust of his hips faltering. I wasn't certain, but I was ninety-nine percent sure that I wasn't the only one who chased a bit of pain with their pleasure.

"Fuck, yes. Just like that." Archer thrust his length back into my mouth, the crown of his cock kissing the back of my throat. I sealed my lips around the base of his erection and when he came, hot jets of his release splattered against the roof of my mouth and the curve of my tongue before sliding right down my throat.

I didn't even have to suck, and I barely had to swallow. Archer's hold on my hair tightened and he cursed my name under his breath, filling my mouth and my throat with the taste and feel of him until he'd had enough. I didn't even realize I'd started humping myself against his leg, and he let me.

He let me pump my cock against his ankle, writhing madly like I was chasing after the fountain of youth and not something as mindlessly simple as an orgasm. But in that moment, it didn't feel easy and it didn't feel thoughtless. Everything that he'd done and that I'd felt since stepping onto that plane had been calculated and directed in order to get me right where he wanted me.

I hated him for it, but I couldn't tell him no.

I didn't want him to stop.

With his cock still in my mouth, Archer released his hold on my head and smoothed the strands of my hair back. He reached down and swiped his fingertips below my eye, wiping tears. My cheeks flamed with heat, but I didn't move, save for my cock, which by that point had a mind of its own.

"Owen," he said my name softly, the syllables scratchy in the back of his mouth. He cleared his throat and slowly eased his way out of mine. My jaw hurt from how long it had been open, and Archer waited until he was free of my teeth to finish speaking. "Put your pants back on."

"What?" I blinked, disbelief flooding my field of vision. I looked down at my cock, at the slick stains against Archer's slacks and shoes. I bet he paid someone to shine them. I wondered if he'd ever had cum cleaned off the expensive leather before. If not, there was a first time for everything.

"Put your pants back on."

"I haven't come yet."

"I know," he said.

I grunted, one eye twitching in the corner as I forced his face into focus. My jaw clicked as I worked it back and forth, every protest right on the tip of my tongue. Every bad word I wanted to call him falling flat before even making it that far.

"It hurts," I managed to admit, once again covering the head of my dick with my palm. The touch was almost too much for me to handle, and I let me hand fly back to Archer's leg for support. "It really hurts."

"Show me."

I swallowed, leaning back and prying my fingers off his leg so he could see.

"Stand up so I can see better," Archer said.

I raised myself on shaking knees until my cock was inches from his face. My erection was nearly purple for how much blood was between my legs, my balls tight and hot against my skin. Archer leaned in, bracketing his hands around my waist to steady me and then he stuck out his tongue.

He moved slow, making it clear what he was going to do, and there was no way I could watch. But my body was moving slow, with all of my attention and need centered between my legs. So his tongue connected with my shaft before I could look away, and he licked one hot and long stripe up to the tip of my dick. He swirled his tongue through my slit, and then he put my cock back into my boxers and zipped me up.

The pressure of my waistband was torture, and when he tightened my belt, the sound of the leather and metal on top of the physical pressure of the constriction had me whimpering and falling back onto my knees at his feet.

"Archer, please," I begged him, grabbing his knees and trying to climb onto his lap. "Please. Please. I have to. It hurts. It fucking *hurts*."

I was dizzy, mindless, panting and desperate. And Archer ignored it all. He petted his fingers down my face, through my hair, against my Adam's apple while I begged and whined. He made soft shushing sounds, nodding as I pleaded for release.

"Archer. Fuck. *Fuck*."

I let my head fall against his shoulder, defeat washing over me as I realized that he wasn't going to let me come. I knew I didn't need his permission. That I could reach between my legs, even there on his lap, and make myself come. But I could have done that at home. That wasn't what had brought me to the airport, and that wasn't what was taking me back to California.

"I know," he soothed, stroking his hands down my back as I found myself settling against his chest, on his lap. "I know, Owen. It hurts. It hurts, but I promise that it won't hurt forever."

I wanted to believe he was talking about my cock, but the burst of agony in the center of my chest had me thinking otherwise. Another tear slipped out of my eye, and I was glad he couldn't see it or the things it meant.

CHAPTER 13
ARCHIE

BRINGING OWEN TO CALIFORNIA HAD ALREADY MADE ITS WAY ON MY very short list of regrets.

I couldn't just fuck him, so the only thing our days together would do was put my heart on the line before shattering it into pieces when he got back onto the jet to go home. I wasn't foolish enough to think that Owen would give me so much as a second thought after our time together, no matter how good I made it for him.

And those were the thoughts I was lost in as I navigated the city streets back toward my house, Owen in the passenger seat beside me, silent and staring out the window.

"Do you really like it here?" he asked as the high-rise buildings of the city gave way to sprawling homes and mansions.

"In L.A.?" I glanced across the car in time to watch him answer with a jerky nod.

"I don't not like it," I said. "I have a good job and good friends."

"Good men?"

"They are," I confirmed.

Owen scoffed. "That's not how I meant it."

"Are you asking after my sex life?"

Flipping on my turn signal, I came to a stop at the intersection, waiting for clearance to make a right on red. Owen's face was almost the same glaring shade as the light and I bit the inside of my cheek to stop myself from laughing.

Was he jealous?

"Considering the first time we got reacquainted was at a sex club, Owen, I think you know the answer to that." My statement to him was a non-answer, and if he wanted to think I was pulling more men than I was, that was on him. I wasn't hurting for part-ners. The emotional connection was what was missing.

The cars around me cleared, and I made my turn, only a few blocks from my house and even more unsure of what that meant for us.

"Maybe I should have thought twice about letting you come down my throat," he muttered.

"I came directly into your stomach," I corrected, pressing the gas. "But I get tested enough to know my status, and I'm offended you would imply otherwise."

"I don't know a single thing about you, Archer."

Fuck, I hated when he called me Archer.

Pulling into my driveway, I cut the ignition and let my head drop back against the headrest with a soft thump.

"Well." I sighed, shouldering open my door. "I assure you that you won't get anything from me. I don't know if I can say the same about you."

It was mean and I knew it. It was unnecessary, but the insinua-tion stung. After he'd already let me get him off as many times as he pleased...as I had pleased, and he had the audacity to question me like that. It made me angry, and while I wanted to take that out on him, I knew he didn't deserve it. The feelings that twisted up in my head were my own problem, not his.

Slamming the door closed behind me, I sucked in a breath of fresh air, knowing that having Owen at my house was a dangerous plan. Especially with the text message thread that I knew would pop up on my phone as soon as I took the device off airplane mode. Flynn was a ringleader, and I wouldn't have put it past him to show up at my house demanding that I produce Owen in all his tragic glory.

Fishing my keys out of my pocket, I heard the passenger side door close, and the rapid sound of Owen's footfalls as he chased after me.

"Hey!"

I ignored him, letting us into the house without a word.

"Hey." His voice was closer, and slightly softer the second time. He grabbed my shoulder and spun me around, his face making it clear the tone had been a ruse. Fury weaved across his features, strung tight between the sharp press of his lips. He kicked my door closed and shoved me into the house in one swift movement. If I hadn't expected his anger, I would have stumbled, but Owen had always been the emotional one, acting on impulse and not logic.

"Don't lay your hands on me," I warned, jerking my shoulder so my shirt would settle back on my arm.

"But it's okay for you?"

"I thought we were both clear on who I am and who you are."

"Yeah, Archer." He spat my name like it was poison. "I know exactly who you are."

I surged toward him, collaring his throat with my hand and pushing him against the closed front door. I heard his breath leave him as his back landed against the wood. His nostrils flared, mouth angling up into a scowl as I reached down with my free hand and tore open his belt.

"Who am I?" I asked. I taunted.

Shoving his pants down to his knees, I forced my hand behind the waistband of his boxers and took his cock into my first. He grunted, eyes immediately slamming closed. He'd been hard since the flight because I hadn't let him come. I'd planned on bringing him home, tying him to the bed, and making him come until he begged me to put him back on the plane and send him home.

"You're a prick."

His cock was hot and slick in my hand. It didn't take much to get him off, and when he came, his knees gave out on him. The only things holding him up were my hands around his dick and his throat, so I tightened them both when I felt him start to slide to the floor.

I leaned into him, nipping his earlobe with my teeth before whispering the correct answer. "I'm the man who makes you come harder than anyone ever has or ever will."

"Still a prick," he grunted.

I gave him a shove against the wall, then released his cock first, followed by his throat. I stepped away and watched Owen's chest inflate with a breath, and I flexed my fist at my side, fingers laced with his sticky and warm release. A flash of shame washed over me, because how ridiculous that I'd just been thinking of Owen as the tempestuous and emotional one when I'd gone and ruined everything I'd planned to do to him because he'd pissed me off with his mouth.

"The guest room's that way." I pointed down a long hallway that branched off left of the kitchen. "Last door on the left."

"No drink, Archer? No wash cloth?" Owen stalked after me, pants undone and cock barely tucked back into his pants. "I bet your guest room has a private bathroom, doesn't it? I can't wait to wipe my dick all over everything in there."

"You can wipe your cock on everything I own, Owen." I threw a scathing look over my shoulder. "You'd hardly be the first."

That comment stopped him in his tracks, and he sucked his tongue across the front of his teeth, expression turning dark. I'd gone too far. But I was so out of my depth with him, I didn't know when to go or where to stop.

"I'm sorry." I held my hands up in surrender. "That was low."

He didn't say a word, just worked his jaw back and forth before giving me a slow nod.

I gestured toward the hallway. "There is an en suite in the guest room. Feel free to shower and use whatever surface pleases you to dry your dick off. Then…if you want, you can join me in here for a drink."

"What's your most expensive bottle?" he asked.

I thought about how much I would have given for a sip of Rob's quiet kitchen whiskey. "I couldn't tell you."

"I'm hungry too," he said.

"You can eat."

He studied me, like he didn't trust me not to rub my dick all over a charcuterie board before serving it to him, then his exhaustion or my persistence got the better of him. Owen gave another nod, then turned on his heel and headed down the hallway. I listened for the tell-tale latch of the door, then the rushing in the walls as the water turned on.

Only when I knew he was safe in the shower did I let out my breath, bracing myself on the counter and the open fridge door to stop myself from falling into a puddle on the floor.

"Fuck."

I pulled the canned spray cheese out of the fridge and shot a healthy serving onto my tongue while finagling my phone out of my pocket and taking it off airplane mode. As expected, my screen filled with notification after notification.

Rob: Bring him to drinks.

Flynn: You know there's no way he'll do that.

Flynn: We aren't even going to see him until his special friend is back on a plane and headed home.

Dalton: You know what that means.

Barclay: He's going to sell the buildings you live in if you don't get your acts together.

Rob: Let us have our fun.

Flynn: Spoilsport. What's it mean??

Barclay: Don't you dare show up at his house.

Dalton: I think it's a great idea.

Flynn: I'm inclined to agree.

Rob: The lot of you are the worst.

I squirted another jet of cheese onto my tongue and tapped out a reply.

Me: Don't you dare show up here.

Flynn was quick to respond.

Flynn: Here? So you're home already?

Shit.

Me: No.
Rob: The plane's been back for over an hour.
Me: I swear I'm never using any of your services ever again if
you're going to keep me under surveillance.
Rob: Good.
Flynn: Drinks at Archie's???
Me: Please no.
Dalton: What will you give us if we let you say no?

The water in the guest room turned off, throwing the house
into absolute unbearable silence. I swiped over to the music app on
my phone and set something playing through the Bluetooth before
taking one more dose of cheese and returning the can to the fridge.

Me: I'll bring him out this weekend, but right now is not the time.

My camera system pinged an alert that flashed across the top of
my phone letting me know there was movement outside. I tapped
it open, finding Flynn's grinning ass in my driveway, ass resting
against the hood of my car. He waved up at my camera and I
mentally gave him the finger.

Me: Tomorrow.
Dalton: I think that's fair.

I watched the camera feed, Flynn's stupid grin as he went between eyeballing my camera and looking down at his phone.

Flynn: Fine. Tomorrow.

I didn't care about anything else they had to say. I turned off the screen, threw my phone onto the counter, and busied myself with drinks and snacks for Owen. He'd asked about my most expensive whiskey and if that was what he wanted, he could have it. I wanted none of it.

I poured myself a glass of red wine and drank half of it, hoping to wash the taste of canned cheese out of my mouth in case I got a chance to kiss Owen again. The combination was less than ideal, but I struggled through.

By the time Owen came out of the guest room, I'd done the best I could. But all sense of self and perseverance died when he stepped barefoot into my kitchen. With wet hair slicked away from his face and a white shirt that clung to him because he hadn't quite finished drying himself off, he looked every inch the debauched dream he'd always been to me. Gray joggers hugged his legs, and for the first time since we'd gotten reacquainted, he looked almost nervous.

I pushed the snack board in his direction. "We can go get dinner later, if you want."

"You don't have to try to impress me," he mumbled.

"Everyone has to eat, Owen."

Producing a bottle of Old Rip Van Winkle from the cabinet beside my fridge, I set the thousand dollar whiskey next to his hand.

"And drink."

He looked at the bottle and pursed his lips. Whether he knew the exact price or not, I wagered he knew it wasn't a grocery store purchase. With a resigned breath, he twisted off the cap and poured two fingers into a glass and swallowed it back like it was a shot of well liquor. I bristled, but bit the inside of my cheek to stop from throwing a biting remark in his direction.

After he swallowed and licked his lips, he looked down at his hands, and I studied the arrow tattoo that spanned the length of his middle finger, wondering what it meant. Wanting to know if he'd ever tell me.

"Well." Owen cleared his throat and turned his attention on me, an unmistakable fire in his eyes. "If you insist on taking me on a date, Archer, you at least better make it interesting."

CHAPTER 14
OWEN

An hour into our meal, I regretted my earlier taunt.

Archer looked utterly unaffected and I was ready to crawl out of my skin and hump his leg until I came all over his shoe.

"Are you quite all right, Owen?" He smirked at me over the rim of his drink, which was water, so basically a promise that my day was barely getting started.

The cock ring he'd fastened around my shaft and sac was tight, keeping my erection hard and my balls painfully full. But it was what I'd asked for, what we *both* wanted. That dangerous kind of tease and torment that got us harder than anything else ever would.

I didn't know why I was built the way I was. Didn't understand why teasing myself around the fringes of an orgasm made them that much sweeter when they finally came. I wondered if sometimes it was rooted in my youth, if I'd just spent so much time listening to Archer talk Mandy through it, then the first time he and I were together. Like, was it some kind of complicated programming I was stuck with?

As far as I could tell, it was a problem for Archer as well. Archer, with his drawer full of butt plugs, and cock rings, and chastity cages. I'd only ever seen those in porn before, not in real life. The hard metal looked heavy and cold, entirely too small to ever contain the throbbing shaft trying to beat a hole through my zipper. When I'd scanned the contents of his sex drawer from over his shoulder, Archer had assured me the cage had an entirely different purpose from the cock rings. One was to make sure I didn't get hard, the other to make sure I stayed that way.

Two completely different kinds of torture, I imagined.

After he'd fitted the cock ring around my still sticky cock, he'd produced a plug no bigger than a finger, which he made quick work of shoving right up into my ass.

"That's not going to do shit," I'd warned him.

But when we sat down at the restaurant and it gave a sharp series of vibrations right against my prostate, I found myself once again proven wrong.

"Just distracted," I answered, not ready to give him the satisfaction of knowing how close I was to crawling out of my skin.

"I can tell." Archer grinned and leaned back—comfortably—in his chair. "You've hardly listened to a word I've said."

"I've heard everything."

"And you're giving me one word answers when I ask you questions," he said. "You're the one who was spouting off about not knowing me earlier. I want to know what kind of man you are these days, Owen."

"What do you want me to tell you?" I asked.

Two quick vibrations against my prostate and I grimaced, lifting my hips off the seat.

"I want to know why you're here," he said.

"Because you invited me."

Archer shook his head, mouth pulled into half of a frown.

Another vibration, this one longer. My cock leaked and I groaned.

"Why are you here?" he asked again.

"Because I want to be," I snapped, my voice loud enough to draw attention from some of the nearby guests. The vibration died down and I exhaled a trembling breath. "I'm here because I want to be, okay?"

"Why, though?"

I knew what he was asking of me, and I hated him for it.

When I didn't reply, Archer leaned in closer, like we were collaborators in on the same little secret. "You can't expect me to believe that I'm the only man who knows how you like to come. Although, the idea of that is doing wonders for my ego."

"The last thing your ego needs is to be bigger than it is."

He arched a brow, the earlier frown now a smirk.

When I thought about all of the things I'd put on the line to be in California with Archer, I didn't have a good answer as to why I'd done any of them. Frankie would hate it because out of everyone in my life, even though he'd come so much later, he was the one who'd borne the brunt of the emotional fallout from Archer's leaving. Mandy's heart would be broken all over again, and when I'd dedicated so much of my life to making sure my sister never shed another tear over Archer Davidson, me being with him behind her back made little to no sense.

"Maybe it's closure I'm after," I finally answered, unsure of a better resolution.

"You think a handful of orgasms from me and a return ticket home is going to wrap things up between us with a nice bow?"

I scoffed. "Only a handful?"

"You're missing the point."

"No." I shook my head, cock pulsing in time with my erratic heartbeat. "I got your point. But, no, I don't think the orgasms have anything to do with it. Maybe being able to leave you on my terms this time is what I'm after."

Archer studied me quietly, jaw working side to side in silence. Maybe, for the first time ever, I'd left him speechless.

"I can give you that," he said.

"How gracious." I rolled my eyes, frustrated at the way he was already able to get under my skin with the simplest of comments. "What about you, Archer? Why did you fly me all the way out here? I know I have a nice dick, but I'm sure this city is crawling with willing partners for you."

"I've never had an issue getting laid, if that's what you're insinuating."

"Then why?" I pressed.

The tip of his tongue darted out, worrying at the corner of his mouth just long enough for me to realize that I was going to regret whatever he said next.

"Because I've always liked the way your face looks when you come."

I swallowed, and an onslaught of vibrations pounded against my already tender and sensitive prostate. Grabbing the edge of the table for leverage to stop myself from sliding onto the floor, I grit my teeth through as much of the pleasure as I could manage. "Stop it," I whispered, glancing up at him from beneath my lashes.

"Didn't you hear me, Owen? I said I like the way your face looks when you come."

The vibrations went steady and I knew I was about to come in my pants.

"Not here," I begged, shoving a hand between my legs and pushing down on my engorged and painful shaft. My dick hurt, my balls hurt, my entire body hurt for how much tension had strung through me.

"Why not?"

"Arch—" I swallowed down the rest of his name when the vibrator went still inside of me.

Something indecipherable flashed across his face and I looked away because the softness in his eyes added another complicated layer to the feelings that had been cycling through me since the weekend before.

"Why not here?" he asked again, reaching into his pants and pulling a black leather wallet out. "You're the one who said you wanted to make it fun."

I had said that, but I'd clearly had no idea what I was asking for.

Archer waved his credit card at the waiter, who was on him in a flash, taking it off to charge whatever ungodly amount of money our meal had cost.

"I don't want to come in my pants."

"What if *I* wanted you to?"

"Do you?" I rasped.

The waiter returned with his credit card and a slip of paper, which Archer signed and handed back. He ignored me while he put his card back into his wallet, and he continued to ignore me when he finished off the water in his drinking glass.

"Are you ready to go?" he asked.

"After you answer my question."

I had no idea how I was going to get out of the restaurant anyway, not with the thickest and hardest erection I'd ever sported in my whole life.

Archer stood and sighed.

"It does seem a waste for you to do it all over your jeans." He leaned down and whispered, "I'd rather you do it at home in my mouth. Let's get out of here, Owen."

Archer grabbed my arm and pulled me up from the table, not giving me any time to hide my cock or get my balance. I stumbled after him to the valet stand, and then happily collapsed into the passenger seat of his car.

We'd just pulled out of the restaurant when my phone rang.

It was Frankie.

I declined the call and turned the phone over so the screen faced the top of my thigh.

It rang again.

"Someone important?" Archer asked.

"A friend."

"Do you need to take it?"

The ringing ended, then promptly started again. Something about the thought of talking to Frankie, of *lying* to him, with my cock hard enough to hammer nails through a two-by-four felt beyond the limits of our friendship.

"Not ideal," I murmured as I accepted the call. "Hello?"

"There you are." Frankie's relief in my ear was palpable, and I wanted to throw myself out of the car and directly into oncoming traffic.

"I'm here." I did my best to mimic sickness, or at least exhaustion, which was a little less of a stretch. The flight had been long and Archer was as much as he'd ever been. Plus, it was a lot of work to be this devastatingly erect for as long as I had been.

"Your sister was worried."

"Just her?" I managed a hoarse laugh.

From the driver's side of the car, Archer watched with one brow raised.

"Of course I was worried too," Frankie said. "You know how I love you."

The volume must have been loud enough for Archer to hear Frankie because, at the last comment, Archer's eyes went wide and his entire head swiveled to face me. I kept my stare focused out the windshield. Let Archer think whatever he wanted about who I was or the things I did. His opinion didn't matter to me.

"I love you." I feigned a cough. "I'm just trying to get some rest. But I'm fine, I swear."

"Don't ghost me, Owen. That's such an Archer thing to do."

I closed my eyes, ignoring the grumbled noise from the driver's seat.

"I'd never," I promised. "I'll talk to you in a couple of days."

"Do you think you'll be up for trivia on Tuesday?" Frankie asked.

I'd told Archer I had to be home on Monday, and then my life could go back to normal.

"I imagine so," I murmured.

"Okay. Call if you need me."

"I will. Bye."

Frankie said bye and ended the call. The beeps from the disconnect were loud, and I let the phone fall into my lap, bouncing off my cock, which was still hard, even with less enthusiasm than before.

"Don't say anything," I said to Archer.

"About which part?"

"Any of it."

I rolled my head away from him to look out the window, ensuring that I couldn't so much as even see his profile. Frankie's offhand comment was a stark reminder of just how stupid I was being. I knew what kind of person Archer was. The same kind he always had been. And after one *really* good hand job, I'd hopped onto a plane and flown halfway across the country for another.

I was as foolish as I'd been at eighteen.

Maybe even worse.

"Answer one question for me," he said softly.

I nodded my approval for him to continue.

"Do you have a boyfriend?"

I wanted to hit him in his mouth for even daring to ask me that. I was many things, but I'd never been a cheater. Though I had coerced him to sleep with me once, knowing he was in a relationship with my sister. Maybe I was worse than I thought. But I didn't want to share any of that revelation with him. That was for me to unpack and sit with when he finished with me and sent me on my way back home.

"The fact you had to even ask me that is proof that you have no idea what kind of man I am, Archer."

I kept my stare focused on the cars whipping past us on the freeway, and he didn't say another word until we got back to his house, when he locked the front door behind me, went right onto his knees and made me come so hard I saw stars and almost confessed that I was most likely, probably, definitely, still very much in love with him.

CHAPTER 15
ARCHIE

WHEN OWEN AND I WERE KIDS, LIKE ACTUAL KIDS, NOT AWKWARD and horny teenagers, we used to sleep in the same bed when we stayed over at each other's houses. Owen had always liked to sleep against the wall and I liked the edge so I could keep my foot stuck out of the blankets so I didn't overheat.

After sucking him off and taking him to bed where I'd fucked him so hard the only thing he was able to say was half of my name and something that sounded like please, he'd promptly rolled himself toward the wall and fallen asleep. Or rather, he'd rolled himself toward the edge of the bed that had faced the wall when we were kids. As an adult with more square footage than I'd ever need, my bed sat centered on the wall, a matching nightstand on either side. But it had always been the left side of the bed tucked under the window when I'd lived at home, and that's where Owen ended his night.

I lay awake after that for hours, the memory of his tight muscles like a hand around my cock, the taste of his cum and sweat on my tongue better than any whiskey Rob would ever be able to afford. And I lay there, counting through the quickly growing list of regrets, knowing two things to be certain.

Owen still hated me, and I didn't want him to leave.

I deserved it, but I didn't *want* it.

I wasn't bold enough to think that I could heal ten years of mistakes in four days, but I still thought I wanted to try. I owed it to myself and it was the least I could do for Owen.

"Maybe we should stay at a hotel this weekend so we can get room service," I murmured, stretching my hand toward where I'd expected his leg to be, only to find it empty. The pillow was cold and the sheets were kicked down to the foot of the bed.

First, I was hit with a shock of panic that had me bolting upright. He'd left me. I should have known. But then I remembered Owen was in California because I'd brought him here, and while I wouldn't put it past him to book himself a commercial flight home to get away from me, I didn't think that was what had happened.

The smell of coffee coming from the kitchen confirmed he was still in the house, and I headed that way, shoving my hair back from my sleep-crusted eyes. I found Owen in the kitchen, wearing nothing more than all of his tattoos and an indecently tight pair of underwear that hugged his ass the way *I* wanted to.

Owen was slim and tanned, hardly muscular but far from soft. He had the body of someone who kept themselves busy, but not at the gym. I wondered how he spent his free time, what his friends were like, what he did on the weekends when he wasn't indulging my whims and wants. He hadn't heard me, so I studied his back, the flaring planes of his shoulder blades and how they jutted out from his spine like wings. The way when he breathed in deep, I could see the outline of his ribs, and how when he exhaled, it looked like the weight of the world on his back.

I wondered if he regretted me again.

Still.

"Good morning," I finally said.

He didn't startle, leading me to believe he'd been aware of my presence after all. Instead, he glanced at me over his shoulder, curled and dyed hair falling into his eyes.

"I used the last of your oat milk for creamer," he said.

"That's fine." I took a step toward him. "I drink mine black anyway. That's for Flynn."

"Who's Flynn?" Owen looked back toward the window in front of him. Another deep breath, another count of his ribs while he held the air in his lungs.

"Ask me what you meant to ask me."

"Is he a boyfriend? An ex?"

"He's my best friend," I said. "Well, one of them."

Owen turned to face me, resting his ass against the counter. He had a cup of coffee in his hands, and on the counter behind him sat the empty oat milk container and my can of spray cheese. My eyes flickered across both objects and quickly back to his face.

"How many best friends do you have?" he asked.

"Four."

"Do they know about me?"

It was too early for the conversation he was trying to have.

"Can I have some coffee before we talk about this?" I murmured, taking a couple more steps toward Owen.

He sidestepped and reached behind him, grabbing a mug of coffee that he'd already poured and passing it off to me. "I was going to bring them back to bed," he said softly, cheeks flushing.

"Do you want to go sit on the couch?" I asked.

He nodded, shuffling toward the living room, but not before grabbing the canned cheese in his free hand.

"Don't think we aren't going to talk about this," he said, tucking it under his arm.

I followed him to the couch and watched the careful way he folded himself down onto the cushion, tucking one leg under his ass and letting the other stretch out in front of him. He set the cheese on the coffee table, then angled his body toward me. His face was expectant, all wide and dark eyes with that soft and sleepy mouth, lips barely parted. I bet he tasted like cum and coffee and me.

"They know you're here," I said.

"Sounds like there's a but coming."

"Before last week, they didn't know a thing about you," I took a sip of coffee to ready myself for the questioning.

"Should I be offended?" Owen eyed me over the rim of the mug before taking a long drink.

"I didn't keep it to myself because I was ashamed of you, if that's what you're thinking."

"Why then?" he asked.

"I didn't want them to think less of me," I admitted.

Never in a million years would I have imagined myself in this conversation, and never would I have thought it would happen on my couch, in my underwear, after a night of the most mind-bending sex I'd ever had since the last time I'd had sex with Owen. There'd been a thousand dreams where I'd been able to use words to repair the damage I'd caused, a hundred more when I'd milked his forgiveness right out of his prostate with the tips of my fingers, but it had never been like this. Raw and honest, and exactly what he deserved from me while being the absolute last thing I wanted to offer.

"Why would they think less of you?" he rasped.

"Are you being serious right now?"

"I seriously want you to answer the question."

I sighed and leaned back, tucking myself into the corner of the couch and finding myself thankful for the buttery softness of the cushions.

I didn't know how to answer.

I knew I wanted Owen. I knew what I wanted him to hear. But I worried the truth would only drive him further away from me. After all, my truth was just that. It was mine, colored by my own experiences and my own understanding of what had happened between us and what I'd done. I couldn't make him agree with any of it or believe it. But he wasn't asking that of me, either.

All he'd asked for was my honesty.

"Because I'm not a good person, Owen. I mean, maybe I am now, but I wasn't then. I was...your sister." I sighed, rubbing at my eyes like the answer would appear somewhere in the dark.

I glanced at him and found him stoic, his expression frozen and giving nothing away. He wasn't going to grant me an inch; instead he sat there content to watch me wade through the quicksand of my own creation.

"Can I ask you a question first?"

He gave a short nod.

"In a perfect world, Owen, what would you have had happen? When you...when you sat down and wrote that letter. When you left it for me...how did you think that would go? How did you *want* it to go?"

His answer would be the piece that had been missing from the puzzle of my life for a decade because, while I'd been left to live with my responses and my actions, I'd never understood the reasons that we'd found ourselves together in his basement. I knew why I'd gone after him, of course. I'd just wanted to make sure my best friend was okay, that he wasn't in pain. Because he'd told me he loved me, told me he wanted me, and all the while those feelings had been growing, he'd been watching me—hearing me—live out those dreams with his sister. I hadn't gone down to the basement planning on kissing him, let alone losing my virginity to him, taking his...

"I hadn't thought that far," he confessed. "I was eighteen and heartbroken, Arch. I just needed to say what I had to say."

"I don't buy that."

"You don't believe I was in pain?" He moved quickly, all sharp and angry angles as he set his coffee next to the cheese and slapped his hand against his bare chest. "You don't think I fucking loved you then?"

"That's not what I meant." I set my coffee next to his and angled my body toward him. "I don't believe that you didn't think that far."

"I told you then I used to fantasize it was you and me." He swallowed, throat working and darkening with every breath.

"So, you got what you wanted," I whispered.

"I didn't understand the fucking cost! I didn't know!"

Owen licked his lips and sucked them between his teeth, stare darting madly around the room, looking at all the furniture that didn't have anything to do with him or me.

Just a diversion from the truths that were finally coming to light.

We'd both done a great job at pretending, apparently. Living in the shadows of half-truths and a whole lot of fucking lies we told ourselves to sleep at night.

"I didn't know," he said again, voice softer. He stared at my knee, at the way my fingers drummed against the bone nervously. "I just knew I couldn't carry it myself anymore."

"You wanted me to break up with your sister," I realized.

"Of course I did," he snapped, and then groaned, like his answer was as much of a surprise to him as it had been to me. "I didn't want to hurt her, but I didn't want to hurt anymore either."

"Owen, why..."

"It was *killing* me."

It still was, if the agony in his voice was anything to go by. I stilled my jittery fingers and turned my hand, palm up. I don't know if I'd expected him to hold my hand, but I knew I hadn't expected him to curl in on himself and lay on my lap, the side of his head nestled in the cradle of my palm. With my other hand, I petted his hair away from his face because I didn't know what else to do, but I knew I had to touch him. I had to keep his skin under mine, had to keep the words coming out between us.

"Mandy doesn't know," he finally whispered, after his breathing had slowed and the tension in his legs had allowed him enough leeway to stretch them toward the far end of the couch.

"That you're here? I figured as much."

"No." Owen rolled onto his back and looked up at me, the unshed tears glistening in the corner of his eyes. "She doesn't know I wrote the letter. She doesn't know that we...she...Arch, she doesn't know any of it."

CHAPTER 16
OWEN

ARCHER LOOKED LIKE I'D SHOWN HIM IRREFUTABLE PROOF THAT THE earth was flat.

"What do you mean she doesn't know?"

There was no stopping the disgusted sound that rolled up and out of my throat in response to his shocked expression. "I wasn't really in a position to say, 'Hey, Mandy, sorry but I fucked the man you wanted to marry and now he's left us both.' How the fuck exactly did you expect that to go after you left?"

"I don't know." He scrubbed a hand down his face, suddenly looking tired. "I honestly didn't think about it."

"Oh, believe me, I know."

"I just…I told her I had an emergency. I'd texted…"

Archer's stumbling words were the answer to a question that had been sitting in my mind for most of my adult life because, after he left, Mandy had come down to the basement, a little flustered and frenzied, asking me what the emergency was. I hadn't known what to say, so I'd answered her—for what was maybe the first and only time where Archer was concerned—honestly, and said no.

"She never talked about you after that," I said quietly, scratching the back of my neck until the tingling memories sank back into the dark corners where they belonged.

"Really?"

"She just…I don't know. I could tell she was hurt you were gone and I think she knew I was hurt you were gone, and that was enough. The why of it never mattered to her."

"I didn't mean for any of this to happen," he said, shaking his head before glancing at me from the corner of his eye. With his hand cradled around the back of his neck, Archer sucked in a slow and sad breath. "Owen, I…"

"I don't need your apology."

"Not that."

"What then?" I grabbed my coffee off the table and took a drink. I needed something to do with my hands, but the coffee had already cooled a little too close to room temperature to not taste like sludge on the swallow.

"I didn't know what else to do. I couldn't go back to her after what we'd done and I couldn't be with you either."

"Because I'm a man?"

Archer threw his hands up in the air. "Because of *her*, Owen."

I took one last drink of my coffee and returned the mug to the table beside the cheese. We still had to talk about the cheese.

"How could I explain that to your sister?" he asked, fingers splayed on top of his thighs and his eyes wide. "How could *you* explain that to her? 'Hey, Mandy. I've been in love with Archie this whole time and I told him that, and then we slept together while you were waiting upstairs. But he loves me back, so you understand, right? You're cool with the whole thing?'"

Even though Archer had taken on a mocking tone with his questioning, the intent of the words landed how he'd planned. Even then I'd known my dreams were unattainable, short of creating an estrangement with my sister and going away with him, which hadn't even been an option then. There hadn't been a future for us. But at eighteen, I didn't think about futures. I thought about the past and the present, and the only thing I knew was how urgently I needed Archer to love me in the way I loved him.

When I didn't say anything, Archer kept talking. "There was no winning, Owen. There was no scenario where that went anyway but badly. And sure, running how I did might have been immature, but it was the quickest fix. It was like...I don't know."

"Cauterizing the wound," I supplied, even though Archer's quick departure had done anything *but*. His abandonment had settled on me and my sister like a festering wound that had taken months, if not years, to fully close. The fact that Mandy and I never spoke about Archer was proof enough that the skin was probably still too tender to touch.

"Basically."

"And what about you, then? You just up and walked out of our lives like nothing?" I stood up and paced to the other end of the living room, hands braced against the small of my back.

"Like nothing?"

The couch groaned when Archer stood, and I could hear the soft sound of his footfalls as he approached, the heat of his breath against the back of my neck when he got too close, and the ache in his voice when he said, "As if I haven't been walking around half-dead since I left your house that night, Owen."

I turned and Archer took another step. My back pressed against his wall and I looked up at him, defiant and sad all at the same time. His features were weary, gentle, but every crease and line on his face telegraphed the truth of his admission. He looked over my shoulder at nothing and licked his lips. A slow drag from one side to the other and back again, accompanied with a small shake of his head like he was in disbelief at everything we'd said to each other.

"What are you saying?" I croaked.

He huffed and raised his hand, hesitating when his fingertips were inches away from my face. From the corner of my eye, I saw Archer flex his fingers and pull back before changing his mind and moving closer. His fingertips landed against my cheek—one, two, three, then his palm cradled my face and there was no stopping me from closing my eyes and leaning into him.

"If I could go back, I wouldn't have left. I know that Mandy, I...

I wouldn't want her to be angry with you, but I couldn't go back and walk away from you another time," he said.

"Arch..."

"I know I walked away from you at Rapture, but I wasn't sure you weren't a fever dream and then you called me, and..."

He didn't need to finish that sentence because we both knew what happened after I had called him to my hotel the weekend before.

"You walked away then too," I reminded him. "You left me asleep in the hotel. You make a habit of leaving me, Arch, whether you want to admit it or not."

He chewed the inside of his cheek, fingers flexing against my cheekbone. His other hand slotted over my bare hip, fingertips grazing the skin of my waist and sending ribbons of fire whipping up my spine.

"Would you rather I stay?"

The question was more than fair, and at the time, it was a no. I wouldn't have wanted him around because I'd been carrying so much anger toward him for so long. But something about the way the morning light filtered in through his windows and the way the coffee smelled on his breath made me rethink all of that.

I still didn't think there was a happy ending for us because everything that had been wrong about us in the past was still wrong now. But I didn't see the harm in closing my eyes and living like a teenager again, living in the present instead of the future for once. After all, I'd already gotten on the plane and I was already in California, in his *house*, and he was so fucking close to me, and his lashes were long and falling closed over his chocolate eyes, and then his mouth was against mine and nothing else mattered.

Nothing would ever matter again besides the way my entire body sparked to life when Archer put his lips to mine. So, I parted them and moaned when he slid his tongue inside. When he tightened his hold around my waist and pulled our chests flush. The hand on my face went back into my hair and I went soft against him, except for the one place I'd gone achingly hard.

In that moment, it was easy to close my eyes and go back to being eighteen in the basement, climbing onto Archie's lap and begging him to put me out of my misery. He was doing it again, but it had a very different flavor than before. He licked into my mouth deeper, groaning when my fingers scrabbled against his hips. Between him and the wall, though, I wasn't going anywhere.

Without warning, he pulled back for a breath, eyes opened. He scanned my face, and I shook my head. He was looking for me to tell him to stop, and even if Mandy walked in his front door, I didn't think I could have found the strength to do it. I grabbed his face and crashed our mouths back together, pushing off the wall and walking both of us to the couch. The backs of his knees hit and he landed on his ass with a huff of breath that shot past my lips, and I climbed on his lap without thinking. The movement was muscle memory it seemed, because our bodies slotted together and it felt like the same kind of blasphemy as before.

"Is that a yes?" Archie murmured, his hands sliding past the waistband of my underwear and kneading my ass until I gyrated against him and groaned.

"I just want to be with you here and now," I said, kissing my way down his neck. He dropped his head back, angling his face toward the ceiling to give me more room and I sank my teeth around his collarbone until he made that sinful grunt I'd been jacking off to the memory of for ten years.

"Harder, then," he murmured, and I let go and bit him again before pulling back and licking over the divots left from my teeth.

"Do you still like when it hurts?"

"I like when *you* hurt me." He dropped his face down and fisted my hair, yanking my head to the side and sucking what would undoubtedly turn into a bruise onto the side of my throat.

"We're too good at doing that to each other," I said, and he slanted our lips back together before I could say any more.

Being kissed by Archie was better than being fucked by anyone who wasn't him, and by the time he got his hands back into my underwear, I was ready to come all over his hand without so much as a single word of encouragement.

I scrambled away from him, partly to get his hands off my cock and partly to get my underwear off. I almost fell onto the table, kicking free of the material, and Archie took advantage of the space to get a bottle of lube and a condom out from a cabinet in the sideboard.

"Do you store lube and condoms in every room?" I asked, coming back toward him as he settled back on the couch.

"Would you rather I use the cheese?"

He rolled the condom down his length, then took my dick into one of his hands and shoved two fingers on his other into my mouth. I thought about babies and baseball to stop myself from coming on the spot.

"Get them wet, Owen. There you go," he praised, dragging his fingertips down the length of my tongue.

I climbed back onto his lap and he wasted no time sinking both of his spit-soaked fingers into my ass. Passing me the lube, he wrapped his other arm around my waist and pulled me down onto his hand.

"Do I want to know why you have lube in the living room?" I rephrased my earlier question, pouring some into my hand and slicking the length of his cock.

"Don't play coy now," he said, scissoring his fingers apart and drawing a sharp gasp from the back of my throat.

He looked smug, and I raised up off of him until his fingers fell free. Instead of waiting for him to rearrange me, or worse, give me time to change my mind about the gentle way we were being with each other, I sat back down with the shiny head of his cock positioned at my spit-stretched asshole.

"I would never," I promised, sinking down onto him.

It wasn't the first time Archie had been inside of me since we'd reconnected, but it felt like it. Every synapse in my body fired off like a short circuit and fireworks flashed in my eyes as I adjusted to the thickness of his erection inside of me. He curled his hands around my waist and I could feel the sweat against his palms, the tremor in his grip.

"Normally, you know…" His words came out barely more than a breath. "I like to make you work for it, Owen."

I shivered, his cock pulsing inside of me as he stretched me, even in his stillness. *Thinking* about the way Archie brought me to the edge over and over again was almost as good as the act itself.

"But I think I'm going to come as soon as one of us moves, so I'm going to need you to get on with it first."

CHAPTER 17
ARCHIE

I WAS HALF OFF THE COUCH, ONE LEG BRACED AGAINST THE CUSHIONS and the other hanging off the edge. Owen was on the floor, covered in sweat with his knees bent and feet flat. His breathing was the loudest thing in the room, even eclipsing the staccato beat of my heart that rattled in my ears.

"That *was* pretty fast," he mumbled before throwing his forearm over his eyes.

I managed a laugh before sliding onto the floor beside him. Without thinking, I reached over, patting the floor until I found his hand. He flipped his, palm up, and threaded our fingers together before either of us realized how foreign the move was. Owen tried to pull back, but I tightened my grip, and he stopped fighting.

After a breath, he gave another tug against my hold.

"Arch." He paused and swallowed, the gulp almost as loud as his breath. "What are we doing?"

"Recovering."

He gave another rough jerk of his hand, but I knew it was coming so I preemptively clamped down on him.

"You know what I mean."

There were multiple answers to his question, one that tasted like the truth on the tip of my tongue and another that felt more like the lie he wanted to hear. But I'd spent ten years with half of my heart living outside of my chest, and I hadn't even realized it until Owen walked back into my life. Even with as much as he hated me the first few times we were intimate, being with Owen was like coming home. He wouldn't believe that if I told him, because all he knew of me was the number of times I'd walked away from him outnumbered the times I'd called for him.

"I know," I agreed.

"I don't know what you want me to say."

"I want you to tell me the truth."

He shook free of my hand and rolled on top of me, one leg on either side, with the clammy flats on his palms pressed softly against my chest. His forehead was sweaty and a chunk of curls stuck to the skin, tangling in his eyelashes every time he blinked. I reached up and brushed it back, and he leaned into my hand with a soft sigh.

He was beautiful and perfect. He was back in my life and I didn't want to ruin it again. I wanted him to stay. No, I *needed* him to stay. But I knew on Monday I would have to put him back on a plane and send him home. He wouldn't stay just because I asked it of him. He didn't owe me that.

He didn't owe me anything.

"I want to enjoy the weekend with you," I said.

Owen's cheeks flushed and he looked down at my softening cock. "You're off to a good start."

"I want you to enjoy being here," I said, softer. "With me."

He licked his lips, pulling them between his teeth and letting his head fall to the side. "You're off to a good start," he said again.

I curled my hands around his waist and let them slide down to the place where his thighs folded into a glorious, olive-tanned softness. His leg hair was dark and curled, coarse against my hands, but I touched him and he moved easily against me like he approved of the way we felt together.

"Are you going to keep me inside all weekend?" Owen murmured, pressing his hand against my cock, just enough to tease.

"I'd like to," I said, eyes falling closed as he pushed the tip against my stomach with the heel of his hand. "But I'm not against going out."

"To meet your friends?"

"Not ideally." My mouth fell into a soft smile. It wasn't that I didn't want the two halves of my world to collide, just that I didn't want Owen to judge me for them, and I didn't want them to know who I'd been before. It was hard enough for *me* to reconcile the things I'd done with the man I'd become.

"What if I want to meet them?" he asked.

Slowly, I blinked my eyes open and brought Owen into focus. He looked serious enough, even with his eyes half closed and his lips half open like he was ready to fuck again.

"Why would you want to meet them?"

"Because I want to know who you are and I don't think you'll be honest with me."

"I haven't lied to you since you got here," I said. I may have been speaking in half-truths, but that was for both our benefits, not because I was trying to hide anything from him.

Owen made a thoughtful noise as he curled his hand around my dick, then his own. The friction of his fingers and his shaft against my skin was heavenly, and I tipped my head back with a groan.

"Which one of your friends would tell me why you have a half-empty can of spray cheese in your fridge?" he asked, giving a lazy stroke from the base of our dicks to the tip.

"Flynn, probably." I groaned. "All of them."

"Will you tell me?"

Owen pointed our dicks toward the ceiling and spit on them before resuming his strokes. I would have answered him anything in the world if he asked on the upstroke.

"I wish you would ask me almost literally anything else."

"Is that a no? Do I have to ask your friends?"

"Owen." My hips rose off the floor and he balanced himself against my stomach with his free hand.

"You used to hate it," he whispered. "You used to make fun of me for eating it."

"That's why I have it," I said, covering my eyes with my hands. In the dark, we didn't have a past and his touch was all I'd ever need again.

"Why, Archie?"

My breath caught in my throat at his use of my name, of my nickname. The one that used to only belong to him before he left it behind. I sat up, wrapping one hand around his shoulders to balance him as he slid back on my thighs from the change of angle. The move brought us face to face and his eyes were wide as mine, and I realized he hadn't meant to call me that. He hadn't meant to send us both back to that couch in his basement.

"Say it again," I rasped.

His pupils dilated and when he licked his lips I could almost taste his tongue against my mouth.

"Why, Archie?"

"Because it reminds me of you," I said. "Because when I am sad and when I'm lonely, and even when I'm happy and with my friends, I think about you. There's not a day...not a fucking day, Owen—"

He cut me off with a kiss, smashing our mouths together to shut me up and picking up the pace with his hand. I curled my fingers around his wrist to stop him because it wasn't fair that he'd asked the question and then tried to run from the answer. I tore my mouth away from his with a gasping breath.

"Every mistake I've ever made was every time I walked away from you," I rushed out, and he slanted his mouth over mine again, tongue digging in deep like he was trying to dig out the rest of my confession before I could speak it.

I jerked my head to the side, chasing another breath, another moment of clarity. He kissed my cheekbone, my jaw, my eyelid, all in search of my mouth.

"I've loved you since before I knew what it meant to love a

man, Owen. Before I even understood how strong my feelings for you were."

He tried to kiss me again, but I evaded him. His fingers around our cocks were almost painfully tight, and he jacked us off like if he could make me come, I would shut up.

"No one has ever come close to you, Owen. No one has ever made me—"

"Shut up," he hissed, grabbing my cheeks and hauling me back to his mouth.

"I love you," I confessed, searching his face for a reaction as best I could, considering how close our faces were. The top corner of his lip twitched and his cock pulsed against mine, then spurts of hot wetness leaked over his fingers and down our dicks.

"I love you," I said again, relishing the way the truth of it settled in my chest like the answer to every question in my life that had ever gone unanswered. "I eat the cheese because I love you, and I walked away from you the first time because I loved you, and I sent a plane for you because I love you, and I'll let you leave me on Monday because I fucking love you, Owen, and I know that doesn't count for anything anymore. But I can't stop it. I can't fucking stop it."

Owen shut me up again, grabbing my face, now with his cum-covered hand, and slanting our mouths back together. He kissed me with as much focus, but ten times more tenderness than the other times, and I went soft against him. Leaning into his hands and his mouth, my aching cock long forgotten between my legs. Owen kissed me like he believed everything I said and that the truth was enough. It was enough to make me believe that maybe, just maybe, he wouldn't get on a plane come Monday, or if he did, he wouldn't block my number as soon as he got back home. My confession didn't make things easier for us, but it did make everything feel *right* in a way that I hadn't experienced since my teenage years.

I took over the kiss, took over everything, taking Owen down to the ground. He laughed and spread his legs, making room for me between his thighs. His hole was still slippery with lube from earlier and my dick was slick with his cum, nosing at his hole like it had any right to be there.

"Do it," he coaxed, lifting off the floor so my tip could notch against him.

"I don't have a condom on." I threw a quick glance over his shoulder at the sideboard that had somehow moved a mile out of reach.

"Do it, Archie," he said my name again and I pushed into him because I'd never been able to tell him no and I wasn't going to start now.

Owen's body spread to make room for me, even as I slowly inched inside because the leftover lube was only so wet. He made the most delicious sounds as I filled him and when I finally bottomed out and fell forward, one hand braced on either side of his head.

"I think that's the most honest you've been with me since I gave you that letter," he whispered.

"How do you do this to me?" I eased out an inch and pushed back into him, drawing a groan from the back of his throat. "How do you lay me bare with such ease?"

"I just asked you about the cheese." Owen gave me a weak smile and an even weaker laugh. A laugh that turned into a moan when I started to move in and out of him with short, measured strokes. "Just asked about the cheese."

"If you want to meet my friends, you can meet them," I promised. "If you want to throw away the cheese, you can. If you want to leave me on Monday, I promise I won't st—"

Owen covered my mouth with his hand before sliding it over my cheek and around the side of my face. He collared the back of my neck and pulled me into another kiss, and like all the other times he'd given that part of himself to me, I could taste the truth on his tongue.

He *was* going to leave on Monday, and he was going to make sure that I kept my word and didn't ask him to stay. But before I could think about the weight of that reality, before I could decide what that future would look like for me, he wrapped his legs around the small of my back, urging me deeper into him.

"Come inside of me, Archie," he whispered, he pleaded, he begged. His eyes shone under the glare coming in from the windows, and he knew I'd never been able to tell him no.

So I didn't.

CHAPTER 18
OWEN

AFTER ARCHIE FUCKED ME ON HIS FLOOR, HE TOOK ME TO THE SHOWER and used half of his hand to make sure my hole was properly cleaned and free of cum. He promptly then bemoaned the absence of his jizz in my asshole, fucked me raw, came inside of me again, then finally pried himself away from me long enough for both of us to get dressed.

His phone hadn't stopped vibrating since we'd sat down at his table with a board of cubed meats and cheeses, the can of spray cheese auspiciously absent from the arrangement. Ignoring me, he glared down at the screen and tapped out message after message before grunting and slamming his phone face down onto the table.

"Is everything all right?" I asked, unable to stop myself from thinking back to when he'd asked me something similar after Frankie had hounded me into answering his calls.

"Just my friends," he said, tossing a block of cheddar into his mouth.

"Are you missed?"

"Something like that."

"You can go out if you wanted." I leaned back and cracked my neck. First on one side and then the other. "I won't wander off."

"They don't want to see me. They want to meet you."

I rubbed my finger against the bottom of my nose and sniffled. "Is that such a bad thing?"

"They're just…a lot sometimes."

Leaning forward, I pushed a cube of white cheese onto a slice of salami and wrapped it up into a neat little package.

"You're a lot sometimes, Archie."

His nostrils flared and his phone vibrated again. With a resigned sigh, he flipped it back over and typed out a message before looking back to me. "I know I don't have a lot of time," he murmured.

"And so many things you want to do before I go home?"

He swallowed and glanced away from me, working his jaw from left to right instead of giving me an answer.

For the most part, things between us had been good since I'd arrived in California. Or rather, since he'd picked me up and we'd flown back to California. A lot of sex, which I'd expected and, honestly, a decent amount of conversation, which I hadn't. Archie and I had talked about some heavy things too, but the mood between us had stayed steady. Sure, there were moments when I was painfully aware of the ten years of silence that existed behind us, and what would most likely be ten more years in the future too…

But I'd lost him before, and I could lose him again.

I had three days and three nights left, and I was going to get my fill.

Literally and figuratively.

Archie didn't want anything more from me than that anyway. At least, that was the lie I'd been telling myself since his confession earlier in the day. The only solace I found in the three words he'd said to me was that I knew they had to be a lie. Archie maybe loved who I was before, or the idea of what we could have been, but not *me*.

When I couldn't get the words or the lie out of my head, I ate my way through half the cheddar and all of the salami. Archie seemed content to watch me eat in silence, ignoring the sporadic alerts vibrating out of his phone. It was a weird thing for me to think about him saying those words to me because there'd been a time when that was all I wanted. When I'd confessed myself to him and hoped for the same in reply.

But he was right. There was no way it would have worked. And much like now, there was no real path forward for us. If for no other reason, that it would have killed my sister.

After finally looking back down to his phone, Archie sighed and opened his mouth to speak at the same time I blurted, "Are we going to talk about the fact that you said you loved me?"

He snapped his mouth closed and scanned my face. I inhaled sharply and let the breath out, dragging my tongue across the front of my teeth.

"Actually, no," I said before he could formulate a response. "Let's not."

"We can talk about it," he said softly. "We can talk about all of it if you want."

"I don't want."

He shoved his hair away from his face, the ends still damp and curling around his forehead.

"My friends are asking if you'd like to come out with us tonight," he said, clearly sensing that I meant it when I said I didn't want to talk about the four letter word in question.

"Where?"

"Rapture."

My mouth flashed into half a smile before falling back into place. Rapture, the private club with the gold-foiled business cards and the private play loft where I'd gotten one of the best blow jobs of my life until Archie showed up in the hallway and knew the other man by name.

That Rapture.

"I know what we did last time I was there. What I did..." I inclined my head to the side. "What do *you* normally do?"

"Honestly?"

I nodded and Archie stood, using both hands against the table to brace himself as he shoved the chair away. As he straightened up, the doorbell rang, and he glanced down at me.

"Anything I want," he said, then he gestured to me. "Are you okay to entertain company like that?"

I'd dressed casually after the shower, a pair of soft and faded jeans with a rip in the thigh and a frayed hem around the ankles in the back from years of being caught under the heels of my sneakers and a band tee from a concert I'd seen on the waterfront two summers before.

"You said tonight."

"I told you they're a lot."

I stood and smoothed my hands down the front of my shirt to wipe away some of the nervous sweat that had already started to puddle in the deep lines over the hump of my thumb. "I'm good," I lied.

Archie gave me a doubtful look, but turned anyway and headed toward his front door.

This didn't matter.

None of this mattered.

They could like me or not, but at the end of the day—end of the weekend, rather—I was getting on a plane and going home. There was no long distance option on the table for me and him, so first impressions with his friends would also be last impressions.

The front door opened, and I listened to an excited crescendo of voices filter inside. Archie tried to get them all to settle down and shut up, but one of his friends laughed and pushed ahead. That friend was the first to make his way into the kitchen and he stopped dead in his tracks after seeing me, lip twitching into what looked like it wanted to be a smirk but didn't quite know how.

Objectively, the man was handsome. Taller than Archie and almost twice as broad with a square, chiseled jaw and short-cropped dark hair. He had a devious look about him, and his lip flew back up into a smug hint of a smile.

"Flynn." Archie came up behind him and shoulder-checked him before brushing past and toward me. "Be nice."

"I'm always nice." Flynn tilted his chin toward his chest and the glint in his eyes gave me the distinct impression that he could be anything *but* nice when he wanted to be. "You must be the infamous Owen."

"You look disappointed."

Flynn stuck his hand out, and I slid my hand into his. His grip was strong and solid, and I held his stare while we shook.

"You're like a little glimpse into Archie's past that I didn't think any of us would ever get," Flynn said.

"No kidding," another man, whose name I'd yet to learn said, coming to stand beside him.

"This is Dalton," Archie said, flicking his finger toward his other friend.

Dalton was just as handsome as Flynn, with a short and well-trimmed beard that worked its way up his jaw toward eyes so dark they looked like coal.

"Nice to meet the two of you," I said, shaking Dalton's hand as well.

Dalton and Flynn exchanged a look that I was nowhere near able to decipher, their attention only broken by the sound of Archie's voice behind me.

"Did either of you want a drink?"

"I'd honestly prefer a lobotomy," Dalton said. "But I'll take gin and some aspirin if you have it."

Archie laughed and I listened to him bang around in the kitchen, unable to join him from the weight of his friends' watchful stares.

"Did you have a long night?"

"You were missed," Flynn said. "Should have gotten into the car."

"Shut up," Archie snapped, setting a bottle of painkillers and a bottle of gin down next to our lunch tray.

Dalton finally looked away from me, taking Archie's seat at the table and twisting the tops off both of the bottles.

"Long night?" I asked, making my way back to the chair I'd occupied before their arrival.

"We normally go out on Thursday nights," Dalton said, grimacing after swallowing what looked to be a rather large mouthful of gin.

"Trophy Doms business," Flynn said with a laugh.

Archie's cheeks flushed red and he pulled out another chair from the table and sat down.

"What now?" I asked.

"He hasn't told you about us?"

"He's told me you're the man I need to talk to if I want to know why he's been eating canned spray cheese," I said. "But other than that, not really."

"It's stupid," Archie said before anyone else could.

"Now you're trying to show off," Dalton interjected. "The nickname was your idea."

"It was Grayson's idea," Archie corrected.

"Who is Grayson?" I asked.

"Rob's boyfriend."

"Who is Rob?" I asked, eyes flickering between the three of them as they bantered back and forth.

"The ringleader," Archie said.

"That's you and you know it." Flynn laughed, then turned to me, expression forgiving. "Rob is another of our friends and his boyfriend called the group of us 'trophy doms' once. Archie thought it was hilarious because he's a patronizing piece of shit who's never been able to make fun of himself, so he ran with it and it stuck."

"The trophy doms," I repeated, smiling at Archie's profile because he wouldn't turn to face me.

"Trophy Doms Social Club, to be precise," Flynn clarified. "And to your other point, he eats the cheese when he gets sad."

Archie shook his head and stared down at his lap.

I wondered if he'd tried to keep them at bay not because he didn't want them to meet me, but because he didn't want *me* to meet them. I'd known these men for all of five minutes and they were ready to lay every secret they knew about him at my feet. It was a lot of power and in the wrong hands—in my hands—it could be dangerous for him.

"We go out every Thursday," Dalton said, blinking slowly and pushing the bottle of gin away. "But we were out a little later than normal last night."

"Where's Barclay and Rob?" Archie asked.

"Rob is holed up with Grayson at his house, like always. And Barclay and Val were there too, last time I checked."

"Grayson tied Val up in the back yard," Flynn added. "Did this fancy thing with the rope around his balls, and—"

"Would you stop?" Archie interrupted, smacking Flynn on the back of his head.

"You asked!"

"I don't mind," I offered, again looking between the three of them. The casual easiness that existed between them, even when I knew Archie wanted to dig himself a hole and die in it, was enviable. I was glad that if he didn't have me, he had them.

"They're a lot," Archie repeated his earlier worry.

"I know." I gave him a reassuring nod, then gave Flynn a lopsided shrug. "But I met Val last time I was in town, and I'd love to hear what kind of trouble the lot of you got into last night."

CHAPTER 19
ARCHIE

ALL OF IT WAS TOO EASY.

The way Dalton and Flynn took Owen into the fold. The way the three of them laughed at inside jokes I already wasn't a part of. The way I was an outsider in my own friend group, with my own...

My own *what?*

I had no idea what Owen was to me besides the man that I'd loved one way or the other for my whole life. That felt like enough and a disservice at the same time, but he wasn't my boyfriend. He wasn't a fuck buddy. He wasn't a one-night stand, and he definitely was more than a friend. Or...was he even a friend?

I glanced at the three of them, Owen in the front seat and Flynn and Dalton in the back. Owen turned around and laughing at something Flynn said, Dalton's hand on Owen's shoulder, pulling him toward them. The three of them had become fast friends, but I wasn't sure that what existed between me and Owen would classify as friendship. If anything, it was a truce. A four-day holding pattern so we could fuck and be done with it.

As if I could ever be done with him.

A handful of days and a dozen orgasms between us, and I knew that Owen was it for me. But I also knew he was going to leave me and move on with his life, and when that happened, I would be alone. Gratefully alone, because no one would ever compare to him and I had never been the kind of man to settle. I wasn't going to start now, and I never wanted to even try.

Pulling into Rob's driveway, I cut the engine.

"I'll be right back," I told the three of them. "Just letting him know we're here."

"He has cameras," Flynn reminded me.

I knew Rob had cameras, but Rob also had kitchen whiskey and quiet. I flipped Flynn the bird and headed toward Rob's front door. Gravel crunched under the soles of my shoes, and the disappointed look on Rob's face when he opened the door wasn't enough to stop my momentum. I pushed past him and marched straight into the kitchen.

"You look like someone shit in your cereal," Grayson said in greeting.

He leaned against the kitchen counter, bottle of water in his hand and hair freshly styled. He had a bruise on his neck, peeking out over the collar of his shirt, the outlines of Rob's teeth still visible against his skin.

"Flynn and Dalton have adopted Owen as one of their own," I said, reaching past him for the bottle of whiskey that Rob kept on the counter.

"Is that really bad?"

"It's a waste," I mumbled.

Rob came up from behind and set a glass beside me, his hand rubbing a soothing circle between my shoulder blades. "Do you want to talk?" he asked.

Grayson finished his water and tossed the bottle into the trash can. "I'll leave you to it," he said.

"You don't have to go," I offered, pouring two fingers of whiskey into the glass and shoving the bottle toward the backsplash.

Grayson hesitated, and then stayed.

"I think bringing him out here was a bad idea," I said.

"Are you not getting along?" Rob rested his ass against the

counter beside me and Grayson propped himself up against the island, facing us.

"It's not even that, I just…"

"You love him," Grayson said.

I bit the corner of my tongue between my sharpest teeth and narrowed my eyes, but answered him with a nod.

"And you don't think it'll work out," he added.

I scoffed. "I know it won't work out."

"This sounds familiar."

"It's completely different than the two of you." I took a swallow of the whiskey and groaned for how good it burned on its way down my throat.

"How so?" Rob asked.

"He's not dominant, for one. Owen is perfectly happy to let me push him against the wall and fuck him until he forgets the alphabet."

"I like that too." Grayson laughed. "That's never been the real problem."

"We're compatible."

"So are Rob and I."

"And yet, I drank this whiskey just out there." I gestured to the pool deck, lit up in golds and pinks as the sun sank toward the horizon. "Letting this guy talk about all the ways you weren't."

"He was stubborn," Grayson said. "And wrong."

"Well, I'm not wrong. Owen doesn't live here. He's only in California because I brought him here."

"He's here because he wants to be," Grayson corrected.

"You don't even know him."

"No one would have gotten on a plane after a one-night run-in with the man who broke their heart a decade ago if they didn't *want* to. That's actually a lot of reasons to *not* get on the plane, and yet…here he is."

"Owen is going home on Monday," I muttered, taking another drink.

"And then what?" Rob asked.

"And then ten more years… I don't fucking know."

Grayson scrunched his nose and let his arms fall to his sides. "That doesn't sound like it's what you want."

"Of course it's not, but Mandy…"

Grayson threw a look at Rob, and I watched Rob mouth the words *Owen's sister*. Recognition flashed across Grayson's face, and I knew they'd talked all about the debacle of Owen, Mandy, and me.

"It's been a long time, Archie. I think she would understand."

"What if I don't know how to explain it?" I finished the whiskey and set the glass down, looking up at Grayson. "I've never known what to say to her about what happened with Owen. With me and her."

"Did you love her?" Rob asked.

"Of course." I was quick to answer, but the words felt insincere as I spoke them. "I mean, I thought I did. I…maybe loved her until I realized that what was between me and Owen…"

"It was different."

I nodded.

"It's all just a mess," I said, sucking in a breath that barely filled my lungs. "I like him being here. In my space, my home. I like that he's in the car with Flynn and Dalton, and I like that they like him more than me."

Grayson chuckled, and Rob shushed him.

"It's fine." I bumped my shoulder into Rob's. "I like all of those things, I really do. And I like Owen. I like him. I…"

"You still love him," Grayson whispered.

"I told him. It's not like it's some big secret." Letting out a long breath, I pushed myself away from the counter. The kitchen whiskey did not prove as quiet or as calming as it had in the past, but I was thankful for the conversation nonetheless.

"You told him you loved him?" Grayson asked.

"I owe him the truth," I said. "After everything else between us."

"You're as hard on yourself about the things you want as Grayson is," Rob said.

"As Grayson *was*," Grayson corrected, reaching out his hand for me.

It was a kind gesture from someone I liked, but wasn't terribly close with. I took it and Grayson pulled me in for a quick hug, wrapping his arms around me and pressing his lips very near to my ear.

"If he's what you want, fight for him. Even if you have to fight yourself," he whispered, clapping his hands against my back and then spinning me toward the front door and calling over his shoulder to Rob, "Let's get out of here."

"Do you want me to get Flynn and Dalton out of your car?" Rob asked when we reached the front door. "I'm happy to shove them in my back seat."

"Or trunk," Grayson suggested. "I have rope."

I huffed out a laugh, rolling my eyes. "I heard about you and your rope last night. And Val."

Grayson made a pleased sound in the back of his throat, the apples of his cheeks flushing a bright red. "He's a fun one."

When we got outside, I found Owen, Flynn, and Dalton all out of the car. Owen had the passenger door open and he leaned against the roof while Dalton and Flynn had come around to stand facing him, still talking. I wondered if they would ever shut up again. I'd known Flynn since college and I didn't think I'd ever seen him as excitable as he'd been since meeting Owen.

"Were you trying to cook us?" Dalton asked, a teasing hint of accusation in his tone. "You didn't even crack the windows."

I felt my pocket and found my keys tucked safely against my thigh. I hadn't even realized that I'd turned the car off.

"Force of habit," I said, pulling them out. "Owen, this is my friend Rob and his boyfriend Grayson."

"Nice to meet you both," Owen said, his earlier shyness over Flynn and Dalton long gone. He looked and sounded like he was ready to further embed himself in the foundation of my life.

"Nice to meet you, Owen, but Archie, are we not friends of our own accord?" Grayson scrunched his nose. "I think I'm hurt."

"Rob will hurt you plenty later," I countered. "Don't worry."

The flush on his cheeks darkened, and his earlier warning rang loud in my ears. Turning to face Owen over the roof of my car, I lowered my voice. "Are you ready?"

Owen licked his lips and answered with a slow nod.

"Flynn, take Dalton and go with Rob," I said, not tearing my stare away from Owen.

"We like you more." Flynn pouted.

"Grayson will put you both in the trunk." I pressed the lock button on my key fob, ensuring the two of them wouldn't be able to get back inside. Owen scratched the side of his nose and lowered himself back down into the car and closed the door behind him.

"You're no fun, Archie," Dalton said, kicking a loose pile of gravel toward my tire.

"You're an infant."

I climbed into the driver's seat and closed the door. After shoving the key into the ignition, I turned to Owen. "Undo your pants and take out your cock."

"What?"

I slapped my hand against the back of his headrest and looked over my shoulder while I backed out of the driveway.

"I said take out your cock."

"Arch." Owen looked out the window. "Anyone in a car that isn't two inches off the ground is going to see."

"When I ran into you at Rapture, you were getting your dick sucked with the door open. I said take out your cock, Owen."

He grumbled, but unzipped his pants and pulled his dick out. He was soft, and I managed a look down at his dick resting against his thigh before I turned left and headed toward the freeway.

"What now, Archie?" he asked, voice rough and low.

The transmission shifted, kicking the engine into gear, almost drowning out the quiet desperation in Owen's voice.

"Just listen," I said, flipping on my turn signal and moving toward the on-ramp.

He dragged his palm down the length of his cock and I made a quiet tutting sound with my tongue against the roof of my mouth. "You don't listen with your hands, Owen."

He grunted, then dropped his hands to his thighs.

"When we get to Rapture, we're all going to get drinks and go upstairs," I told him, hitting the gas as I crested the ramp onto the freeway. It was a Friday night and I only had about three hundred feet before I hit traffic, but the speed gave me enough exhilaration to keep talking. "I need to know how much you're willing to play."

"In what way?"

"Any. Every."

I had no idea what the night was going to hold, but I needed to know how far Owen would let me take things. Grayson's words were still loud in my ears, like he was sitting beside me with a bullhorn shouting the warning at me over and over again until I took action. He was right. If I wanted Owen, I would have to fight for him. I would have to show him why I was a choice worth making.

"Would you fuck my friends?" I asked, arching a brow. "Would you suck them off?"

He swallowed, head barely moving left to right. Relief flooded my chest, and I let out a slow breath. "I don't share my toys well. So I'm perfectly happy with that answer."

"I don't want *them*," he said. "I'm fine to be around other people doing stuff. I don't even mind doing things...with you... around other people, I just..."

"Message received. Don't worry," I promised. "If I asked you to sit at my feet, would you do it?"

"I never have..." he trailed off, but his cock thickened and spasmed, lifting off his leg before landing back against his jeans.

"But you don't hate it."

"Apparently not."

"What if I made you rub your dick against my shoe, against the couch, against the wall?" I asked, "What if I asked you to hump inanimate objects to keep yourself hard until I decided I wanted you to come?"

Owen dropped his head against the headrest and closed his eyes, hips rising off the seat with a sharp thrust. He clearly liked that idea and the tightness between my own legs proved that so did I.

"Do you think I could make you come just from talking?" I reached over and curled my fingers around his thigh, giving him a rough squeeze. Owen let out a breathy moan and answered with another twitch of his cock. Precum leaked out the slit and pooled against his leg.

He rolled his head to face me, eyes hooded and dark, then his answer took my breath away. "I don't think there's any end to the things I'd do for you, Archie."

CHAPTER 20
OWEN

ARCHIE TALKED ME INTO A FRENZY AND BY THE TIME WE REACHED THE parking lot at Rapture, I was ready to blow, but when he told me to put my cock away and get out of the car, I was far from surprised.

This was the game between us, the push and pull of pleasure and need. He liked to make me hurt for him, and even after all this time, I liked the pain. It wasn't typical, but neither were we.

"I'm not a submissive," I reminded him as we rounded the back of the car to head toward the looming steps that led into the club.

"I know you're not," Archie said thoughtfully. "But I *am* a Dom."

I bit the tip of my tongue until it hurt, using the forced silence to think about what those very short and simple words meant for me. For us.

He chuckled, mouth pulling into a wry grin before he stretched his hand out for mine.

"Are you ready?" he asked.

I didn't think I was, but I slid my hand into his and let him guide me up the stairs and inside. It was dark and loud, and Archie pulled me close to him, his lips warm and wet against my ear.

"I'm glad you're here with me."

My heart skipped, but before I could reply, he was leading me up the stairs to the private loft that his friends seemed to favor over the dance floor. He stopped in front of the playroom I'd been in with Val the first night I saw him again. The door was closed this time, and Archie stared at the knob, the small green panel indicating the room was open for use.

"I thought you were a ghost," he whispered, pulling our bodies together. His back rested against the railing and mine against his chest. Archie reached one hand around, softly pawing at the dangerously hard erection he'd made me put back into my pants. "I never thought I'd see you again and there you were, coming with my name on your tongue like it was just yesterday."

"Leave the poor man alone," Flynn interrupted, coming up to the top of the stairs and shouldering past us with Dalton on his heels.

"Mind your own business," Archie shot back.

Dalton laughed and gave Flynn a shove, then Grayson and Rob were cresting the stairs, Grayson's observant gaze tracking over Archie and me, lingering just for a beat on Archie's hand and the bulge between my legs. When he looked up, he licked his lips and smirked, then headed after the others. Rob looked over my shoulder, his expression wary, but otherwise indecipherable.

"What was that about?" I asked after they'd gone.

"He doesn't want me to make a bad decision," Archie said in my ear.

"Is that what I am?"

"I don't know, Owen." He squeezed my cock and used his hips to bump me toward the door. His own cock was hard against my ass, and I groaned on reflex. "You tell me."

Archie walked after his friends, leaving me in the hallway in front of the private room. His departure didn't feel like a dismissal, but the intent of his words was clear to me. He was in this with both feet, and he needed to know if I was too. And I mean, I was for the next few days. Because what was the point of being in California with him if not to enjoy everything he had to offer, but after Monday...

There wasn't anything for us to *be* in.

Adjusting my erection behind the waistband of my underwear and my jeans, I went after him and the rest of his friends. The trophy doms. It was a ridiculous, if not fitting, name for the group of them. They were undoubtedly rich, unfairly classy, and unnervingly commanding. Not that I hated any of those things about any of them, especially not Archie, but they were a lot when they were together. I admired Grayson's ability to hold his own around them, even though I expected there was more to their story than met the eye.

"I don't think I caught your name last time I caught your load," a voice said in my ear, and I startled. Turning with one hand against my heart and the other still over my dick, I found a friendly and recognizable face topped with a well-coiffed mop of blond hair.

"Val." I smiled. "I'm Owen."

"Nice to *meet you*, meet you," he said with a grin. "I've heard your name and I want you to know if I'd known you were Archie's—"

I cut him off. "I'm not Archie's anything. We're not...It's complicated."

He threw a glance over his shoulder toward the group of men gathered in the corner of the loft.

"I know what it's like to be complicated."

"They all speak fondly of you," I said, falling into step beside him and walking toward the far corner where Archie and the rest of them had taken seats. There was another man there I didn't recognize, but his stare searched Val out like there was a string between them that no one else could see.

"And I'll always say the same about them. I'm sure I'll see you around, Owen."

We'd reached the group, and Val headed past me, going straight to the fifth man I assumed must be Barclay.

"How are you doing?" Archie asked, reaching up and brushing his fingers against the top of my hand.

"If you want honesty, I can't think about anything besides my cock."

He reached behind him and pulled a pillow out from behind his back and tossed it on the floor beside his feet. "I know I said inanimate objects, but you can use my leg if it gets too bad," he offered.

"I told you I'm not a submissive."

"There's nothing submissive about getting off, Owen. We all do it." Archie gave a dismissive shrug and pointed toward the St. Andrews Cross in the opposite corner. "Did you want to watch?"

There were two men over near the cross, and they didn't look to be part of Archie's friend group. One man, older and blonde with gray hairs peppered near his temples, worked with quick skill to spread a much younger man in front of the cross. With his arms up and his legs out, his body mirrored the X-shape of the furniture, a thick and black leather blindfold covering his eyes matched the heavy-looking black cage around his cock.

"Who are they?" I asked.

"Everybody knows somebody," he said. "That's Richard and his husband, Sam."

I watched Richard select a riding crop and use the folded leather tip against the inside of Sam's thighs. The attachment points on the cuffs rattled, audible over the low hum of conversation and the reverberating bass from the dance floor. The two of them were captivating to watch. Richard moved like he knew Sam's body as well as his own and watching Sam moan and writhe against the cross only served to make my cock harder than it already was.

Rapture should have been a scary place for me because, while I was down for rough sex and the occasional spanking, a lot of what happened was extremely far out of my comfort zone. I didn't know what I would do if Archie tried to put my cock into one of those cages, but I also knew it felt like a natural extension of the things we already did together.

"What are you thinking about?" Archie asked, again brushing his fingers against the top of my hand.

The pillow still rested at his feet and I stood beside it, rooted in place.

He knew what I was thinking about.

"Is it the crop?" He leaned forward and pulled my hand into his lap. He was hard, and he lifted off the couch to push himself into my palm. "The cage? The blindfold?"

"It's the trust," I said, looking at the way my fingers curled around his length of their own accord. "The knowing."

Archie licked his lips, the tip of his tongue lingering in the corner of his mouth while he held my hand steady over his cock. Slowly, he nodded up and down, like his head weighed a thousand pounds, carrying the understanding of my answer.

"Get on your knees then, Owen," he rasped, the side of his shoe kicking out against the pillow.

Precum leaked against my underwear, the material long ago soiled and sticky with the wetness, only getting wetter when my knees hit the overstuffed cushion of the pillow at Archie's feet.

"Do you hate it?" he asked, fingers still tangled with mine, cock throbbing beneath our hands.

I had to take a beat to catch my breath, to quiet the frantic hammer of my heart and the pulsing organ between my legs that hurt for how eager it fought against the constraints of my pants. Archie's fingers were sweaty against mine, but his hold was firm and steady when I felt anything but.

I should have hated it, but as my muscles settled into the pose, I became aware of a flurry of new sensations. The tight heat in my balls raced up my spine and through my ribs like I was supported and held in place by something bigger than myself, bigger than Archie even. And I wanted to hate it because it was him and because I hadn't been raised this way. I'd never wanted these things with anyone but...

I'd never wanted this with anyone but him.

I closed my eyes, covering my face with my hands and trying to make sense of the revelations that were unfolding in front of me, one after another after another. Had I always wanted this, even without realizing? Was this feeling right here what I'd been chasing? I had never been on my knees for Archie before—it wasn't even something we'd talked about. But if I allowed my mind to go back to the beginning, back to the nights where I'd hid outside Mandy's bedroom door and listened to the two of them be intimate, wasn't *this* what I'd always wanted?

I'd wanted his attention, his praise. I wanted him to control my cock, my orgasms, and wasn't this, wasn't being on my knees for him all part of it?

"It's all right," Archie said, voice soft and low. He stroked my hair back behind my ears, and his touch felt like electricity, sparking parts of myself awake that I never knew existed before that moment.

"What the fuck?" I whispered, the words catching in my throat. "What the fuck? What the *fuck*?"

"It's okay to not hate it," he assured, fingers still twined through my curls. "It's okay to not hate *me*."

I let my hands fall onto my lap and I went further to the floor, my ass hitting my heels. My cock still pulsed and twitched against my leg, not even the slightest bit deterred by the absolute cataclysmic explosions happening in my chest.

"What now?" I croaked, staring down at my hands, palm up on my thighs.

From across the room, I could hear leather against skin. I heard the soft whimpers of an orgasm being teased and denied, and closer still I heard the familiar sound of someone getting their cock sucked. I let my eyes close because experiencing all of my sensations at once was too overpowering, too consuming.

"You tell me," Archie answered. "What do you need to stay right where you are?"

There wasn't a single thing I needed that I didn't already have, and there wasn't enough money in the world to get me off my knees and away from Archie in that breath. With his hand in my hair, fingers trailing down to my face, the shell of my ear, I leaned into him and relished the quiet hum of approval that he made.

With the shock of the act and the pose wearing off, my arousal once again took center stage. Painfully aware of the throbbing, desperate cock between my legs and the orgasms happening around me, I knew there was only one thing I needed, and I needed it like air.

"I need to come." I cleared my throat and angled my face toward his.

Archie's cheeks were flushed, even in the dark of the room. He edged his leg toward me, placing the sole of his shoe onto the pillow and nosing the toe underneath my balls. I gasped, falling forward and steadying myself against his calf for support, which earned me another hum of approval.

"I need you to come too, Owen," he said, bracing his hand around the back of my head and holding me against his leg.

It should have been embarrassing and demeaning, but it wasn't. It was kindness and grace. It was Archie giving me exactly what I asked for as soon as I asked for it. It didn't matter that there were people around us, and I didn't care what they would think, to see me on my knees on the floor, humping another man's leg to chase my orgasm.

"You've waited long enough," Archie said, drawing his ankle in a circle that teased a pressure shift against my dick before drawing it back. I groaned, fingers digging into the back of his calf as the waves of arousal washed over me. Shuddering, I pressed my forehead to the top of his knee. My breath came in harsh pants, too loud and nowhere near deep enough to fill my lungs.

It didn't take more than the slightest movement for the edge of my orgasm to come into sight. How did Archie always do it? How did he know what to say? How to move? How did he get me there easier than anyone else ever had? Than anyone ever would?

As cum spurted from my cock, soaking through my jeans and

wetting Archie's slacks, I couldn't help but think it was the biggest unfairness of my life that the one man I wanted above all else was the one man I couldn't have.

"Right in your jeans?" He looked down at me with a smirk, like he was equal parts embarrassed and aroused by me coming in my pants after dry humping his leg on the floor of a public kink club. "That's impressive."

"Is it?"

Heat flooded my cheeks and I rested one against his calf, looking toward the railing instead of the scene being put on in the corner. It was almost a sensory overload, with the smells and the sights, the sounds, all of it too much for the heavy ache that felt like it would never leave my balls. Even after an orgasm and even with the uncomfortable stickiness of my cum drying against the cotton of my underwear and the denim of my jeans, I was still hard, still ready to give Archie another orgasm.

"I mean." He chuckled under his breath. "It's a good start."

Groaning, I shifted to ease the friction between my legs.

"You can take it out if you want," he said softly, barely audible over the sound of someone else shooting their load with as much flair as I'd ever heard anyone muster in their lives.

"What?"

"You can take it out," he said again. "No one here is going to care."

"Should I be insulted by that?" Even as I asked the question, though, my dick throbbed with interest at the idea of being put on display like that.

"They respect me too much to look at you without my express permission, Owen." Archie reached down and cradled the side of my face in his hand, brushing a chunk of my hair back behind my ear.

"Because you're a Dominant," I murmured.

He nodded, and there was enough permission in his request that I made quick work of my fly and the waistband of my underwear. Getting my cock away from the sticky material had me gasping in immediate pleasure, and I bit down on Archie's kneecap to quiet myself as to not make a scene.

"No one can hear you and nobody cares," he assured me. "Nobody cares about your orgasms but me."

I groaned and fisted my dick, giving a slow pull from root to tip. My erection was still sensitive from the first orgasm and the way my skin stuck and pulled from the drying cum and the clammy sweat on my palm was enough to make me grimace in discomfort. I let my hand fall away with a sigh, knowing I would have to wait it out to come again.

"Why did you stop?" he asked.

"It hurts."

As if to disprove my point, my dick jerked, a pearl of precum beading on the tip.

"I know," Archie agreed, jerking his chin toward my hand. "That's the point."

"Archie."

"We can stop," he offered, leaning down so our faces were only inches apart. "But I don't think that's what you want. I think you like to hurt for me, and I *know* I like to make you hurt, so I'm not understanding why you're not touching yourself right now."

He was right, and I hated him for that, but I didn't have enough willpower to even entertain the idea of stopping myself from doing what he asked. I made a tighter fist around my cock and pulled up from the base, whimpering as my fingers crested the flared crown.

Even in the dark of the club, I could see the way Archie's nostrils puffed out, the way his pupils dilated, and the way his own dick tented the soft and rich material of his slacks. He palmed his bulge, adjusting himself before turning his attention back between *my* legs.

"If it hurts, you can tell me," he murmured.

"You like when it hurts."

"*You* like when it hurts," he parroted back to me. "Now give me another orgasm, Owen. Tell me when you're close."

Screwing my eyes closed, I fought against the nerves and the need to stop touching myself. Every sensation was too much sensation, down to the callouses on my palm that rubbed my shaft like sandpaper. Cradling my balls with my other hand, Archie lifted his foot, which I didn't even realize I'd been sitting on. The toe of his shoe pushed toward my hole, pressed up against my hand and my balls, sending a new flurry of arousal through my body.

I cried out, and he made a pleased sound, nodding for me to continue.

But the longer I touched myself for him, the further away my orgasm felt. I grew frustrated, sweat beading at my temples and tension wrapping itself around my tired wrist.

"I can't," I whined, not stopping even though I wanted to.

"Nonsense."

"Archie, I can't."

"You absolutely can, and you very much will," he said, like it was that simple. That easy. Archie looked away from me then, turning his attention back to Richard and Sam on the cross.

The dismissal infuriated me, but the anger only served to push me toward proving *myself* wrong. Archie wanted me to come again. *I* wanted to come again. But more than that, I wanted his undivided attention. How dare he look away when I was right there on my knees for him, erect and swollen cock in my hand.

"Archie," I rasped his name, the emotions tangling with my physical arousal and building like storm pressure in a thundercloud.

He raised a brow but didn't look back to me.

I spit on my cock and tightened my grip, stroking faster until I pushed past the point of stopping, past the pain and the resistance. The beginning waves of my orgasm felt like stepping into a meadow after being lost in a forest. It was calm, and beautiful, and awe-inspiring all at the same time.

It was relief.

"Archie, I'm close. I'm go—"

"No, you're not."

He grabbed my bicep and gave my arm a sharp tug, tearing my hand away from my dick. It was almost like a movie in rewind, the glorious comfort I'd just stepped into was gone in a flash, and I was back in the forest, in the dark and discomfort once again. A frustrated sound tore out of my mouth and I punched the ground with my fist as the promise of my release evaporated into the ether.

"Why did you..." I could barely make words for how angry and desperate the move had left me.

He hummed and dragged his thumb across my cheekbone. There was wetness beneath his touch, and I didn't know if it was sweat or tears. Probably both.

"Because you're gorgeous like this." He licked the pad of his thumb, expression turning positively feral.

My brain was scrambled, thoughts making little to no sense as every spare drop of blood in my body had centered itself between my legs. I didn't even think I needed to touch myself at that point, but I also knew if he asked me to do it again, I would.

The ease of my submission to him should have terrified me, and I hated to find that it didn't. He was still the same Archie I'd known for my whole life. There were only so many things between us that could change, my desire to feel his wrath upon my body clearly not one of them.

"Okay," he said under his breath, attention finally fully focused on me. "Get up."

"Are you serious?"

Archie stood from the couch and hauled me up with him, not even bothering to put my cock back into my pants. He pulled me down the hallway toward one of the playrooms and shoved me inside, closing the door with his foot.

I hadn't paid much attention to the room the first time I was in there, and my focus was too shot to pay it any mind now. What I knew was Archie walked me to the far wall where there was a full length mirror, then he shoved my pants to my knees and took my cock into his own hand. His other hand rested around my throat, not constricting, just holding me in place.

"Look at yourself," he whispered in my ear, pulling up my length with little concern or care for how much his hand hurt me.

I blinked myself into focus, looking at us both in the mirror and almost coming on the spot. I looked like a disheveled mess, sweaty and flustered with my pants around my knees and my cockhead as purple as a grape. Behind me, Archie looked far more put together, still dressed entirely, but his dick pushed against my back with an urgent ferocity, and I could see the frenzy in the dark pools of his eyes.

"Do you see it?" he asked, stroking and pulling my cock like it was a toy.

"See what?" I wanted to rest my head against his shoulder. I wanted to slide onto my knees and curl up into a ball. Every muscle in my body trembled and ached for how tightly I'd been wound.

"How fucking gorgeous you are." He nipped my earlobe and growled. "How fucking mine you are."

The words were my undoing, my orgasm slamming through us both without so much as a warning. Cum shot out of my cock like a cannon blast, splattering against the mirror and finally taking out my knees. I went to the ground with a shout, and Archie moved with me, easing the fall before my knees hit the floor. The tightness of his grip didn't waver and neither did his speed, and I sobbed, entire body bucking against him, even though in the very darkest parts of my mind, I had no real interest in getting away.

And that...

That was the one thing in my life that I wasn't sure about anymore.

CHAPTER 21
ARCHIE

IT TOOK THE REST OF THE NIGHT, AND SIX ORGASMS, BUT OWEN'S BODY had finally given out on him just before four a.m. His lips formed the word *please,* but no sound came out, his eyes fell closed, and he almost immediately started to snore.

I adjusted myself against the headboard to watch him, relishing the way his tanned and tattooed skin offered such a sharp contrast against my sheets, beneath my hands. If there was anything I'd ever wanted in my life, it was this, it was him, and a weekend wouldn't be enough. A weekend with Owen would be enough to show me how good life could have been if I hadn't been such a stupid and immature prick after college. The sight of him, lips parted and thighs sticky with cum, was enough to make me forget all of the reasons I'd acted the way I had back then. It was almost enough to make me forget why there still wasn't a future for us.

I loved him. I'd told him as much, but words were words, and words didn't mean anything. Words were just useless tools that kept me up at night, questioning every choice I'd ever made. I watched Owen sleep for two and half hours, unmoving except for the drool that slicked down his chin and pooled on the pillowcase.

Carefully extracting myself from bed after realizing sleep was never going to come for me, I made my way into the kitchen where I brewed a cup of coffee and carried it into the back yard. I brought my phone with me, debating the idea of doing something absolutely catastrophic like calling Mandy, but my fingers knew better and dialed Flynn instead.

He didn't answer, so I called him again, and he finally picked up with a yawn and a muttered curse.

"You better be dying," he grumbled.

"It feels like it sometimes."

"It didn't look like it last night." Flynn yawned again. "Not with that pretty little boy of yours coming all over your Zegna slacks."

I sighed and closed my eyes. "I don't know what the point of any of this is."

"You love him, and you're also the most masochistic Dom I've ever met in my life, so I think we both know the point."

"This has never been the kind of pain I enjoy." Slowly, I opened my eyes and watched the puffy white clouds break the sky line between the dark purple of the night and the orange-pink of the sunrise. "A nipple twist here and there, Flynn. I'm not an emotional masochist."

"Are you sure?"

No, unfortunately, I wasn't.

"Honestly, Archie." Flynn yawned again. "This call sounds like you ran out of your emotional support aerosol cheese."

"It's not aerosol," I protested.

"Are you out of it?"

"No. But I can't eat it when he's here."

"He's *there*?" For the first time since he picked up the phone, Flynn sounded awake. "And why are you on the phone with me?"

"I couldn't sleep."

"Thank you for making that my problem, by the way." Flynn sighed. "You're a sad, little, lost boy, aren't you?"

"That's a little more patronizing than I would have liked, but the sentiment isn't terribly far off."

"When does he leave?" he asked.

"Monday morning."

Forty-eight hours.

I had two days and two nights left with Owen before he ran back home and never looked back. The irony of him getting the chance to leave me for once wasn't anywhere close to being lost on me, and I took a careful sip of my coffee.

"Do you want him to stay?"

"I don't want him to go," I said. It felt different, but in a way I couldn't explain.

"Have you given him a reason to not go?" Flynn asked.

I snorted, scrubbing a hand down my face. "I gave him six last night."

"Anyone can give him orgasms, you idiot. Have you given him a reason to stay with *you*?"

"Am I not a reason enough on my own?" Even as I shot the question back at him, I knew it was stupid. There was a time when I might have been enough as I was for him, but that time was a distant memory. "Don't bother answering that."

Flynn laughed. "Are you sure?"

"I'll put some pants on and come up with something."

"Put them on and *keep* them on. Remember, Archie, sex with Owen was what got you into this mess in the first place. Don't let it happen a second time."

The warning came a little too late, but I appreciated the sentiment just the same.

Flynn yawned yet again, so loud it caused me to tip my head back and follow suit. "Can I go back to bed now?" he asked.

"Yes. Thank you."

"That's what friends are for, asshole."

He hung up on me.

I set the phone down on the arm of the chair and stretched my legs out, crossing them at the ankle. It was amazing how fast the sun moved in the morning. How many times had I sat out here alone and watched the sunrise, thinking about the man who was currently dead to the world in my bed? More times than I'd ever be able to count, but I didn't think I'd ever thought about him being in my actual bed. Whenever I thought about Owen, I had imagined us a completely different life where we were both other —better—versions of ourselves. I had no idea where we lived or what we liked, but we loved each other and that was always enough.

Just one more way dreams were crueler than reality. Maybe I was an emotional masochist after all.

Owen slept through two full cups of coffee, and when I made my third, I made one for him as well and carried it back into the bedroom. The room was dark, thanks to my blackout curtains, and I sat on the edge of the bed. At some point, he'd rolled onto his back, one arm folded over his stomach and the other stretched toward my side of the bed. I didn't want to read too much into that, but it was hard to not imagine him, half asleep and reaching for me.

Maybe he'd been dreaming about me.

I situated myself against the headboard again, using the remaining minutes of his sleep to make a mental catalogue of his tattoos. For some reason, the one that kept pulling my attention was the single arrow on his middle finger, pointy end alongside his fingernail. I reached out and traced my fingertip to the end, then went lower, toward the sheet that barely covered his happy trail.

"How long have you been watching me?" he asked, sleepy.

"Not as long as you're thinking," I assured him.

He pushed the sheet down lower, revealing his flaccid cock and the dark tuft of hair around the base of his shaft. I yearned to touch him, but Flynn's biting commentary was still sharp in my ears. I tightened my grip around the coffee that I'd brought for him and pulled my other hand back toward my lap.

"Tell me about that tattoo," I murmured.

Owen rolled onto his side, propping himself with one hand under his head, his elbow resting on the mattress. The sheet somehow slipped lower, offering me no grace when it came to my willpower to not fuck him back into the floor.

"Which one?"

"The arrow on your finger."

He huffed out a soft laugh. "Why that one?"

"I don't know."

"Would you believe I had forty dollars and fifteen minutes of free time?" he asked.

I handed him the coffee, and he took it with a happy little moan that went straight to my dick. I really needed to get my head out of my ass if I wanted to keep my dick out of Owen, because he made it damn near impossible without even trying.

"I'd believe that's half the story." I picked my coffee back up from the nightstand and took a sip, waiting for him to answer.

"Of all the tattoos, Arch." Owen pushed himself onto his ass, leaning back against the headboard with his shoulder brushing mine. He turned slightly and pointed at me with his first finger, the other three curling back around toward him, which brought the arrow on his middle finger level with his chest. "Anything that's your fault is also mine."

"Owen."

He let his hand fall with a shrug. "I needed the reminder sometimes that you weren't the only villain in my story."

"You didn't do anything wrong," I said.

"We both know that's not true." Owen closed his eyes and raised the mug to his mouth. Taking a tentative drink, his shoulders sagged and he nodded. "But it's okay. I think the tattoo is a much better deal than the spray cheese."

"Can we not?"

"After all this time, Archie?" Owen laughed, taking a larger swallow.

"I told you last night why I have it."

"Flynn told me this wasn't the first time you've gone on a cheese bender."

"I'll kill him." I rubbed my fingers across my forehead, fighting back the tension that simmered just beneath the surface. "I already told you, it's a stupid thing I did because it reminded me of you."

"It's not stupid." Owen leaned over me and set his coffee down on the nightstand, then set mine down beside it. He took my face into his hands, and I would have given him all the money in my bank to know what thoughts went through his head when he looked at me.

Nervously, I swallowed, but he didn't stop his appraisal. I could feel every fingertip as they pressed into the soft skin of my cheeks, against my jaw.

"It's not stupid," he said again.

"You're my biggest regret," I whispered.

He moved to pull back and I grabbed him, curling my hands around his wrists and keeping his hands in place.

"That's not the compliment you think it is," he said.

"Not what we did." I shook my head, eyes falling closed. "Never that."

"What then?"

"Leaving."

"This again, Archie?" He let go of my face, straightening his fingers, but I didn't let go of him. I pulled his wrists together, hauled him half onto my lap.

"Can we just pretend?" I asked. "For the next two days, can we just pretend we're different people?"

He rolled his eyes. "Why? What good will that do either of us?"

"No past between us, no future that…if we're other people, the future isn't out of reach for us," I rasped, letting go of his hands. "We're just two people who can be together."

Owen didn't pull away. He just let his hands fall half onto my lap, half onto the mess of sheets between us.

"Never mind," I said quickly, practically shoving him off of me. I grabbed my coffee and climbed out of bed, heading for the window. I yanked the curtains open, casting the room under the unforgiving glare of the sunlight. Maybe that was what I needed. A reminder that no matter how much I wanted to be someone different, I was still Archer Davidson and this was the real world.

My ex-girlfriend's younger brother, the love of my fucking life, was still in my bed, my cum still inside of him.

"Archie."

"It was a stupid idea."

Owen crawled out of bed, his soft footfalls growing louder as he closed the space between us. He rested his chin on my shoulder and wrapped one of his arms around my waist. It was new and somehow so familiar. The feeling of a daydream that had haunted me for ten years come to life in my very house. My bedroom, of all places.

"It wasn't stupid," he whispered, pressing his lips against the side of my neck. I turned to face him, relishing the way his lips dragged across my skin as I moved. Owen tilted his mouth up and licked his way over my lips, my jaw, and around to my ear. He loosed a quiet moan, then smiled and whispered, "I'm in."

CHAPTER 22
OWEN

IT WAS NICE TO PLAY PRETEND.

Moving around Archie in his giant bathroom like we'd been doing it for years came naturally as breathing. The way he caught my eye in the mirror while we brushed our teeth, and how he passed me a hand towel without even looking when I was finished washing my face. It was easy and comfortable, and the drive into the city felt so much the same.

He held my hand, our fingers twined together on top of his center console as my foot tapped in time with the bass drum beat in the song he had low on the radio. With the windows down, I could smell the concrete and the smog, but hints of the ocean whipped through the air and I knew we were somehow close to the beach. He hadn't told me where we were going, though, and even as he pulled off the freeway and headed up a narrow winding road into the mountains, I wasn't sure.

"Did you come to The Getty last time you were here?" he asked when we reached the parking lot kiosk.

"I went to the beach and I went to Rapture," I said. "I checked out the hotels my sister—"

I snapped my mouth closed, not wanting to talk about my sister when we were supposed to be pretending she wasn't anyone important to us. Archie threw a sideways glance at me, but didn't ask any questions.

"I didn't go to The Getty," I finished. "Do you come here often?"

"Not as much as I used to," he said.

I waited for an explanation, but he didn't offer one so I let the car fall into silence while he drove through the parking garage. It wasn't until we boarded the tram to take us the rest of the way up the mountain that I asked him to clarify. "I feel like there's a but."

"No buts." He squeezed my hand and turned his attention out the window. "It just feels like a different life sometimes. Back then."

"You came here when you were lonely," I guessed.

"I came here when I didn't have anywhere else to go."

Archie gave me a plastic smile and hauled me between his legs, bringing our mouths together. He gave me a quick, chaste kiss, then let me rebalance myself as the tram pulled up to the museum.

"Jesus," I muttered, stepping out of the air-conditioned tram and into the warm southern California heat. "This place is massive."

"This isn't even half of it."

"Is it all…" I gestured at the beige tiles that ran underfoot, up the stairs, and up the walls.

"It's travertine," Archie said with a shrug.

We walked together up a set of shallow stairs, past a fountain and onto a promenade that held more buildings and the most beautiful view I'd ever seen. I could see the ocean, the city, the mansions that sprawled between the two, and the sky above and all around us. The sight took my breath away, and Archie side-stepped behind me, wrapping his arms around my waist and resting his chin on my shoulder. It was the same hold I'd offered him earlier, and it brought up the same illicit feelings in the deepest parts of my chest.

"What is your favorite exhibit here?" I asked.

Archie's smooth cheek rubbed against my stubble, and I closed my eyes to the view so I could feel him, which was exponentially more necessary.

"The illuminated manuscripts," he whispered.

"Will you show me?"

Archie hummed, letting out a breath that dropped more of his weight onto my shoulder. It felt *right* to be there with him that way, and we stayed like that for so long I lost count of the heartbeats between us.

"We have the whole day," he finally said, "Do you want to eat? Have some wine?"

"It's so nice outside."

He hummed again and pulled me toward a kiosk on the far end of the courtyard.

"We can picnic," he promised, buying a charcuterie box and a bottle of white wine. I took two small plastic cups from the vendor and waited while Archie collected the food and the wine. We couldn't hold hands, but we walked close back toward the edge of the courtyard and further down toward a sprawling grassy area.

We sat down and stretched out, and Archie poured me a glass of wine. As soon as his hands were free, he took my hand back into his and I had to admit, this was the best game of pretend I'd ever played.

"Tell me about yourself," I said, angling my face toward him without making eye contact.

Archie raised our joined hands to his mouth and brushed a kiss across my knuckles before returning them to the grass.

"What do you want to know?" he asked. "That's such a broad question."

"What's your favorite color?"

Archie chuckled and took a sip of his wine. "Navy blue. You?"

"Orange," I said. "Like, rusty fall orange. Not pumpkin orange."

"That's fair. What's your favorite movie?"

I had a thousand. "The Dreamers," I said.

"I don't think I've seen that one."

"We can watch it together," I suggested, even though I knew we never would. "What about you?"

"The Big Lebowski," he answered.

I turned to face him fully then, letting my brain strip away the facial hair, the tired eyes, and the expensive clothes. I saw the man beside me as the boy he used to be, with his bold words and fumbling hands, and a lifetime of promise sprawled out ahead of him.

"I believe it."

Archie laughed at that, throwing his head back and finally letting go of my hand, but only to get himself something to eat. He rolled a cube of cheese into a slice of salami and plopped the whole thing onto a cracker, which he passed to me. I ate it gladly, watching the way his fingers rolled the salami before he took a bite for himself.

"Is summer still your favorite season?" he asked.

The answer was no, but I didn't want to tell him that. Summer had been my favorite before because summer meant late days and long nights, sitting on the porch with Archie while my sister was at work. It meant ordering pizza and sitting in my back yard and counting fireflies, and late night swims in the lake that lay just beyond his property line.

"I don't think I have a favorite season anymore," I said instead of telling him the truth. "That was a pretty childish thing, don't you think?"

He scoffed, taking another swallow of his wine.

"I love the spring here," he said. "It's not humid like at home, and it's basically seventy degrees all night and all day. It doesn't stay light super late and it's enough time to get used to the darker sunrises."

"That all sounds reasonable."

"The winter is nice too, though," he went on. "For being in bed under the covers."

"If I had blackout curtains like you do, I don't think I'd ever get out of bed regardless of the season," I said.

Archie rolled his eyes, plucking another cheese cube from the tray. "It's the curtains that paralyzed you, not the sheets?"

"Should I have been impressed by the thread count?"

"*I* am even impressed by the thread count and I sleep on them every night." He flicked his finger toward my wine and I took another drink, which prompted him to top me off.

"I was impressed by the thread count," I assured him. "But more so by the man beneath them with me."

"Are you trying to flatter me?" Archie winged up an eyebrow and leaned in closer.

"Is it working?"

His voice was low and dangerous when he answered me, "Come a little closer and find out."

It was impossible to not, and when Archie's lips pressed against mine, I could taste the spice of the salami and the fruit of the wine against his skin. I opened my mouth, tilting my head to the side and letting his tongue dip inside, drawing a low moan from the back of my throat. He reached up and cradled the side of my face in his hand and I leaned into him, parting my lips even more to make way for him.

The shrill squeal of a toddler shattered the moment and stopped Archie in his tracks. We both went still and pulled away, just enough for me to see the dark flush that crept up his cheeks and the way his eyes had gone completely dark.

"Owen."

He said my name like it meant something, and I shook my head to stop him from saying any more. We weren't supposed to be ourselves on this date. This was supposed to be pretend, and the way he looked at me felt very, very real.

"What's your favorite kind of cheese?" I asked, hoping to break the moment even further because I didn't know what else to do.

"Would you believe me if I said the spray kind?"

"Not for a second," I rasped.

He smiled and let his hand fall away from my face. "Raclette."

I chuckled and pulled back farther, taking down half the

contents of my wine glass in one swallow. "I don't think I've ever had it."

"It's in fondue."

I shot him an annoyed look, then finished the rest of my wine. "I don't know what about me makes you think I've ever had fondue in my life, Archie Davidson."

He settled back onto the grass, bending one of his knees and straightening it back out after it made a satisfying crack. "I love that you're calling me Archie again."

I opened my mouth to snap back at him, but realized he was right. I couldn't remember when I'd made the switch, but at some point, something had shifted and he'd become Archie in my head again. That said more than I wanted to admit, so I swallowed back all the feelings the shortened version of his name brought up for me.

"I hate that all your friends call you Archie," I admitted, grimacing as the words left my mouth.

Archie laid his hand on my thigh, giving me a squeeze before going in for another bite of meat and cheese.

"I started going by it after I moved out here," he said.

In the marrow of my bones, I knew why he'd made the change, but asking him and receiving confirmation felt like a point of no return for us, so I didn't ask him out loud and he didn't offer to share.

"I like Swiss cheese," I said instead, preempting his rebuttal of the cheese question back onto me. There had been a time when I leaned into spray cheese like it was a drug, but I hadn't eaten it for years because every time I picked up a can, I could hear him taunting me over my affinity for it.

"Swiss and raclette." He huffed a breath out of his nose. "Do you want to have fondue? We can go tonight."

"If you want."

"I'm asking what you want. You have a day and a half. I want to make sure you're getting your trip's worth."

The truth of the matter was I wanted to spend the next day and a half with him. It didn't matter to me what we did or where we were. I would have been happy to stay in bed with him until it was time to climb the rickety stairs back up onto the plane, but the withdrawal from sex would be worse than when I'd given up the cheese.

When I'd given up him.

"Where is your favorite place in L.A.?" I asked.

"Rob's back yard," he said, quick and decisive. It was an unexpected answer that had me smiling.

"Why?"

"Because he has more expensive liquor than me and a salt water pool."

I tried to not picture Archie's life without me. But I could see him when I closed my eyes, clear as day, in an expensive back yard with a glowing pool and a glass of whiskey. All his friends and all of their boyfriends swimming together naked and God knew what else. It made my stomach simmer and burn with an unexplainable jealousy that I'd never felt before.

"What was your last serious relationship?" I asked him, desperate to get my mind off the pool.

He made an unhappy sound in the back of his throat and poured more wine into both of our cups. "You don't want the answer to that one," he said.

I took that to mean that even if it wasn't recent, it had been very serious, and that ended up making me feel worse than the pool had.

"Tell me more about the pool," I changed the subject back, giving myself whiplash, but it was better than drowning.

"How about we just finish our day here, go get some fondue, and then I'll take you to his house so you can see for yourself?"

"Is he going to mind?"

Archie laughed, using his first finger and thumb to pull a red grape off the stem on the corner of the charcuterie plate.

"That's never stopped me before; I don't know why it would now."

CHAPTER 23
ARCHIE

I F I COULD ADD AN ENTIRE LIFE I'D NEVER GET TO LIVE WITH OWEN'S hand in mine to the quickly growing list of regrets in my life, I would. But it felt like an overstatement and understatement all at the same time. The jingling cadence of his laugh when I hopped the fence in Rob's back yard immediately burned itself into my memory, and I knew it was a sound I would come back to often after Owen was gone.

"Are you sure he's not going to be mad?" Owen asked when I flipped the latch on the gate to let him in.

"He won't be mad."

Grayson might be mad, though, but that was a problem for Rob and not me. I was entirely too fond of Grayson, and endlessly pleased that Rob had managed to get his head out of his ass long enough to not fuck that whole relationship up. The two of them were perfect together—in practice, not on paper. Rob needed someone to keep him in line sometimes, and Grayson was more than up for the challenge.

Because of how much I liked Grayson, and only because of how much I liked Grayson, I fished my phone out of my pocket and texted him to let him know we were at Rob's, immediately prompting a reply *from* Rob in the Trophy Doms Group Chat, which had become the bane of my existence.

Rob: No skinny dipping.
Flynn: What? Where?
Archie: You outed me in the group chat.

I glanced up in time to watch Owen's slender fingers pop the fly of his jeans and pull down the zipper.

Rob: Same sentiment.
Dalton: Did you commit B&E?
Barclay: Not this again.
Archie: If the fence is scalable, it's hardly breaking and entering. It's practically an invitation.

Owen shoved his pants down to his ankles and stepped out of them. In a threadbare band t-shirt and his underwear, I wanted to take him right there on the lounger, but the whole point of this endeavor had been to take him on a date. To...to give him a reason to stay that wasn't the best orgasms of his life. Bringing him to the pool might have been a horrible idea.

Flynn: We have the code to the front door, you idiot.
Dalton: Jumping the fence makes him look cool.
Barclay: Nothing makes him look cool. Are you sure I can't get out of this chat?
Flynn: I'll add you back.
Flynn: So, are you saying Archie and Owen are at Rob's?
Rob: They are.

I watched Owen dip his left foot over the edge of the pool and into the water. Waves rippled across the otherwise still surface and he smiled before sitting down on the edge of one of the lounge chairs.

Flynn: I want to swim.
Barclay: I doubt they're swimming.

Flynn: They better be.

Archie: This is what I get for offering GRAYSON the courtesy of letting him know we'd come over. I didn't want him to end up with his dick smashed against the glass in the playroom, thinking no one was home.

Rob: Quite considerate.

"Who's more interesting than me?"

Owen's question tore my attention away from the conversation in hand, and I set my phone on a table face down, ignoring the incoming flurry of vibrations.

"Not one single soul," I said, stepping toward him.

"Are you going to strip?" he asked.

Yeah, this was definitely a horrible idea.

"I don't think I should have brought you here," I said, reaching back to tug my shirt over my head and off.

"Why not?"

"I'm trying to…" I dragged my tongue across the front of my teeth and looked past him to an overgrown bougainvillea at the far edge of the yard.

"Not fuck me?"

Snorting, I rolled my eyes. "You make it hard."

"That's never been a bad thing before."

"There's more than just *that* between us, Owen," I said, finally turning my attention to his face. He studied me earnestly, elbows resting on his knees and his fingers tapping together in front of him.

"I know," he agreed. "There always has been, though. You don't have to abstain to prove it."

"I don't want sex to be the first thing you think about when you think about me."

Owen smirked. "That's not a bad thing."

"But it's not the only thing."

"No," he said softly. "It's not the only thing."

The sentence didn't end with any sense of finality, and I

couldn't shake the feeling there was a *but* coming, so I jumped up and walked toward the house before he could continue on with it. The back door had a keypad that matched the front, and I pushed the four digit code and let myself in.

From the lounger, I heard Owen laugh and then settle, and I closed the door behind me, not daring to look back at him. Rob's house was silent, save for the low hum of the air conditioning unit that kept the entire space at an entirely too cold 68 degrees. My nipples almost immediately hardened, and I wiggled my shoulders, hoping to relieve some of the nerves that had already started to take root in the base of my spine.

"Kitchen whiskey," I muttered to myself.

After pouring a shot and wasting Rob's money by swallowing it back without even tasting it, I braced myself against the sink and let my head dip low between my shoulders. If Owen looked in, he'd be able to see me. I wondered what he would think. If he would think I was flustered over pretending to break into Rob's house, or if he would know I was distressed over him and the unfairly rapid passage of time.

The air conditioner switched off, and the house lapsed into a deafening silence. The door opened and then Owen's body heat pressed against my back, a welcome shift from the coldness of the house. His arms wrapped around my front and his cheek rested against my back between my shoulder blades.

"Are you pretending that we're breaking up in two days?" Owen kissed my spine. "Because that doesn't sound very fun."

"It's not," I rasped, covering his hands with my own.

"Then why are you doing it?"

"It's hard to stop," I admitted. "I know I said I wanted to play pretend, but there's not a single person on this planet that I'll ever love more than you, and that's the honest-to-God truth."

"I don't think you've ever had to pretend to love me."

He grabbed my hips and gave a tug until I turned around and faced him. We were a mismatched pair, him with no pants and me without a shirt, none of our skin touching in the places that it mattered. Like always, something between us, keeping us apart.

"I used to pretend to *not* love you," I admitted, kissing his forehead. His curls smelled like my shampoo, his skin like salt from the hours we'd spent in the sun.

I grabbed his hand, remembering the way he'd squeezed me and pulled our shoulders together while we hunched over one of the illuminated manuscripts at the museum earlier. The room was cold and Owen's hand against mine was like holding a fire poker. He was burning. He *burned*. For me.

And I for him.

"What are we doing, Owen?"

"I thought we came to swim," he answered, but the humor in his voice fell flat. He cleared his throat. "You know, when I fell in love with Frankie—"

I cut him off quickly, turning us both so it was his ass pressed against the kitchen sink. I didn't glare at him, but I towered enough to show him how much I meant what I said, "I don't want to hear about the way you loved another man."

"You may not want to, but you need to," he said, and then he waited.

He waited and I finally, begrudgingly, nodded for him to go on.

I could still taste the whiskey in my throat, licking like fire as it settled in my stomach, which was already tumultuous just from being in Owen's presence.

"I fell in love with him and he was nothing like you. At first, it felt like a blessing. He was so patient with me, so full of grace when the cracks in my heart showed."

"Owen."

The only thing worse than hearing about how he loved another man was hearing about how much I'd hurt him before that man came along to repair the damage.

"But I fell out of love with him just as slowly." He grabbed my chin between his thumb and forefinger, pulling me down so he could look me in the eye. "I never fell out of love with you."

"Of course you did."

"I hated you," he said, eyes wide. "I hated you so hard and for so long, but I never stopped *loving* you, Archie. And I haven't stopped now, and I don't know what that means for me."

I'd heard enough.

I crashed my mouth against his, grabbing his face and taking a step back from the sink so I could get my hands under his thighs. Owen jumped, wrapping his legs around my waist and his arms around my neck. He angled his head so I could deepen the kiss, the breath leaving his lungs when I walked him back against the fridge.

He'd never stopped loving me.

He'd never stopped loving me.

He'd never stopped loving me.

And that didn't change anything. It had no bearing on the entire country between us or the history with Mandy. It didn't change the fact he was leaving me on Monday and we had less than thirty-six hours left. I still didn't know if it meant these moments with him would be my last, because if he'd loved me the whole time and iced me out the way he had, I didn't expect that to change.

We were still *us*.

Owen's cock throbbed against my stomach, pressing against his underwear and all but begging to be released. He humped himself against me, much like he'd done the night before at the club, but with a different kind of desperation. He was almost frantic, like the threat of this being our last time together hung over us like the blade of a guillotine. I matched his energy, balancing him against the fridge and freeing one of my hands so I could get my cock out of my pants.

I didn't have lube, but I didn't care. I knew that was unfair and would hurt us both in the end, but with Owen, I had an unchangeable one-track mind, it seemed. I was so focused on the wet heat of his mouth and the softness of his body that I didn't hear the beeping of the front door key pad. I didn't hear the door being opened. All I heard was the way Owen breathed and moaned and moved against my body, every muscle begging for what I wanted to give him.

I even missed the click-clack of someone's expensive shoes making their way across Rob's floor, and I could have ignored their presence entirely if I'd tried harder.

"Shit," I cursed into Owen's mouth and turned, trying to keep my dick and the swell of his ass out of view.

I slowly dropped him to the floor and glanced over my shoulder, finding a very unamused Grayson standing in the entry, his arms folded in front of his chest. Rob was behind him, a smirk playing across his lips, and farther back, Flynn, looking like he'd just seen the greatest show on earth.

"Don't stop on our account," Flynn said.

"Ignore him," Grayson snapped, even though there was hardly any heat in it at all. "But please tell me which one of you is going to clean Owen's assprint off of the fridge?"

"It's a fingerprintless fridge," Rob said, and I buried my laugh into Owen's curls.

"For fuck's sake." Grayson leveled a glare up at him that did nothing but make Rob swat him on the ass. "Go get your trunks on and get yourself in a better mood."

"It's where we *eat*," he protested.

"Like you've never fucked in here," I wagered.

Rob laughed again, and Grayson huffed. "I'm going to rename the lot of you The Participation Ribbon Pricks, I swear to God."

But he laughed, even as he pretended to push Flynn out of the way and head toward the stairs.

"My plan's foiled," I whispered, pressing a kiss against the side of his head.

"Your plan was to take me on a date and take me swimming at your best friend's house," Owen said. "You've taken me on a date, and we're not entirely waylaid on the last part. There's hope for you still."

I didn't see Flynn stripping out of his clothes until I caught a glimpse of his bare ass streaking out of the house and onto the pool deck. I did, however, get an eyeful of his ball sac when he launched himself into the air and tucked his legs against his chest, hollering *cannonball* so loud that I didn't even hear whatever Owen whispered up at me that had him looking like the house had collapsed around him.

"What did you say?" I asked, stroking my fingers across his cheek.

He shook his head and reached down to adjust his erection, even though his underwear wouldn't do anything to hide him.

"Nothing." He smiled up at me. "Let's get into the pool before Flynn splashes all of the water out."

Grayson came down the stairs, pineapple print swim trunks hanging low on his hips. He stretched his hand out for Owen, clapping his fingers to get attention.

"Come on, Owen. On the way out, we're going to talk about all the places you should never put your ass, starting with a stranger's refrigerator."

CHAPTER 24
OWEN

S<small>UNLIGHT BLASTED THROUGH THE GUEST ROOM WINDOW, CASTING A</small> golden glow across Archie's bare chest. The sheets were tangled around his thighs, his half-hard cock resting thick and plump against his thigh.

And I was terrified.

The night before, and the very early morning, spent at Archie's side and surrounded by his friends was a glimpse of a life that was so beyond out of reach for me. Tomorrow I would be on a plane back home and our lives would once again separate. The past days and nights with Archie would be memories, albeit nicer than the previous ones, but memories just the same.

It felt like it had been days since I checked my phone, since I'd even thought about my actual life back home. Rolling away from Archie, I climbed out of bed, careful to not wake him. He didn't even snore or stutter, and I let myself watch the steady rise and fall of his chest while I put my pants on. My phone sat heavy in the front pocket, and I waited until I'd slipped out of the guest room to pull it out.

I had a couple text messages from Mandy, nothing urgent, and I answered her back, letting her know I was feeling better and that I would see her soon. I had another batch of messages from Frankie, and I offered him the same platitudes I'd sent my sister.

"You look stressed."

A voice distracted me, and I fumbled my phone, barely managing to catch it before it landed on the floor. Getting my wits about me, I recognized Archie's friend Flynn in the kitchen. He had on a pair of black basketball shorts and nothing else, just a messy mop of brown hair and some scruff along the angle of his jaw. He held a coffee mug in both hands, and his stare was narrowed in on me.

"I'm fine," I said.

"Rob doesn't keep spray cheese in the fridge like Archie does."

I huffed out a laugh and looked down at my feet. Flynn stepped to the side so I could get to the coffee pot, and I shuffled toward him. I caught the scent of the pool on him and a hint of cologne that smelled like more money than I had in my checking account. It was a sharp reminder of just how different he was, how different Archie was...from me and the life I'd built in his absence.

"He used to make so much fun of me for the cheese," I said. "He'd never eat it when I offered."

"I don't blame him."

"I don't know when he started eating it."

The coffee pot whirred to life, warming the water and getting ready to brew.

"Probably as soon as he got to California," Flynn said. "I've known him since we were in grad school and he's always had a taste for it, but only when he's stressed or sad."

There was a part of me that hated to think of Archie stressed *or* sad, but there was a larger part of me that took some comfort in the fact that his abandonment had hurt him too. I'd always imagined that he left and never looked back for me because he didn't care. Because I didn't understand how someone could do what he did if you cared for another person? But with my return flight home so within reach I could see it, my perception changed. I was getting ready to leave him, and the distance would kill me this time.

For years, I thought he'd walked away from me because he was weak and scared, but as I readied myself to do the same thing, I knew better.

"If he would have told me about you sooner, I wouldn't have spent a decade teasing him about his trash taste in cheese." Flynn chuckled softly and the coffee pot finally started to spurt into the mug.

"Why do you think he didn't?"

"Because he's a fool for you. Absolutely head over heels, and he clearly always has been."

"I doubt that," I muttered.

"He's gone for you now," he went on with a shrug, like we were talking about something as casual as the weather. "It's going to kill him when you leave."

"This was never supposed to be a thing," I said. "This was four days and…"

"You believe that?"

"Why wouldn't I?"

"I don't know what your perception of us is." Flynn stepped out of the way while I finished making my coffee. "But I can't imagine you see us, see him, as anything other than millionaire playboys with too much money to burn and an endless waiting list of men to take to bed."

I snorted. He wasn't far off base.

"Archie has…I don't even know if I should be telling you this." Flynn glanced toward the hallway that led to the guest rooms like he was worried about getting caught.

"Did you want to go outside?" I asked.

He furrowed his brow and let out a soft sigh. "I'm not trying to spill Archie's secrets. He's my best friend, I just…"

"I get it." I jerked my head toward the door. "It looks nice out. We can talk outside, no secrets required."

Flynn followed me out to the pool deck, where I shoved some discarded clothes from one of the loungers so I could sit down. There were pants and towels and empty bottles of alcohol, and Rob's back yard looked more like a college rager than a group of thirty and forty-something year-old men getting together on a Saturday night. A stab of longing pierced through my chest, and it felt like jealousy at first. I wasn't sure if I was jealous that Archie had so many friends or that they had *him*.

After we'd both settled onto chairs with coffee in hand, I stared out toward the bushes at the far end of the yard. I didn't know what Flynn had wanted to say to me, but I figured it would be easier if he didn't have to face me while he did it. I could tell the decision to speak freely weighed on him, and I respected how closely he held Archie's confidence.

"None of us are saints," Flynn finally said, and I nodded. "We've all had our hearts broken a few times. It comes with the territory, you know."

He gestured to the pool, to the house, to the extravagance of the life they lived. I thought about my one bedroom apartment and my Goodwill couch. I thought about my ramen dinners and my car that was two hundred miles past needing an oil change because I didn't have money for it.

"All of us except Archie," he corrected.

I turned my head toward him, finding his attention focused on the tree line as well. After my conversation with Archie at the museum the day before, where he'd started to talk about the last serious relationship he'd been in and stopped, I'd been dreading the story. I wanted to be glad that Archie had found a love so massive that it was painful to relive the loss of, but that spear of jealousy burned and thickened and turned inside of my chest.

"Okay," I said, because there wasn't anything else to say.

"He's only been in love once."

It was impossible to breathe, impossible to swallow.

I nodded, and looked down at my coffee, finding my reflection in the dark and still surface as I steeled myself for the rest of the story Flynn was sharing.

"It nearly fucking killed him, you know?"

I closed my eyes, jealousy bursting like a volcano behind my ribs.

"Archie is Archie, though. He knew, but he didn't know. He's a little aloof sometimes. But by the time he realized what he'd lost, it was too late for him to get it back because he's stubborn. And he's so righteous. Acting like he would bear the burden to save the person he loved from having to shoulder it."

"You don't need to tell me this," I said, desperate for Flynn to stop.

Tears prickled the corners of my eyes and I wanted to scream and throw the furniture into the pool for how envious I was that Archie had loved someone the way I loved him. I thought about the lonely nights as a teenager when he'd been with my sister, and the better nights when she'd been gone and we'd been together. Just as friends, of course, but he was so close to me and he always smelled so good. He smiled so nice, and there wasn't a single person in the world back then who'd made me feel as good as he did.

I loved Archie before I'd known what it meant to love another person, and I loved him still. Even with his expensive home with his fancy clothes and his luxury car, he was still the too tall and too skinny boy that I'd secretly fallen in love with as a teenager. He was the one thing I'd wanted back then, and even though time had healed that wound, it hadn't taken away the way I wanted him.

If this trip had done nothing else, it had proved that time and time again.

"You're missing the point," Flynn said.

The sliding door opened, and we both looked toward the house. Archie filled the frame, half dressed with his hair askew and his eyes half closed. I didn't realize he'd looked frantic until he saw me and then *didn't*. His shoulders relaxed and his lips curved up into a softer line instead of the terse frown he'd worn. My breath caught in my throat, and I blinked as quickly as I could, hoping to hold back the tears that had threatened to spill at the beginning of Flynn's confession.

"I'm going to buy Rob curtains," Archie said, scrubbing a hand down his face. He was trying to play it casual, but as he came toward us, his movements were jerky, like whatever fear he'd carried hadn't quite left him yet.

I spread my legs open and Archie plopped down between my thighs, leaning back against my chest with a content little sigh. The pose was awkward, but he was still warm from sleep, and I set my coffee down next to a half-drunk whiskey bottle so I could hold him against me.

"What were you two talking about?" he asked, angling his head up to face me as much as he could manage. I kissed the side of his head. "I didn't mean to interrupt."

"I was just telling Owen how insufferable you used to be. Back when we first met."

He scoffed. "Hardly."

"He said you were stubborn, actually. Righteous."

"Don't tell all my secrets," Flynn admonished.

Archie wiggled against me and I wrapped my arms around his chest to hold him still.

"I was getting ready to tell him how you keep everything so close to the chest that I didn't even realize how heartbroken you've always been until two weeks ago when he walked back into your life."

In my arms, Archie's entire body went rigid as a board.

"What?" I asked, looking toward Flynn with wide eyes.

"I didn't realize. Honestly, I didn't put it together until he put you on a plane and brought you here."

"Shut up, Flynn," Archie said, almost a plea, even if there wasn't any real fight in it. Just resignation laced with a little bit of fear.

Flynn stood up and stretched, cracking his back with a heavy breath. "I didn't realize what it was back then."

"What are you even trying to say?" Archie's tone was exasperated, but trembling. In my arms, his muscles twitched, and I tightened my hold around him.

Flynn shot Archie a scathing look, then flicked his stare toward me. "It wasn't until I saw the way Archie loves you that I realized it's what he's been doing all along."

He raised his mug and clicked his tongue against the roof of his mouth, and went back into the house, leaving Archie and me in the lounger.

"What does that mean?" I asked.

Archie wiggled out of my arms, shaking his head. Turning to face me, he sat cross-legged, unable to meet my eyes. I shifted back so my spine was straight, and I waited for him to explain.

"Archie." I licked my lips. They were parched. "Tell me about your last serious relationship."

He exhaled and angled his head to the side, looking up at me with earnest and tired eyes.

"Owen, come on."

"It's not a big ask."

I didn't want to fight with him, not on my last day in California, but I wanted to know the truth. I deserved to know the truth.

"It was you," he whispered, giving me a weak shrug. "The last relationship, the last person I loved, the last person I wanted to build a life with. They're all you, Owen. It's you. It's always been you."

CHAPTER 25
ARCHIE

OWEN LOOKED AT ME LIKE HE'D SEEN A GHOST.

"Archie, what? We never…"

"I know." I scrubbed a hand down my face, not sure of how to explain. I glanced into the house, finding a grinning Flynn staring out the window with Grayson beside him. Grayson gave a thumbs up and Flynn mouthed an apology. I would deal with them later. I had more pressing things to attend to.

Namely, Owen.

"I just…in my head, I guess I…"

Shit.

Fuck.

"It was me," he said softly.

"I mean, technically my last relationship was your sister, but—"

He held up a hand and I snapped my mouth closed before I said something even more regrettable. The silence between us stretched on long enough that I debated flinging myself off the chair and into the pool, if only to drown and put us both out of the misery my confession had just thrown at us.

"In my head, it was…it was you, Owen," I admitted. "I had so many ideas and dreams, fantasies about what life could have been like, what it would have been."

"But you left me," he said.

"You were my friend, and I didn't..."

Why were words so damn hard?

I'd talked my way into every bed I'd ever wanted to get into. For my entire adult life, I'd used nothing but words to get myself —and others—off. I'd even finessed my way through multi-million dollar real estate deals and now that the things I said actually mattered, I couldn't string a coherent sentence together to save my life.

"I didn't realize that I loved you until you told me that you hated me," I said. "I hate you, Archer, you said."

"If we're being honest, I've said it a lot."

I pushed a self-deprecating breath out of my nostrils and shoved my sleep mussed hair away from my face. Owen watched me so patiently, so steadily. I didn't deserve any of it, but I'd take it all.

"Rightfully so," I agreed. "I've said the same thing to myself too. More times than I can count."

"But the facts are still the facts, Archie."

I reached for his hands, grabbing them tight so he couldn't leave. I couldn't bear him leaving me.

"Facts can be changed," I said. "They can be spun."

"This isn't a fucking business deal."

"I know!" I snapped, pulling him closer. His knees came alongside the outside of my thighs, our hands held between us. He threaded his fingers through mine like he was just as desperate to stay with me as I was with him. "This is so much more important than any deal I've ever made."

"You can't spin this, Archie." The corner of Owen's mouth twisted downward into a sour-looking frown. "There's nothing that we can say to my sister to make this okay."

"It's been years. She's getting married. It's not like..."

There was no way this transgression could haunt me for the rest of my life. I didn't believe for one second that Mandy would begrudge either Owen or me for being together. She was in love with someone else, building a life with them that didn't have anything to do with me or him. I would just have to talk to her. I would have to explain, which was something I should have done a very long time ago.

"Archie," he protested again.

"I'll talk to her," I said, breaking our hands apart and raising mine in a small gesture of defeat. "I'll call her and apologize, and I'll tell her the truth."

"Don't you dare."

"She's getting married to someone else," I reminded him.

"Exactly," he said. "That's why it's not the time."

"It's the perfect time," I countered. "She's head over heels for someone else or she wouldn't be getting married. We can put the past behind us so you and I can finally stop living in it."

"It's not that simple!" Owen swung a leg over the lounger and stood up, walking away from me with his hands bracketed on his hips. I spun on the seat, facing him but not getting up to go to him. Fisting my hands at my sides, I dug my nails into the clammy skin of my palms to ground myself. A quick glance over my shoulder at the house thankfully showed an empty window, Grayson and Flynn nowhere in sight. I didn't want them to witness this. Didn't want them to see the worst parts of me on display again, because Owen made me needy and he made me desperate. He took me apart in ways no one ever had before or would again.

Didn't he see that?

Why wouldn't he understand that life had given us a second chance and it was worth fighting for? That it was irresponsible of us to get to the edge of this cliff and turn back because we were too scared to jump off.

He turned on his heel and stared at me, then looked up at the sky and sighed. After a handful of minutes, he came back, inserting himself between my knees. I curled my hands around the backs of his thighs and rested my head against his stomach. My pulse hammered in my head and his happy trail tickled my ears, but I held him tighter and, with a reluctant sigh, he threaded one of his hands through my hair.

"It's not that simple, Archie," he said again, this time with a sigh. His hand went limp against the top of my head, and I dug my fingers into the backs of his thighs.

"You're wrong." I pulled my head back so I could look up at him. "It's been complicated for long enough, but it doesn't have to be, not anymore."

"You're not listening to me."

Owen slowly untangled my arms from around his legs and put space between us. I shook my head, biting my lips between my teeth until they ached.

"Don't do this," I begged.

He swallowed and looked up at the playroom window, then back down at me as he pulled his cell phone out of his pocket.

"My best friend is threatening to come by my house because it's so unlike me to isolate the way he thinks I am. Every time I get sick, he brings me soup, he always..." He snapped his mouth closed and held his phone in the air before letting his hand fall down to his side.

"Always has," I finished for him, finding myself sick with jealousy over the man who'd had so many years to take care of Owen when it should have always been me.

"I'm lying to my sister."

"You've been lying to her for years." I finally stood and took a step toward him, hands raised again in surrender. "Aren't you ready to stop? Don't you want to tell her the truth, Owen?"

He shook his head, a tear tracking down his cheek. I took another step toward him.

"I'll tell her," I offered. "I'll tell her the truth of the whole thing. From then to now, because if she knows how long I've loved you, she has to—"

"Archie, stop." He closed the space between us and shoved both of his hands against my chest. I curled my fingers around his wrists so he couldn't pull away and tugged him closer. He lost his balance and stumbled into me.

"If she knew you loved me and that I loved you too, she'd want us to be together," I rasped.

"You don't know a single thing about her."

"I know I was going to you that night. She knew your feelings mattered to me."

"She didn't know how much," he whispered.

"She didn't know a lot of things back then. Neither of us did. But we know now. I know now, Owen, that I don't want to live this life without you anymore."

"Please don't do this."

Another tear fell from the corner of his eye, then another and another. He shook his head, bleached curls flying the faster he moved. Like if he disagreed with me enough, I'd stop. But that just proved he didn't know a thing about the man I'd become. I'd gotten through school, gotten rich, built my whole life around the relentless pursuit of the things I wanted. Owen was the only thing I'd never chased, the only thing I'd ever willingly let go. But now that I had him back, even if only for a handful of days...

Well, I was a different man than I'd been before.

"I love you, and I know you love me. I *know* you do, Owen." Even to my own ears, my voice sounded tight and urgent, nearly desperate.

"The last few days have been great."

I dug my nails into his wrists to shut him up. I knew where he was going and I hated it. I didn't want any part of it. I wanted a ball gag from Rob's playroom that I could shove into his mouth and strap around the back of his head so he wouldn't say all of the things I knew were coming.

"But I have a life, Archie. And you're not in it. You haven't been in it for years. You can't just..."

I tapped my finger against his temple. "I'm right here."

I pressed against his heart. "I'm here."

He grimaced and looked at the way my fingers splayed out across his sternum.

"I wouldn't trade this weekend for anything in the world," he whispered.

"But you are. You're trading it for another ten years of nothing."

"More than ten years," he corrected.

No.

I couldn't stand for that. I walked us both back until his shoulders hit the wall. The second floor of the playroom above us jutted out, casting a sharp line of shade that had us both shivering from the cold.

"I'll talk to your sister," I promised. "I'll apologize and explain."

He shook his head

"And I'll apologize to you," I said. "Again and again. Every day for the rest of my life, but I'm begging you not to do this."

"I'm not trying to hurt you," he whispered, screwing his eyes closed. "I'm just trying to do the right thing."

I dropped our foreheads together, swallowing down the whimper that threatened to burst out of my chest. "Paying me back for leaving you then isn't the right thing."

He grunted, bumping me with his forehead until I opened my eyes.

"This doesn't have anything to do with our past," he muttered. "This weekend, this morning. It just put everything into perspective for me. This is your life, Arch. It's a good life."

"It's empty."

My ribs cracked, my sternum spider-webbed like he'd taken a sledgehammer to my chest. There was no way this was happening. No possible way that after three days of absolute and mindless perfection, I was losing the man I'd pined after my entire adult life. It had been careless to walk away from him when we were teenagers, and I'd be damned if I let him do the exact same thing to me but as adults.

"Owen." I lifted my hand from his chest and flattened it back down, touching him over and over to make sure he was real and he was still in front of me. And then, so carefully, he took my face into his hands and dragged his stare over every crease and line and angle. He had to have seen my tears because I could feel the salty wetness covering my cheeks, my chin, and the hollow of my throat.

"I'm sorry," he said softly, so low I barely heard him.

"Don't make the same mistake that I made back then," I begged. "Walking away from you was the worst decision of my life, Owen. I'm begging you to give me a real fucking chance to show you this can work."

He exhaled and closed his eyes, pressing our lips together in a delicate kiss. I knew he'd done it to shut me up, but I took advantage. I licked the seam of his lips until his mouth opened, and then I dove in. Fully and wholeheartedly, because that was what he deserved from me, what he deserved from everyone. I moaned into his mouth, pushing him against the wall and stretching my tongue as deep as I could reach, like I was maybe, hopefully the only person to ever kiss him so deeply.

He held my face tight in his palms, kissing me back with as much frantic intensity as I gave him. And it wasn't long until our bodies got the better of us, and when his hips bucked against me, I acted fast. Reaching into his pants, I fisted his cock, swallowing down any protest he could have offered. And I kissed him while I jacked him off, loving the way he sniffled and whimpered and moved because of how good it was with me.

It was so good with me.

He had to see.

He had to understand.

He came quickly with a garbled cry against the corner of my mouth, and I didn't stop stroking him until his little moans turned into painful whimpers. His cum coated my fingers and my tears covered his, and I could tell by the tension that radiated out from him that it hadn't been enough.

I'd failed him yet again.

"Please, Owen." I licked the taste of him off my lips, leaning back enough to see his tear-streaked face. "Don't do this."

"I hate you for this, Archer." My full name came out barely more than a strangled cry. "I hate you for reminding me just how fucking much I love you."

THINGS HADN'T GOTTEN BETTER WITH ARCHIE.

After the argument at Rob's pool, everything was tense and awkward, and when I asked him to push the flight to Sunday night instead of Monday morning, he obliged. He hated it—I could tell, from the tightness that spread across his shoulders and the jerky way he helped me carry my bags down to the car, but he didn't fight me on it. I was under the impression there was too much going on in his head to protest, and I didn't know if I liked that or not.

What outcome had I been after in the first place?

I hadn't meant to pick a fight with him, but as our little pretend weekend drew toward its end, the crushing weight of reality had started to settle, and I didn't see the point in dragging anything out for any longer than we already had. Archie and I had shared a few great days, but that was all it could ever be.

The flight home was miserable after I'd fought Archie on the tarmac about accompanying me back home. The way his cheeks burned dark and his eyes filled with frustrated tears was something that would haunt me as long as the rest of our cursed memories. He'd let me kiss him, though, or I'd let him kiss me, and it was sad, and bitter, and salty, and far from the kind of goodbye either of us deserved.

I didn't eat or drink anything on the plane, choosing to instead keep the taste of him in my mouth for as long as I could. And I took a cab home from the airport, pads of my fingertips set softly against my lower lip until I was on my welcome mat, fishing my keys out of my pocket.

Before I could get the key into the lock, my front door swung open, revealing a Frankie, a worried accusation painted across his face. He took in my appearance, from what was undoubtedly my splotchy cheeks and red-rimmed eyes to the backpack slung over my shoulder and the slump in my spine, then stepped out of the way to let me into my apartment.

I dropped the bag just inside the door and went straight to the couch, collapsing without a word. When he sat down beside me, I toed off my sneakers and shifted, leaning into him instead of the arm. Without a word, he wrapped his arms around me and I buried my face into his chest, finally letting all of the tears I'd held back at Rob's house fall.

I soaked his shirt, the wetness covering my face so thoroughly I knew every trace of Archie had been cleansed from my lips and my skin, so when Frankie offered me water, I didn't hesitate to drink it. I had more tears to cry, I knew. I would need the hydration. Frankie didn't say anything. He just stroked his hand down my back in a way he'd done long ago, and he waited for me to speak first.

"I was with him," I whispered, sniffling and wiping my nose with the hem of Frankie's already ruined shirt.

"Him?"

I flung myself out of Frankie's arms and tucked my body into the corner of the couch. He handed me back the water bottle, and I washed the rest of Archie out of my mouth.

"I was in California," I muttered. "With Archie."

"Archer?"

"Arch—" I stopped myself. There was no point in correcting Frankie, because although for a few days he might have been

Archie to me again, that's not who he was. Not who I needed him to be. I could forget Archer. I could hate Archer.

I *needed* to hate Archer.

"Where do you want to start?" he asked.

"When I was in California looking at wedding venues for Mandy, I ran into him. Totally on accident."

"Alright." Frankie cocked his head to the side and waited for me to go on. It was only fair that he judge me the way he was. Frankie was the one who'd borne the brunt of the aftermath of whatever had existed between Archie and me. He was the one who'd been so patient and kind as I'd picked up the pieces of my life and tried to understand who I was without my best friend, the man I'd fallen in love with. And he'd loved those bits and pieces of me like I was whole, and...

Well.

"We hooked up. I won't go into the details, but we stayed in touch when I came home and he flew me out for the weekend."

"I'm sorry. He *flew* you out? What does that even mean?"

I sighed. "He's pretty well off. Sent a plane and all that."

"Sent a plane?"

"Frankie, this story is going to take a lot longer to tell if you make me repeat everything twice."

The corner of his mouth twitched and he arched a brow, again waiting for me to elaborate.

"A private jet," I clarified, chuckling under my breath when Frankie's eyes went wide. "He's loaded. All his friends are rich as fuck."

"So you weren't home sick, you were in California. With him."

The disdain dripped off his words, especially the last two and I closed my eyes to avoid his stare.

"I'm sorry I lied to you, but I didn't know what to say."

"You could have said, 'Hey Frank, I'm in California making some stupid fucking decisions. See you Sunday.' That would have been a good start."

"This is why." I pushed myself up off the couch, needing to get space from the intensity of his vitriol. "This is why I didn't tell you, because I knew how you'd react."

"And wasn't that a sign, don't you think? My best friend would *hate* this for me, so maybe I should think about that before I do it?" Frankie didn't stand up, but he angled his body toward me as I walked to the other end of the room.

"I was clearly not thinking with my head," I snapped.

"You were. Just the wrong one."

I sucked in a breath and let it out slowly, mouth pulling into a smile as Frankie started to laugh from the couch. The tension snapped like a glow stick, and he stood up and crossed the room toward me, arms open. The entire side of his shirt was covered in my tears and my snot and my spit, and I went right back into his arms like they were the only home I'd ever known. Because for a time, they had been.

"What happened after that?" he asked, resting his chin on the top of my head.

"Nothing bad, not like you're thinking." I mumbled into his chest before turning and pressing my cheek against his sternum. "He told me he loved me. He said he wanted me to stay."

Frankie went still.

"I told him I couldn't."

"Why not?" he asked.

"Are you serious?" I tipped my head back to look at him. "You were just reading me the riot act for going in the first place and now you're asking why I didn't stay?"

"I read you the riot act before I got the facts."

"You still don't have all the facts," I said.

He looked at me like he wanted to strangle me.

"Even if I wanted to stay—" I started and he cut me off.

"Did you?"

"Did I what?"

"Did you want to stay?" he asked softly.

"Yes, but… it doesn't matter." I cleared my throat and took both of his hands in mine.

"Why not?"

"His life is there. Mine is here." I gestured toward the sparsely furnished but well-loved apartment that I'd spent years making into my home.

"People can relocate," Frankie reminded me.

"He would never."

"There's two of you," he said.

"I don't want to leave you...or Mandy."

"There's the real issue, Owen." He gave me an extremely stern teacher look that let me know he'd sussed out the truth without me even having to confess it. "It's not you and I know it's not me. It's her."

"He broke her heart."

"He broke your heart too, and you obviously forgave him." Frankie shook his head. "And Mandy is getting married, so she's clearly over it."

"Archie isn't the kind of man you just *get over*."

"Do you love him?"

The change in his line of questioning gave me whiplash, and any biting reply died in the back of my throat. I swallowed, blinking rapidly to fight against the fresh wave of tears that threatened to spill at the thought.

"That's a yes," Frankie said for me.

"I didn't say that."

"You didn't have to." He let out a breath, his own shoulders giving out.

"Do you hate me for it?" I asked.

"If I didn't hate you for loving him then, I couldn't very well hate you for it now," he said, reaching his hand out for me again.

I took it, and he kissed the tops of my knuckles, walking us both back to the couch. I sat down with a tired groan, and Frankie pulled me against him, adjusting us both so my back rested against his chest.

"Tell me about your trip," he said softly against my ear. "Tell me about the man who has always held your heart."

"That's not fair to say," I protested.

"I've always known it, Owen," he assured me. "Even if you haven't."

I swallowed and settled against him, unable to stop myself from comparing the fit of his body against mine to Archie's and finding all the ways it was lacking. Not that it was any fault of Frankie's, he just wasn't Archie, and that was the first time I felt the gravity of the decision I'd made.

"I wonder if he felt this way," I choked out, screwing my eyes closed and balling my hands into fists at my sides. "If he hurt this badly when he walked away from me."

"I'm sure it was the same or worse. Everything is amplified when you're young. When it's the first of everything," he said.

"I had a really nice weekend," I rasped. "We went out with his friends. He took me on a proper date."

"Had he ever done that before?"

"A date?"

Frankie nodded against the top of my head.

"No, we never had. Back then we'd just been friends, he'd been with Mandy, it wasn't..." I trailed off, and Frankie was quick to pick up the change in my mood.

"Where did you go?"

Thinking of our date, I chuckled, fingers going tingly at the memory of Archie scaling Rob's fence like we were teenagers again.

"We went to a museum and had a picnic, then we broke into his friend's house to go swimming."

I thought about Flynn, and Dalton, about Grayson, and the rest of them. I told Frankie about all of them and the lecture from Grayson on not having sex in other people's kitchens. Frankie laughed at that and tightened his arms around me when I talked my way to Sunday morning, to the fight by the pool and the fraught frot before I asked him to change my flight.

"It's obvious," Frankie said, long after I'd finished, "that you need to go back to California."

"I can't," I still argued with him. "Not with Mandy here. Not with the history..."

"Has Archer called you since you left? Texted?"

"I don't know. I haven't even turned my phone off airplane mode," I admitted.

"He's probably frantic."

"You don't even know a thing about him," I said.

"I know that he's in love with you, and I would be worried sick about sending you back across the country after the story you just told me." Frankie shoved his hand into my pocket and pulled out my phone. He switched it off airplane mode and held it in front of us both while it rattled incessantly with vibration alerts.

I grumbled, watching Archie's name flash across my screen no less than half a dozen times.

"He chartered the flight," I said. "He knows it landed safe."

"Owen, I loved you once as a partner and I love you now as my closest friend, so I'm saying this with all the love in my heart."

"Don't." I took my phone out of his hand and tossed it onto the table. It was still vibrating, the screen flashing with every alert that popped up onto the screen.

"Learn from his example, Owen. Don't let history repeat itself when it's so damn obvious the two of you are meant to be together."

CHAPTER 27
ARCHIE

I KNEW IT WAS FLYNN TRYING TO BREAK INTO MY HOUSE BECAUSE HE'D never been able to get the key into the lock on the first try in as long as I'd known him. It wasn't like I even had a fancy keypad panel like Rob, but then again, maybe that was the problem.

An actual, physical, key was too plebian for him.

"God, it stinks of wine and desperation in here," he announced, kicking his way inside.

It was dark, yes, but I hadn't been holed up long enough for the place to smell like anything besides the lemon verbena cleaning spray I used in the kitchen. It was Sunday night, maybe Monday morning, and of course it was dark because unlike the rest of my filthy rich friends, I splurged on blackout curtains. And after I'd taken Owen to the airfield, I'd come right home, closed them all, and thrown myself onto the couch in a well-deserved state of melancholic misery.

I hadn't felt sorry for myself in almost ten years, so I was well overdue another round of self-pity.

"This feels like grounds for dismissal from your little club." Grayson's voice filled the room and I closed my eyes again with a tired sigh. "This is far from trophy-winning behavior."

"I don't think you can dismiss anyone from a club you're not part of," another voice chimed in, and I dared to look toward the door, wondering what sort of circus Flynn had brought with him.

"Wesley, do you remember Archie?" Grayson flicked his hand between the owner of the unidentified voice and me.

"Should I?" Wesley asked.

"Probably not." Grayson laughed and pulled a plastic grocery bag from behind his back. "You were positively inebriated the first time you met him."

That indirect introduction clicked the pieces into place and I recognized Wesley as the doorman from Rob's little residential living experiment in Mid-City. Wesley was also Grayson's best friend and roommate, if I remembered correctly.

"This is for you." Grayson stood behind the couch, dangling the overloaded bag a foot from my chest before letting it fall. It landed hard and loud, a painful clattering of metal against my sternum.

"What the fuck?" I sat up, managing to shove the bag into my lap as I moved. It tipped and four cans of spray cheese rolled out on the floor. "God, you're both assholes."

"It's your comfort food." Flynn shoved my legs onto the floor and sat down next to me. Grayson cocked his hip against the back of the couch and stared down at me, Wesley hovering beside him like he wasn't sure where to go or what to do. I couldn't blame him for that. I didn't know either.

"I don't need comforting."

"The state of your home says otherwise," Grayson said.

I shot a glare up at him. "You've never even been here before. Maybe I like the dark."

"I don't doubt that," Wesley said softly, eyes focused on the curtains across the room. "But when Grayson and Rob were being idiots…it felt a lot like this."

"I don't even know you," I reminded him, twisting off the security seal on one of the cans of cheese.

"I know *you*, though," Flynn said, and I glowered at him while

I shot a swirl of cheese onto my tongue. "But what I don't know is why you're still here."

"Because Owen left me, obviously."

I threw the can of cheese at him and folded my arms in front of my chest. Owen left me and I'd come home and cried about it because I didn't know what else do. If he'd let me get on the plane with him, I would have had almost five hours to talk him out of leaving me, but he'd blocked me on the stairs and kissed me like he wanted to bury me six feet under with his goddamn tongue, and I couldn't fight him.

I hadn't cared about what Owen wanted or what he'd needed the first time we were together, the absolute least I could do was try to manage something different now. And if Owen wanted to leave me, if he wanted to spend the rest of his life away from mine... well, I'd find a way to give him that. It was apparently a deal I couldn't talk my way to the dotted line on, a first. But a fifth when it came to the list of my life's regrets.

"You never struck me as the quitting type," Grayson said.

I flipped him off and Wesley laughed.

"He doesn't want to be with me. I'm not going to force him."

"If you believe that, you're a fool," Flynn said.

"It's what he told me. I asked him to be with me, I took him on a stupid date like you suggested, and he used his words and he told he hated me for it. " My breath caught in my throat. "I tried to give him a reason, but none of them were enough. And he wanted to go, so he's gone."

"I've only had one real boyfriend before," Wesley said. "But that feels like a copout to me."

"Again, do I even know you?"

He shrugged. "If Colin said something like that to me and I knew it wasn't true, there's no way I would let him just leave me."

"Is Colin your boyfriend?" I asked.

Wesley nodded.

"Owen isn't my boyfriend. He's a man that I spent a weekend

fucking, and then he got tired of my shit and wanted to go home, so home he went."

"If we weren't in mixed company, I would smack the shit out of you, Archer Davidson," Flynn admonished, and I glared at him a second time for good measure.

"Sometimes getting hit is all it takes to put things into perspective," Grayson mused.

"No one is giving me a spanking," I snapped.

"Oh, God." Wesley covered his face and turned away. "Were we talking about spankings? I'm so confused."

"Owen did not want to leave you," Flynn said.

I arched a brow, the proof of that lie visible in the gaping absence of the man in question.

"He loved you," Flynn said, voice softer. "Loves you. He loves you more than he knows what to do with sometimes. But he loves his sister too, and he carries a lot of that burden."

"How do you even know all of that?" I asked.

"He told me and Dalton."

That night in the car, I realized. The three of them laughing like fucking idiots and they were talking about me the whole time? That tracked.

"What then, Flynn? What do you propose I do?"

"Put on clean clothes, for starters," Grayson offered, not even paying attention to me. He was intensely focused on his phone, tapping away at something clearly more important than me.

Which was fair.

He slid his phone back into his pocket, and my own phone vibrated almost immediately.

"Then go to the airfield, get on that fucking plane, and go bring him home with you."

Pulling my phone out of my pocket was a reminder that Owen had been ignoring my messages since I'd left him on the tarmac. I'd even tried to call, but it had gone straight to voicemail. Though, I supposed voicemail was a good sign because it meant he hadn't blocked my number.

Yet.

"He's not answering my messages and I don't know where he lives," I told them, tapping open the itinerary Grayson had apparently arranged on my behalf.

"Do you know where he grew up?" Flynn asked.

I thought of the long summers and that final goodbye in the basement of Owen's childhood home and nodded.

"That's where his sister lives. He told us."

"No." I shook my head, letting my phone call onto my thigh. "I'm not going to Mandy's house to look for Owen."

"If you want to be with him, you're going to have to talk to her eventually," Flynn said. "You might as well get her blessing off the bat."

"She hates me."

"How do you know?"

My eyes rolled back and I groaned, minutes away from throwing the three of them—and all of the spray cheese—out of my house.

"Just go." Flynn shoved my shoulder and I let the force of it push me over onto my side. Grayson snorted a laugh and fisted my collar, hauling me back up. "Just take a shower, get dressed, and go. Then find out for yourself one way or the other. If shit hits the fan, come home and I'm sure Val will let you shoot some of this cheese up his asshole."

"That sounds horrible."

"I mean, yeah. It probably would be, but you know what I mean."

"If I agree to this, will the three of you leave me alone?" I asked.

"For now," Grayson said.

Flynn huffed a laugh and agreed with the sentiment.

"Fine." I stood up, shoving the grocery bag of cheese onto the floor. "I'll go."

An hour later I was at the airfield, and five hours after that I stood in front of Owen and Mandy's childhood home. It was Monday, just before dinnertime, and while I studied the wreath on the front door, a late model car pulled into the driveway. Owen and Mandy's parents had never had a wreath on the door. They'd never even had flowers in the front yard, but now there was a planter box overflowing with vibrant marigolds.

"Can I help you?" A delicate, if not tired, voice asked from the driveway.

I thought I'd forgotten the sound of Mandy's voice, but hearing her talk for the first time in a decade offered me a rush of feelings as intense as when I'd seen Owen for the first time. I turned, hands shoved in my pockets and expression as downcast as I could manage without looking sullen.

"Archer?"

"Hey, Mandy."

Her shoes tapped against the cracked concrete as she walked around the front of her car and came to stand in front of me. She was as tall as she'd been in college, just as put together and beautiful as I remembered her. But time was a funny thing, and it was weird to look at her with eyes that now favored men. Mandy had been breathtaking, all dark curls and wide obsidian eyes, and of course she still had those features, but I found myself longing for the sharper angles of Owen's jawline, the broader set of his nose compared to her more elegant slope.

She still had great tits, though.

"What are you doing here?" she asked.

I scratched the back of my neck, nerves very close to getting the better of me. "It's kind of a long story. Can I come in?"

"I don't know, Archer." She looked over her shoulder to the front door. "My fiancé isn't home."

"I prefer men, Mandy. It's not like that."

Color flooded her cheeks and something settled in the tightness of her jaw.

"I know you do," she said, words clipped. But then she sucked in a deep breath and let it out, her massive tote bag sliding down her arm toward her wrist. I reached out and caught it before she lost her grip on it, and for that she gave me what almost passed as a grateful look.

"Let's sit on the porch," she offered, turning away from me and making her way up the cobblestone path that cut through the front yard. There was a bench under the front window, taking the place of what used to be a swing.

I set her bag down by the door and sat on the bench, looking up and finding the telltale eyebolts still screwed into the exposed beams. They were rusted beyond repair, it looked like. Proof somehow of how much time had gone by.

"I hear you're getting married," I said, not sure where to start.

She gave me a tired look from the corner of her eye. "Where did you hear that?"

"Can I backtrack first?" I asked, scrubbing a hand down my face. I should have shaved. Not because I was trying to impress her, but because I felt more like myself when I was put together. And even though I had showered and put on clothes, I didn't feel balanced. I didn't feel right. But a voice in the back of my head told me that didn't have anything to do with the hair on my face.

That was all Owen.

"You don't need to," she said. "We don't need to revisit the past."

"At least let me apologize, then."

That earned me a sardonic laugh. "An apology from you hasn't meant anything to me in a very long time, Archer. I assure you, it's not necessary."

"It means something to me," I said.

She gestured for me to go on.

"I'm sorry, Mandy. I'm sorry that back then, I didn't know I was in love with your brother."

That confession wasn't what she'd expected, and her head

snapped toward me so quickly, I thought her neck might break in half from the force of it.

"I didn't know a lot of things back then. But the night of my graduation, the night I left, I did know it was wrong of me to go the way I did. Without even saying anything. No explanation."

"Was it also wrong of you to fuck my brother that night?"

My heart slammed so hard against my ribs I worried the bones were ready to shatter.

"He said you didn't know," I whispered, shame washing over me like a tidal wave. Which, at that moment, would have been a blessing. Anything to end the conversation that I'd never imagined myself having with one of the two people I'd hurt so beyond measure and so unfairly.

"If he really thinks that, then he's a fool." Mandy made a thoughtful sound in the back of her throat. "You'd been gone so long, I went downstairs to check on the two of you, and I...I heard...well, I don't think I heard everything, but I heard enough."

My body collapsed in on itself, my elbows going to my knees and my face falling right into my hands. If there'd been a time where I'd ever felt more shame than after her confession, I would have been hard pressed to recall it.

"Oh, my God, Mandy. Why didn't you say anything?"

"Back then?" She gave a cruel laugh that tapered off into something sad. "What would I have said, Archer? And to who? You were gone and Owen was a disaster. He tried so hard to pretend he wasn't..."

Mandy let out a long breath and leaned back, stretching her arms and legs in front of her.

"I gave him an out because, even though I was in denial, I understood what had happened. I told him you said you'd had a family emergency. That you'd gone to say goodbye to him, and then..."

"Mandy."

"You said you loved him back then," she said. "What about now?"

"It's complicated."

"It shouldn't be."

"I ran into him on accident when he was in California a couple weeks ago, and it was like not a day had passed, at least not for me. Though, that's not really true. I'm aware of the time that's passed—"

She cut me off with a hand on my leg. The small diamond in her engagement ring sparkled, and her touch felt as unwanted to me as saying goodbye to Owen had been.

"I do love him still. More than I have words for, and I tried to get him to stay with me, but he had me put him on a plane yesterday. There's no way I can let go of him again. At least not without a fight."

Mandy's lips twisted into a wry grin "Yesterday?"

That was when I remembered he'd been lying to everyone about where he was, but I could ask for forgiveness later. If he'd even talk to me, of course. There were enough lies and silence and secrets between the three of us, I didn't want any more of it.

"He was with me for the weekend," I admitted. "Was supposed to come home today, but we argued yesterday and he wanted to go early."

"You know, I knew he was in California." She let out a small little laugh as she pulled her hand away from my leg. "I checked him on my phone, whatever that app is."

I shook my head, knowing how much Owen would hate being caught by her when he'd tried so hard to keep her in the dark.

"I just didn't know he was with you," she said.

"He was happy, Mandy." I didn't know why, but it was important to me that she understood that. I knew my feelings in the situation didn't matter, but his? Maybe his did. "It was only for a few days, but he was so happy and things were so good, and I just…"

"You just what, Archer?"

"I'd just like for him to come home now."

Mandy leaned over toward her purse and pulled out her phone. She tapped around until a map came up on her screen, a little circle with Owen's face in the middle of it popping up on the other side of town. She showed me the screen, but not long enough for me to get a read on the exact location, then she turned the screen off and dropped her phone back into her purse.

"Yeah, Archer. I'd like that for him too.'

CHAPTER 28
OWEN

EVEN AFTER I'D CALMED DOWN, FRANKIE HOVERED LIKE A HAWK. He told me he was worried about me running headfirst into dehydration, what with all the crying and snotting I'd been doing, paired with all the ejaculating he was sure I'd done over the weekend. He wasn't wrong about any of it, but hydration was the last thought in my mind as he called for takeout Vietnamese from our favorite Pho restaurant down the street.

My phone stayed quiet on the table, and Frankie didn't push me about that. Thank God.

Twenty minutes later, there was a knock at the door, and my stomach rumbled in response, but when I opened the door with my wallet in hand, I didn't find a delivery driver.

I found my sister, looking tired around the eyes and red in the cheeks.

"Oh," she said weakly. "You're alive."

It would have been so easy to stick with the lie that I'd been feeding her all weekend, but the fight with Archie had taken everything out of me.

"Do you want to come in?" I asked.

"Are you going to get me sick?"

I shook my head and stepped out of the way.

"Because you're not sick, are you?" she asked, coming inside and kicking out of her flip-flops.

I shook my head again as Frankie chimed in from the couch, "He's sick in the head, Mandy."

She leveled an accusatory glare across the apartment at him. "Did you know the whole time?"

"Just found out today or I would have told you the truth, you know that."

"Thanks for ratting me out," I grumbled, shoving the door closed behind Mandy.

"You were going to tell her the truth anyway." Frankie gave my sister a sympathetic smile. "Did you want me to go?"

"You can stay." Mandy sat on the couch next to Frankie with a weary groan. "So, what was going on?"

Frankie pulled his lips between his teeth and stared out the window.

"I was in California," I said.

"I was in California," she mocked. "I know you were in California, Owen."

My body went ice cold, palms immediately starting to sweat. "How did you know?" I whispered.

"I knew because of that ridiculous app you made me download that shares our locations with each other."

I let out a breath and my chin fell against my chest.

"But even if I hadn't checked the app, Archie is home."

"What?"

"Well, maybe not home for him, but he's here." The corner of my sister's mouth twisted into what looked like half a smile and half a frown, like her brain couldn't single out the emotion she wanted to feel, and I didn't blame her for that.

"What do you mean he's here?" I brushed past her legs and sat on the coffee table, leaving her facing me from one side and Frankie on the other. Frankie's eyes had gone wide, his attention narrowed onto my silent and dark cell phone beside his feet.

"I mean Archie Davidson showed up on my porch after work

with a whole lot of very interesting things to say about you, little brother."

In that moment, it was impossible to not think that there had to be an easier way. If I would have just agreed with Archie when he talked about wanting to be honest with my sister, for one. We could have done it together, presenting a united front, our hands joined. With that thought, I looked down at my palm, sweaty and pale white with half-moon divots gouged into the surface.

I'd done that.

I'd done all of this.

"Like what?" I managed to ask.

"What do you think, Owen?"

"I never meant to lie to you, Mandy."

"Wrong." She cut me off, slashing her hand through the air and leaning forward so her face was only inches away from mine. "You didn't just mean to do it, you planned to do it. And you planned it more than once."

My eyes were wet with tears and my throat was parched. I wasn't entirely convinced I wasn't on the cusp of a heart attack.

"It wasn't like that."

"No?"

I shook my head.

"Do you think I'm a child, Owen? Like I'm some stupid little girl who can't handle the truth about her college boyfriend taking her little brother to bed?"

"Amanda."

"He didn't tell me about it," she said, shaking her head like she was disgusted with me. "Or rather, he did. But I already knew about it."

Every word out of my sister's mouth was the swing of a sledgehammer against the foundation I'd built my life on. I'd built my life on a lie, though. My relationship with her too. I'd dedicated so much to her because of what I'd done and the future I'd stolen from her. With all of that crumbling, what did I have?

"How did you know?"

"I have ears, Owen. And a college degree. I'm not an idiot."

"Why...why didn't you say anything?"

A flash of undeserved resentment flared up the base of my spine and directed at my sister for not speaking up sooner. She had to know that I'd acted how I did, that I'd done the things I'd done to pay her back for the biggest mistake of my life. And she had just let me. She had willingly and actively taken advantage of my guilt over sleeping with Archie for the first time.

"Archie asked me the same thing." She looked up at me with a sad smile, then she shrugged. "It was embarrassing."

"And you just...you let me live the last ten years like you didn't know about what happened between us?"

"At the time, I didn't think bringing it out into the open would have been better for either of us. For any of us. And I got over him, Owen. I thought you would have too" Mandy twirled a loose curl around the tip of her finger before letting it fall. She leaned back against the couch, some of the earlier anger going with her and her mouth pulled down into a frown. "None of us did the right thing, Owen. But that doesn't mean we can't start."

I scrubbed a hand down my face and Frankie kicked me in the hip.

"I know. You're right."

"I know I am," she answered with a quiet laugh. "But what does the right thing look like to you?"

"It looks like I don't lie to you anymore."

"That's a good start. So, tell me the truth."

Next to her, Frankie choked, a laugh catching in the back of his throat. Mandy and I both shot him a sharp glare and he waved one of his hands in apology, even as he kept sputtering and spitting up everywhere.

"That is the truth," I said, shoving Frankie's feet off the table and onto the floor.

"I'm sorry," he choked, standing up and taking my water bottle with him. "I'm sorry, it's just..."

"Do you remember when we were really young and we used to play Truth or Sucker Punch?" Mandy asked.

I grabbed the outside of my left arm, the memory of my older sister's horrible game all too clear in my mind.

"That wasn't a fair game. You were stronger," I protested.

"And it taught you never to lie to me, but we quit playing."

"We stopped playing because you got too cool to hang out with your little brother," I said, letting my hand fall into my lap.

"I clearly shouldn't have stopped because you've spent the past ten years lying to me which, by the original rules, means I should be able to beat you to death." She cracked her knuckles like she was serious, and I worried that she might be.

"Come on, Mandy," Frankie interrupted, flipping the half-empty water bottle and catching it around the base.

"I love you, Frankie. I think you've always been great for Owen, but this doesn't involve you."

"I'm his best friend," he reminded her. "It does involve me because he involves me."

"With all due respect—" she started but I cut her off before she could say something to Frankie that all of us would regret.

"I shouldn't have lied to you," I told her, and she tapped her fingernail against her thumbnail while I talked. "But I was doing the best I could at the age we were."

"Your best was shit."

"Your best wasn't much better," I snapped.

"His best has been dedicating his entire life to making sure you didn't get hurt because of him," Frankie interjected, leveling an accusatory finger at my sister. "He's buried down everything he feels for that man because of you. He went to California for you, and he walked away from a man who fucking loves him because of you. I don't know what else you want from him, Mandy."

"I wanted the truth!"

"The truth is that I love him," I said, stepping between my closest friend and my sister before she got a chance to revive the game that had kept me up afraid some nights. "I love him and I love you, and I don't know what to do."

"I love you." She shoved me in the chest. "I just want you to be happy."

"I don't think I would be happy flaunting Archie around you, Mandy."

"Then don't flaunt him. It's not..." She let out a frustrated breath. "Are you being deliberately stubborn?"

"Yes," Frankie answered on my behalf.

"I need you to know that the weekend after Archie disappeared, I fucked Chad Walker."

"I'm sorry, what?"

Frankie let loose another laugh, and I didn't know who to look at first, her or him.

"I was at a summer kickoff party and I slept with Chad Walker."

"Why are you telling me this?" I asked.

"Because it's normal, Owen. It's a normal reaction to lash out and then move on and get over shit. And Archie hurt me, but I've been over it for a very long time, and it doesn't sound like you're over it."

"He's not," Frankie said.

I would have to deal with him later because it very much felt like my best friend was taking my sister's side in something when I would have really expected him to have my back.

"You're not over it because you're still in love with him and he's in love with you, and..." She stood up and adjusted the strap of her purse over her arm before going to the door and sliding her feet back into her flip-flops.

"And what, Mandy?"

"I'm meeting Mark for dinner and we aren't going to be home until late."

I blinked slowly, trying to decide if she'd been body-snatched or if I had just imagined the whole conversation we'd had up to that moment.

"That doesn't feel relevant to this conversation," I said.

The doorbell broke me out of the stupor, and Freddie rushed past me.

"Finally. That must be dinner."

I stared blankly at the door while he collected the bag of food and paid the delivery driver. He carried everything into the kitchen and started separating the food out onto the counter.

"And Archie is at the house," Mandy said quietly, sending a rash of gooseflesh down the back of my neck.

"I don't know what that has to do with me."

"Everything, Owen. It has everything to do with you."

CHAPTER 29
ARCHIE

THE BASEMENT HADN'T CHANGED MUCH IN TEN YEARS.

Mandy had replaced the furniture, but the couch was still about five years too old to be current. The TV mounted on the far wall was obviously the model before the one that graced the mantle in the living room. How a place could be so much the same and so different at the same time was beyond me, but I took my time and pondered it while I stared at my reflection in the dark mirror surface of the screen.

After Mandy and I finished talking, she'd told me to go downstairs and wait for Owen. I didn't have much faith that she'd be able to get him to come talk to me, but it was worth a shot. After all, I had flown all the way across the country to talk to him.

No, I was tired of all the lying.

I'd flown across the country to bring him home with me.

The front door opened and my heart flew into my throat. I wanted to jump up and meet Owen at the stairs, but if it wasn't him…

Footsteps grew louder and the door to the basement opened, and I'd know the sound of him anywhere. The way he carried himself. Owen slowly descended into the basement, stopping when he reached the carpeted floor.

"This is a change," he said.

I allowed myself to look over my shoulder. The basement was relatively dark, the lamp from when we were kids in the corner casting an orange glow for a few feet before falling into shadow. But I could still make out his features, the puffiness around his eyes. He'd been crying, which meant all hope wasn't yet lost for me.

For us.

"I have to admit I hate it."

He chuffed out a sad laugh and came to sit next to me on the couch, falling into the already well-worn cushions with a sigh. "I don't have a letter for you this time."

"That's probably better." I flipped my hand palm up onto my thigh, and without much delay or thought, Owen threaded his fingers into mine. I grabbed him back, tight, staring down at the way his tattoos and tanned hands contrasted with my paler skin.

"It just ruined things last time."

"No." I shook my head. "It gave me the best gift of my life."

"Shut the fuck up, Archie."

I tugged his hand and turned to face him. "It's true. You and... I'd go back if I could, you know. I'd handle it differently. At least, I like to think I would. But I can't imagine living the life I've lived and knowing you the way I do now and not fighting a little harder."

"That's bullshit and you know it."

He tried to pull his hand out of mine, but I held on tighter.

"If you don't see how unmistakably and uncontrollably in love with you I am, then you haven't been paying attention."

"And what am I supposed to do with that?" Owen raised our joined hands into the space between us, his fingers clamped as solidly around my hand as mine were around his. "With this?"

"Be with me." I took the time to enunciate every word so there could be no confusion as to what I wanted from him. What I wanted *for* him.

"How?" His voice cracked on the single syllable, taking my heart with it.

"Come to California," I told him. "Move in with me, or let Grayson find you an apartment of your own. You can get a job. My friends already adore you and we can finally just be together."

I hadn't even finished speaking before Owen started to shake his head, one tear, then another sliding down his cheek. Using the thumb on my free hand, I wiped them away, fighting the urge to pop the digit into my mouth for a taste. I'd already tasted his spit, his sweat, his cum, and it felt appropriate to add tears to the mix, but I didn't. I had to believe I would get another chance to lick them from his cheeks.

"I have a job here," he said. "I have friends...I have a friend."

"Frankie." I remembered him from the call in the car, and I knew from the way Owen had handled him how much he meant.

"Frankie," he agreed.

"You can get a new job. Frankie can come visit," I said. I hoped the fact I had a private jet at my disposal hadn't been lost on him in the less than twenty-four hours that we'd been apart.

"*You* can get a new job," he shot back, eyes squinting into angry and narrow slits. "*Your* friends can come visit."

"Are you asking me to move back home, Owen? Because I will. Don't fucking tempt me."

"You're being ridiculous."

"Nothing means shit to me if I don't have you." I stretched my fingers apart and shook out of his grasp. Blood rushed through my hand from all the places his grip had been restricting it, and as I stood, I shook my hand out at my side. "My house, my job, my friends, my *life*. It's inconsequential now if you're not a part of it."

I realized, as I raised my voice at him, just how tired I was.

I hadn't really slept at all after he left and before he left...well, I hadn't slept much then either because I'd done everything in my power to get my fill of him in the few days we had together. I was fairly certain the last thing I'd eaten was spray cheese, and maybe a handful of peanuts on the plane. I was running on fumes, and for the very first time since I'd seen Owen again, I was scared.

It was an uncomfortable and unwelcome feeling that curled

itself around the base of my spine, threatening to unfurl its tendrils and spread through my body like tentacles. The fear would paralyze me, which might be better than the alternative because running and acting too quick wouldn't get me anywhere good either.

"You don't even know what you're saying," Owen muttered, and I spun on the balls of my feet to come back face to face with him.

"That's where you're wrong because, for the very first time, it's all clear." I tapped my temple in demonstration. "Everything makes sense for the first time."

"You're thirty years old, Archie. You can't just give up your whole life and move back here."

"Of course I can."

Owen snorted and rolled his eyes, letting his head fall against the back of the couch. He studied the ceiling like he'd find the answers there, and I sat back down beside him with an exhausted grunt.

"What's the point of this?" he finally asked, voice barely louder than the hum of the lights.

"Who says there's supposed to be a point? I love you, Owen. Can't that be enough?"

He pressed a hand to the front of his chest with a pained grimace.

"Everything hurts right now, Archie." Owen twisted his eyes shut and rubbed his sternum until the tension started to leak out of his expression.

There was only one time in my life I'd ever felt as helpless and I'd been seated in the same spot in the same room, but back then Owen had writhed on top of me, all desperate and sad, and I felt all of those things and more."

"How can I help you?" I grabbed his wrist and pulled his hand away from his chest. "How can I stop it?"

The smallest whimper tumbled out of his mouth and he spun,

flinging one leg over my lap and setting down. He straddled me, cheeks slick with tears, and he pressed our foreheads together.

"Kiss me again," he whispered.

It was like my mouth was the only thing I could give him and the absolute last thing he wanted. But, just the same, I took his face into my hands and slanted our mouths together. His lips parted without question, the taste of his tears salty and sharp against my tongue. Between our bodies, Owen tried to get into my pants, and my protests were weak.

It wasn't long until he had both of our cocks in his hand and then my hand in his and my hand around us both. He moaned into my mouth, hips pressing forward, and with my free hand, I steadied myself with a firm grip around his hip. My fingertips dug into his ass and when he began to move, it took all my strength to not throw him onto the carpet and fuck him into the floor.

"It still hurts," he whimpered, thrusting his cock through the loose hold of my fist.

"Please don't ask me to do this again."

Before he could say anything to that, I kissed him again. Letting my tongue dive deep into his mouth to silence any other pleas or protests before he could bring them to light. It was like being kids all over again, but finally I knew better. And so did he, but he was blinded, and...

"Then I'll do it myself," he grunted, swatting my hand out of the way and fisting his dick. He grabbed me around the back of the head with his free hand, and I mirrored the pose, holding him as still on top of me as I could manage. His knuckles dusted over the tender length of my shaft with every stroke of his hand and I gritted my teeth against the wave of sensation that brought.

"Not yet," I whispered.

But not because I was trying to delay his pleasure, not because I was trying to give him the one thing we'd always done best. I wanted him to slow down. I wanted him to stop because he was desperate and frantic, and that curl of fear at the base of my spine told me this was going to be the last orgasm of his that I'd ever get to see.

His hips jerked at my words, and I screwed my eyes closed.

"Say it again," he begged.

"Don't come yet, Owen." My words were thick with tears and my head ached for how hard his forehead pushed against mine. "I know you want to. I know you think you have to, but you don't. You can hold out longer."

"No, I can't, Archie."

"You can do anything you want." I wasn't talking about the orgasm anymore. "But more than that, you'll do anything I say, won't you, Owen?"

Another pained gasp.

"Don't come yet," I gave him the command slowly. One word after the other after the other. "I'm not ready for you to come."

"It hurts." He pushed the words out from between clenched jaws, sweat slicking between our skin. "It fucking hurts. It hurts, Archie. I need it."

"No."

I released my hold on his head and grabbed his face, fingers and thumb dipping into the hollows of his cheeks. I positioned his head so we were still face to face, mouths brushing against each other.

"You listen to me, Owen, and you listen good."

He grunted in the back of his throat, hand moving quick and splattering sweat and precum against the front of my shirt and the swollen head of my cock.

"Ten years was a long fucking time to go without this."

"Don't do this," he protested.

"I don't want another ten years," I said. "I don't even want another ten days, ten hours, unless I know we're under the same roof and I can take your come whenever I want it."

"That's not fair."

Owen's breath stuttered, puffing against my cheek.

"If you said yes, Owen, I'd make sure that you never hurt again unless we both wanted it, and fuck." I wrapped my fingers around his so we both held his cock in the same grip. "I'd make it hurt so fucking good, Owen. I'd bring you to the edge over and over for the rest of our fucking lives—"

He came before I could finish, shooting hot and wild jets of cum against our hands and our clothes. I slanted our mouths together, relishing the taste of his cries and his release, and more than that, his love. It was perfect and it was the only thing I wanted for the whole rest of my life. But as his cum cooled on my fingers, I could feel him slipping further out of reach.

"This doesn't have to be hard," I promised, our mouths still so close together I could taste his breath. "It doesn't have to be...we can do it together."

Without a word, Owen climbed off my lap, history repeating itself before my very eyes. I zipped my flagging dick back into my pants, doing my best to not smear his cum all over the wool blend of my slacks.

"Do you want me to get on my knees and beg you, Owen? Because I will. I'm not above it."

"I know you're not." He wouldn't meet my stare, and I thought that if I could just get him to look me in the eyes one more time, I could convince him to stay, to give us a real chance. "But that's not where I want you."

"Where, then?" I asked.

"I want you in California, Archie." He shook his head, bleached curls bouncing as he stared at the floor. "I want you to go home."

CHAPTER 30
OWEN
SIX MONTHS LATER

MANDY SMELLED LIKE LAVENDER, MOST LIKELY ON ACCOUNT OF HER bouquet which had sprigs of the purple blooms scattered around the white roses and baby's breath. She had some stems tucked into the loose braid of her hair, and when she floated around the room, she carried the soft scent with her. But when she caught my stare from across the room, her face turned serious. I went still, stumbling over my own feet as the intensity of her look stopped me in my tracks.

"What did I do wrong?" I asked when she got within earshot.

Her expression immediately softened, but she rolled her eyes at me just the same. "You know what you did wrong, but this isn't about that," she said.

I sighed, looking down at the ground and focusing on the shined black tips of my dress shoes and the delicate, rhinestone-studded straps of her heels that peeked out from beneath the hem of her dress.

"What then?"

She studied me quietly, using her bouquet to smack me in the chest, jostling more of that lavender smell into the air.

"You know what? I was wrong. I do want to talk about what you did wrong."

"Mandy."

"It's been six months," she accused.

"I have a calendar. I know."

She hit me again with the bouquet. "Do you know I talk to him every week?"

I did not, in fact, know that Mandy talked with Archie every week, and I could have gone the rest of my life *not* knowing that. It felt unfair in a way I didn't have the class or the skill to articulate.

"That's great, Mandy," I said instead.

"He got me a new car for a wedding present."

"Am I supposed to be impressed?" I was impressed, but also annoyed, and I wouldn't give her the courtesy of knowing about either. It didn't surprise me in the least that Archie was trying to buy his way into our lives, but what surprised me was that Mandy had fallen for his tricks.

In the days and weeks after Archie's visit home, he'd tried just about every trick in the book to get back into my life, but I'd fought him tooth and nail the whole way. Even with Mandy's blessing, which had come less than three days after Archie went back to California, I hadn't felt right about it. Something with the expectation that one of us just give up our life to move across the country felt presumptuous and entitled. And there was a voice in the back of my head that screamed at me every time I fought him, that told me I was being stubborn for no reason at all. That I was only hurting myself by trying to hurt him.

But still.

And the weeks dragged into months, and I was too focused on helping Mandy finalize her wedding plans to deal with much else. I'd found that in the absence of a self-imposed obligation to help her, I truly enjoyed being someone she could rely on. As time progressed, so many things changed, but the one thing that remained steady was Archie's insistence that I hear him out again.

At least once a day he sent me a message, even though I had long ago started to leave them ignored. I didn't know what to say to him because his persistence was like a fine grit sandpaper wearing me down so slowly I didn't even notice I'd begun to soften. By the time I realized that I looked forward to his daily messages, it had been five months since I'd seen him last and even though that was nowhere near ten years, it felt like too much time had passed for me to make it up to him.

"He asks me about you," Mandy said, and I covered my throat with my hand to hide the flush that burned toward my chin.

"And what do you tell him?"

"I tell him that you're not the same since you left him," she said, staring at me down the slope of her nose.

"Since I left him," I muttered.

"You did. Even if I don't understand it."

I inhaled a rattling breath, pasting on a fake smile as there was no way I would ruin the biggest day of my sister's life by publicly lamenting my own bad decisions.

"I don't want to talk about him today," I said.

Her stare flickered over my shoulder, a small smile falling across her face as she took a step away from me.

"Then how about you talk *to* me?"

Archie's voice behind me was like a bucket of ice water being dropped on my head...in the middle of the desert.

Mandy gave me a quick jerk of her head, then turned back toward her wedding party. It took me a solid minute to find movement in my legs, and when I finally brought myself around to face Archie, my knees almost gave out anyway of their own accord.

Archie looked better than he ever had, in a finely tailored tux made of material so expensive it almost glimmered under the market lights that were strung zigzag above their heads to light the dance floor. He'd always been tall and slim, but the dark wool accentuated the shape of him, and Archie subconsciously pressed a hand against the buttons of his tux, catching my stare and holding it.

"What are you doing here?" I rasped, unintentionally mirroring his pose by pressing my hand over my middle, but on my end it was to settle my stomach and not throw up all over our shoes. His probably cost more than my entire outfit had, and that was just a rental for me.

"Your sister invited me," he said.

"Sure. But what are you *doing* here?"

"Your sister invited me," he said again, this time cocking his head to the side and winging a brow up in the air.

"She's a traitor."

"She wants you happy," he said.

"And she thinks you have anything to do with that? You're just a bad habit at this point, Archie."

My blood boiled, starting at the tips of my fingers and working up through my body until my spine was on fire and threatening to sear through my muscles and my skin. I'd tried so hard and for so long to quit the man in front of me, but somehow he still had his hooks in me. No matter how far away I swam, he was able to reel me back in with a look or a phrase, and it felt so unfair for him to have that control over me after so long.

"Come on, Owen."

Archie sounded tired and it was then I noticed the dark bags under his eyes. At first, I thought they were a shadow, but when he stepped toward me and brought himself into the light, I realized their shading remained unchanged. Maybe he wasn't the only one who felt trapped at the end of someone else's line.

At that moment, the music took a decidedly more romantic turn, and I knew my sister had a hand in the change of pace. Archie smiled quickly, then held his hand out for me and stepped back, almost into a bow. "May I have this dance?"

I loved when Archie told me no. Our entire relationship had been built upon it, which was ironic considering the instances I told him no were the times when things began to crumble and wither.

"Fine."

I put my hand in his, and Archie hauled our chests together, bringing our mouths inches apart. He smelled so much like I remembered. It brought me an unexplainable sense of comfort that dulled the fire in my bones, and I allowed myself a deep breath of him as he slid his hand around my waist to hold me like a proper dance partner would.

Our feet moved in time like it was our thousandth dance, not our first, and when he brushed his nose against my temple, I let my eyes fall closed. I let him lead. He must have noticed a shift in my demeanor, because the arm around my waist wrapped tighter, the grip on my hand turned less sweaty.

"You look nice," I muttered, which earned a low laugh in my ear.

"I look like a man obsessed," he whispered, giving me a whirl around the dance floor.

"With what?"

"With the one thing he can't have."

"You're rich, Archie," I reminded him. "You can have anything you want."

"Evidently not."

I squeezed his fingers and let him lead me around the dance floor again.

"I meant what I said," he went on. "I've meant everything I've ever said to you. I would bring you here, I'd give it all up, I'd split the time...whatever you want Owen, as long as part of what you want is me."

"We can't split the time," I said.

Archie's graceful footsteps faltered, but he recovered just as quick and without any mention of the stumble. I didn't call it out because, if I did, I would have had to admit it was the first time I'd given him an inch since the last time we'd been in the same room together.

"We can do anything we want," he corrected.

"It's not practical." I rested my cheek against his shoulder, my resolve slipping with every breath. Now that Archie was with me again, it was hard to remember why I hadn't wanted to give into him. Why I'd fought him in the first place. Had it been the entitlement and the assumptions? Or had it been an inexplicable drive to continue to punish myself for a mistake I'd made at eighteen?

Not that Archie could ever be a mistake.

The rest of it, though...

"As you so often like to remind me, I have enough money that anything can be practical," he said.

I laughed, relaxing into his arms. The song changed from one slow dance to another, and Archie righted his grip around me and kept us moving around the outskirts of the dance floor.

"Your friends will think I'm a whore," I said.

"My friends will think you're in love with me," he said.

"I don't want to be a kept man."

Archie made a victorious sound in the back of this throat that I ignored.

"I would keep you so hard you wouldn't even remember what it was like to not be kept, Owen." He brushed his lips against my temple, and I tilted my head back to look up at him.

"You know what I mean," I warned.

"And you know what *I* mean."

I didn't have a response to that, so I returned my cheek to his shoulder and let the silence blanket over us as he continued to steer us through the rest of the song and into a third one. I would have to have a conversation with my sister later because, while I'd never been married before, I knew this many waltzy romantic songs in a row was not a part of any wedding DJ's repertoire.

"It all feels stupid now that you're here," I whispered. "The past six months, sending you away, ignoring the text messages."

"All of the spray cheese and lack of shaving," he added.

I scoffed, glancing up at him again and raising my fingers to trace over the dark circle that hinged one of his eyes. The wrinkles around the edge of his lash line fanned out as he smiled, leaning into my touch with the slightest incline of his cheek.

"Tell me more about that."

"Grayson brought me a whole bag of it," Archie explained. "I think he and Flynn meant it as a joke, but once I started to actually eat it, they got worried."

"It's not fit for consumption, Archie, you know that."

"You used to eat it," he said quickly. "All the time, and when I was first in California, it was the easiest way to make my mind think of you. On the porch at your parents' house, on that swing with our feet up and you always had that spray cheese going."

"It was a horrible habit," I interjected, "Just like you."

"Some habits are harder to break than others," he murmured, head tilting a little more to the side and his lashes falling a little more closed.

"Some are impossible," I whispered back, leaning my head to the other side so our mouths were very nearly in alignment.

"Maybe best to stop trying then," he said.

"Probably," I agreed, and then Archie pressed our lips together in the softest and most tentative kiss he'd ever given me.

I didn't know if it was because we were in public at my sister's wedding or if it was because he just truly felt that uncertain about my reaction, but his mouth against mine was like a relay switch sparking to life. I grabbed him around the back of his head and licked into his mouth with a rough moan. The dominant attack caught him off-guard, and Archie brought us to a standstill, curling his hands around my waist and deepening the kiss.

The record scratched and whatever song the DJ had been spinning came to a stop, immediately replaced with something more up tempo, but neither Archie nor I paid it any mind, too lost in each other to care about anything else.

CHAPTER 31
ARCHIE

After the reception, Owen brought me back to his hotel room.

It was impossible to ignore how often our lives played out in parallels, but this time it was my back against the wall, Owen's hungry fingers tearing my shirt open, button after button.

"Those are mother of pearl," I managed to murmur as he slammed his mouth against mine, kissing me until neither of us could breathe.

"Never mind," I said when he broke away for air. "It doesn't matter."

"I know," he agreed, shoving the straps of my suspenders off my shoulders and down my arms. I stripped the rest of the way out of my shirt, reaching for his bow tie at the same time he went for my fly.

"I love being here with you," he rasped, shoving my pants down to my ankles.

I toed out of my shoes, hoping that I didn't scuff the leather, but not caring about it enough to stop and undo the laces, and we stumbled backward together until the backs of my knees hit the bed and we both went down.

Owen had more clothes on than I did, tangled in his pants and the sleeves of his shirt, so it was easy enough to roll him onto his back and pin his hands above his head. His hips lifted off the bed, slacks still restraining his thighs and underwear covering his cock.

"In bed?" I laughed and ground down against him, just happy to have the weight of him beneath me again.

I'd stayed in touch with Mandy because, at the end of the day, I liked her as a person. And by the grace of some sort of higher power, she'd found it in her heart to forgive me for what I'd done to her when we were in college. I also knew that if Mandy liked me, that would help make things easier if I ever got Owen to give me the time of day again, but it was a side effect, to be honest.

Sure, when Mandy invited me to her wedding I hoped that I'd be able to convince Owen to talk to me again. He'd been ignoring me for months, but my messages and my goals had remained consistent. I loved him. I wanted him. And I wasn't going to give up on either of those things without one hell of a fight.

"With you in California."

A soft smile settled across his mouth and I went still, not entirely certain I'd heard him correctly. "What?"

"I don't make a lot of money," he said.

"I do." I shoved the waistband of his underwear behind his balls and cradled his sac in the palm of my hand.

"I don't have any friends out here."

"I do," I said again, shoving his underwear and pants out of the way. There had to be lube somewhere in this goddamn hotel room of his or I was going to lose my mind. "You can have all of them. All of it. Owen, are you saying what I think you're saying?"

"I've been miserable without you," he said, cheeks flushing dark. "I'm told I've been insufferable and no fun to be around at all since you left."

"We can't have that."

He shook his head. "No. I don't think we can."

With one hand still bracketing his wrists over his head, I dipped down and pressed our lips together in a soft kiss.

"Everything that I have is yours," I promised him.

"Am I rich now?"

Owen smiled against my mouth and I nipped his bottom lip until he groaned and arched up into me. "So rich," I assured him.

"Scrooge McDuck rich?" he asked.

I chuckled and let go of his lip, angling my head up so I could scan the room for a bottle of lotion, or lube, or anything that I could use besides spit to spread him open and make sure he understood just how much of myself belonged to him.

"I've never counted his coins," I murmured. "Please tell me you have lube here."

"In the bathroom. In my toiletries bag."

I smashed a kiss against his mouth and climbed off the bed, fingering out of my socks as I stumbled into the bathroom.

"Take off the rest of your clothes," I called over my shoulder to him.

The lube was thankfully easy to find, and when I made it back to the bed, Owen had arranged himself against the pillows like a god, all golden and spread apart for me with his long and hard cock in his fist.

"If everything that's mine is yours," I said, pouring a generous amount of lube over my achingly hard dick, "then everything that's yours is mine. Right?"

"Right."

His lashes fluttered, and I pressed one knee into the bed, climbing back between his legs, my cock and my fingers slick with lube.

"Then take your hand off my dick, Owen."

"It's been months," he protested.

"Then a couple more hours won't kill you."

"Hours?" His eyes went wide, the protest falling short when I pressed one of my fingers right into his hole.

Fuck.

He was so hot and tight, and it had been so long since he'd been wrapped around me that I'd almost forgotten how much his body felt like heaven.

Moving between his legs, I used my shoulders to spread him

wide, then pushed my tongue alongside my finger between his cheeks. Owen grabbed my hair, yanking hard against my scalp, but I wasn't anywhere close to giving in or being done.

"Don't touch my cock, Owen," I reminded him again, dipping my tongue inside.

I added another finger, making a loud and sloppy mess of his hole until sweat slicked down his thighs and caused his legs to slip and slide against my arms and my shoulders. A quick look up showed his balls so high I could barely see the shape of them and his cock so hard it bounced against his stomach with a loud slap when I pulled at it.

"That'll make me come," he panted.

"Better not."

He was harder than I'd ever seen him, but I was harder than I'd ever been too. His hole was soaked in spit and already puffy around the rim, and when I aligned the head of my dick, I slid inside with ease. Owen shouted when I seated myself fully inside of him, a thick spurt of precum oozing out of the tip of his dick and into his happy trail.

"I missed how good this hole feels," I praised his body, peppering kisses along the sharp angle of his jaw until I reached his ear.

"I'm so sorry," he whispered.

"What for?"

"Everything." Owen shook his head and closed his eyes. I tapped my fingers against his cheekbones until he opened up, revealing a curtain of unshed tears below his irises.

"We've both done stupid things," I assured him. "But we can stop that now. Right?"

He nodded.

I eased my hips backward, shivering at the way his body tried to grip my length as I pulled out and slid back in.

"You're going to be with me now, right?" I asked, setting a pace so slow it had to be as torturous for me as it was for him.

"Yes," he whined, one of his hands going for his cock before he shouted his frustration and fisted the sheets instead.

"Touch me," I said.

He let go of the sheets and curled his hands around my head, fingers threading into my hair as he held my face directly above his. The muscles in my arms trembled as I tried to hold my balance and fuck him at a snail's pace so I could drag the moment out a little while longer.

"I need you to know." Words were hard because my orgasm sparkled around the edges of my vision, threatening to pull me under without so much as a warning. "My biggest regret is the ten years I wasted. The ten years I could have spent making you come."

Owen gasped and whimpered. Even though it had been months, I recognized the tension in his body, the twitch at the corner of his mouth. I went still and pulled out, leaving his hole gaping and hungry for my dick. His hold on the back of my head tightened before he flung his arms to the sides and cried out.

"I'll make it up to you, though." I teased my head back into his channel, letting his ring close down around me before pulling all the way back out.

"You don't...don't have to."

"But I want to."

In and out.

In an out.

An inch, an inch, then two, then one, and three, and one.

"I'm going to come up with a thousand new ways to own your body," I promised, taking his earlobe between my teeth and giving it a tug. "A thousand new ways to make your orgasms hurt in all of the best ways."

I'd get him a cage, a plug. I'd get sounds. I'd try every tool and toy out on him that both of our hearts desired, and I would make him beg and cry and plead and whimper until he didn't have words. Until he didn't have thought. Until he had the only thing that mattered.

Me.

Until he had me.

And I would spend the rest of my life making sure that I was the only thing he needed. I would take care of him in all the ways I should have, and all the ways I wanted to.

"I need to come, Archie. You're killing me," he whined, hips pumping as I thrust into him again.

This time four inches, six inches, one inch, one inch, all the way home.

"Not yet."

Maybe it was selfish, but I wanted to come first. I wanted to see his face when I spilled inside of him, while I found my own pleasure in depriving him of his own. I wanted him to know how much I loved him when he gave that to me.

"Archie."

"Not yet." I buried myself deep, my thrusts turning into nothing more than feral rutting. The back of his head angled up against the headboard, the sound of our wet skin slapping against each other loud enough to echo off the walls of the hotel room.

"Archie," he rasped my name again.

"Not yet." I let my lips dance across his, feather-light. Sweat dripped from my forehead, splattering onto his curls and sliding down onto the pillow. He brought his hands back, this time grabbing my shoulders, like he was trying to change the pace of how I fucked him to get him over the edge. "You can last a little longer, can't you?"

He shook his head, lower lip quivering.

"I know you can," I assured him. We were both right at the precipice. It wouldn't be long now. "I know it hurts, but you can hold out a little longer."

One of his eyes opened, revealing the white of his eye and his lashes fluttered like he was trying to keep himself conscious. "For you."

The words were barely audible, but they were the right ones, and they were everything.

"For me, yeah."

I buried myself to the hilt and let the ferocity of my own orgasm drag me beneath the surface of coherency. A guttural shout broke the silence, and somewhere in the back of my mind I knew it was me. I was the one who I had cried out like I'd finished a marathon or won a battle. And in a way of thinking, I had.

Owen cried openly, tears slicking down his cheeks and mixing with the sweat, and I was alert enough to lean down and lick him, dragging the hot flat of my tongue from his jawline to the crook of his nose. My entire body hurt, my orgasm still ripping through me as I poured spurt after spurt into the deepest parts of Owen's body.

One of his fingernails pierced the skin on my arm, and the shock of pain only served to draw another pulse of cum out of my cock.

"Come for me, Owen."

I'd barely gotten the words out before hot bursts of Owen's cum splashed against my stomach, even my chest. I shifted my weight and took him into my hand, drawing every drop out of his balls until he went from begging to come to begging to *not* come.

Only then did I collapse, half on him and half on the bed, shivering as he reached for me and started to draw mindless shapes and swirls over the small of my back. My cock was still inside of him, pulsing in time with the frenetic beat of my heart, and I sighed, content to rest in him and on him until our breathing returned to normal.

"Did you mean it?" he asked me a while later, fingers working their way from my spine into the short hairs at the base of my neck.

"I've meant everything I've ever said to you," I promised. "But what part are you asking about?"

"About it not mattering that I don't make as much money as you."

"Money isn't anything. It's just extra." I pressed my palm against the center of his chest, spreading my fingers so I could feel his heartbeat in every point of contact. "This is what matters. This is what it's all for."

"And the orgasms," he added weakly, bumping me with his shoulder to push my weight off of him.

I rolled onto my back and searched for his hand, grabbing it and bringing it to my mouth where I kissed his knuckles.

"And the orgasms," I agreed. "Definitely those too.

EPILOGUE
OWEN

THREE MONTHS I'D BEEN LIVING IN CALIFORNIA AND I'D HAD MORE orgasms in the last ninety days than I had the last ten years of my life. Sometimes I wondered if Archie's master plan involved keeping my balls so empty and my cock so tender that I'd never even have the energy to think about moving back to Brixton. I didn't want to tell him it didn't matter—sated or starving, he was it for me and I wasn't ever going to go back to a life without him.

But as I found myself in his kitchen...*our* kitchen, rather, with my soft cock on day two of being imprisoned in the tight confines of a black plastic chastity cage, I debated my own dedication to staying with him forever. Two days wasn't a long run, by any stretch of the imagination, but Archie had been doing everything within his power to keep me as turned on as possible for every second that had passed since he latched the small lock into place.

Saturday had been fine, all fun and games as my dick pressed at its cage, making me grunt and grimace in pain as I found myself unable to get anywhere close to hard. Saturday night, Archie had kept waking me up, with his fingers slick with lube and teasing at my asshole until I was humping against him like a man desperate for penetration. He'd give me a finger, then two, then he'd feign a yawn, roll over, and go back to sleep.

I'd woken up at two in the morning to the soft shaking of the bed and the furious jerks of Archie's arm beside me.

"Are you awake?" he'd whispered, hand flying up and down his length with enough lube to make it loud and wet.

"Yes."

"Good," he rasped, back bowing off the bed. "I'm coming, Owen. Oh, shit."

Archie trailed off as he spent all over his stomach, and I rolled onto mine with a needy moan. I didn't bother trying to quiet my frustration as I rutted my hips into the sheets, trying to chase out any sort of friction that could bring me off. It was nowhere near enough, the cage keeping me small and soft, the locking ring mechanism at the base strangling my balls and keeping my orgasm at bay.

"Please let me come," I whined.

Archie mounted me and, for one fleeting second, I thought he was taking pity on me. Instead, he used his sticky fingers to fuck his cum into my ass, then he turned over again and went back to sleep.

Sunday morning rolled around, and Archie had gotten up before me, serving me coffee and toast in bed. He'd teased his finger over the exposed slit of my dick while I ate, and I worried there'd be permanent marks left on my shaft once he finally took mercy and let me out of the cage. My cock had never felt so desperate to get hard as it had since he'd locked it up, and my body had never felt the urge to offer him anything and everything under the sun to get me there.

"Can I come now?" I'd asked softly after finishing my coffee.

Archie took the empty mug with a smile and dusted his lips across mine in the barest tease of a kiss. "Not yet, Owen," he said.

Climbing off the bed, Archie took the mug and plate into the kitchen and I followed behind, not bothering to get dressed. The cage had me feeling covered and exposed all at the same time, and I joined Archie at the sink, glaring at his hand as he shoved it into the mug to wipe it clean.

"When?" I asked.

"Later today," he said.

"When later?"

Archie chuckled and turned, cupping his palm over my imprisoned dick. His skin was warm and wet from the dishes, a little soapy.

"I'll let you decide," he offered, mouth twisting up into a devious smile. "You can get it off now, but I'm going to make you come as many times as *I* want. Or you can wait until later and we can make you come as many times as *you* want."

I covered my face with my hands, pressing my fingertips into my eyelids. Archie offered me a choice between two kinds of torture and leaving the decision up to me felt horribly unfair. Of course I wanted it off right that second. I actually worried I was going to come all over his hand the second my cock was able to swell to full hardness. But the threat of letting Archie control how many orgasms followed that release? That was...something else entirely. And the thought of leaving my poor dick locked up until whatever time in the day he decided was long enough and being the one in control of my orgasms afterward? Maybe a sweet reward after two days of torture.

But...

There were things about Archie that made him perfect for me, and his cruelty around getting me off was one of them.

"You choose," I muttered, letting my arms fall limp at my sides.

"What was that?"

"You choose," I said again, grinding out the words.

He answered that with a thoughtful hum in the back of his throat.

"I think I win either way," he whispered. "Because I know once you get past four orgasms, you never want me to stop anyway. It's like your tipping point into oblivion."

"This is the most perverse game of chance I think I've ever played."

"How about we meet in the middle?" Archie cocked his head to the side, hair falling across his forehead.

I reached up and brushed a chunk of soft brown strands behind his ear. He angled his head the other way, leaning into my hand with a borderline sadistic smile.

"What's the middle?"

"We take it off after lunch." He puckered his lips toward my palm, blowing a kiss against the heel of my thumb. "And I make you come as many times as I want."

"You pretty much said that was what was going to happen anyway," I grumbled.

"Good, then we're in agreement." Archie slid his arms around me and pulled me close, the plastic cage bumping into his hip as he brought our bodies together. "Now kiss me."

As always, I never told him no.

With a slight turn of my head, I pressed our mouths together and parted my lips for his tongue. Archie moaned, licking past my teeth and into the depths of my mouth, kissing me like we'd been doing it our whole lives and not just three months.

Three months.

Time moved quickly when we were together.

It wasn't more than two weeks after Mandy's wedding that I moved to California without much more than the clothes on my back. I'd gotten onto that plane again and closed the distance between us for what we both hoped to be the very last time. Archie paid for movers to come and pack up my things because he couldn't bear the thought of me being away from him for even one more day. And, to be honest, neither could I. Frankie came out when it was finally moving day, meeting Archie's friends and helping me get settled. He wasn't Archie's number one fan, and he definitely didn't like Flynn, but after about a month, he'd stopped giving me shit for the quick relocation.

I was grateful that Archie wasn't the jealous type because Frankie's friendship meant more to me than my romantic relationship with him had, and being able to maintain that meant a lot to me. Even with Frankie across the country, we talked every day and he was still my best friend. We'd all gotten settled into this new kind of routine, and I'd found a new job doing the same thing but making twice as much money because that was just what happened in California. Archie had vowed that I didn't have to work, but he'd stopped fighting when I insisted that I wanted to.

He gave me absolute free reign over his house once my things got delivered, but I didn't have the heart to mess up the space he'd curated for himself. I'd kept my band posters tucked away in the back of the closet until I came home one day and found them re-framed and hung behind the back of the couch. Neither of us said anything about it, but I'd sucked Archie's cock with twice as much vigor as normal that night as my way of saying thanks.

It continued on a lot like that while I got settled, finding little bits and pieces of my life integrating into his almost flawlessly. We started using the kitchen and eating at home. I took to feeding his friends—my friends now—at least once a month, sometimes more. All in all, it was the start of a life I'd never even realized I wanted until it was almost out of my grasp for a second time.

I had bad dreams some nights, when I would wake up after dreaming about telling Archie to leave me again, but him never coming back to me. Thankfully, the warmth of his body and the softness of his sheets would always calm my fears and ease me awake, wrapping me up until my heart rate returned to normal and my mind remembered where I was.

Right where I was always meant to be.

"Go get on the bed," Archie murmured against my lips. "Get on all fours."

"I thought you said after lunch."

"I thought we agreed you would do what you're told." He nipped at my lower lip and gave me a gentle push toward the hallway.

We had, in fact, never agreed such a thing, but we had both learned, over time and trial and error, that it wasn't the worst thing in the world for me to lean into my submission a little.

Sometimes. I was by no means a collar-wearing yes, sir-no, sir kind of submissive, but I didn't hate kneeling for him occasionally, and I very much liked giving him enough control to send my soul into an absolute other stratosphere every time he got me off.

"You're lucky I love you," I huffed and turned toward the bedroom.

Archie slapped my ass. "I know I am."

Back in the bedroom, I arranged myself on the bed as he'd asked, nearly blacking out when he climbed onto the bed behind me and spread my ass cheeks apart.

"What are you—"

He cut me off before I could finish the question, spitting straight onto my asshole and pushing both of his thumbs past the tight and unprepared muscle.

"Sssh. Sssh. Ssssh," he soothed, fucking his thumbs in and out of me in tandem.

I dropped my face against the pillows, fighting my eyes as they threatened to roll all the way back into my head.

He went from two thumbs to one, the sound of the lube bottle opening piercing the silence like a gunshot. To the spit, he added a generous amount of lube, then the second thumb was back. Archie hooked his digits into me and then pulled me open, pressing the head of his cock against the small gape he'd made.

"Let me in," he coaxed, pulling back without coming close to getting inside of me.

"You're trying to kill me."

"Is that what this is?" Archie laughed again and finally pushed the head of his cock into my body. Even with what felt like half a bottle of lube covering my crack, the thickness of his cock paired with both of his thumbs had me feeling full enough to burst. I whimpered, ready to protest, but he eased his hips forward, fitting more of his thick length into me.

"Jesus, Owen," he whispered, clearing his throat. "You're so tight like this I'd think *you* were the one trying to kill me."

"Not without a prenup first," I groaned, and behind me, Archie went still.

"You'd marry me?" he asked.

I hadn't even meant to say it. I hadn't even been thinking about it, but we both knew the answer was a loud and resounding yes.

"Never," I lied.

"I'd marry you too," he said, like he hadn't just heard my denial as clear as day from beneath him. "I'll have my attorney draft a prenup on Monday. What do you want?"

"Everything," I lied.

"It's yours."

"I don't really want it," I told him. He started to fuck me, thumbs still lodged inside. My pulse thrummed in my balls as heavy and insistent as a bass drum, and my dick fought against the hard plastic constraining it. The pleasure shot through me, taking my breath as I choked out, "I just want you."

"I'm yours."

"Please, Archie, can I come right now?"

He made another noise, quickening the pace of his thrusts. The stretch intensified and I shivered, body fighting to get away from him.

"It's not after lunch," he said.

One of his hands left me because he petted down the small of my back, but my hole still ached from being tested and held wide.

"What's inside of me?" I asked, trying to look over my shoulder and see.

"My cock," he said, snapping his hips forward for good measure. "Three of my fingers."

"Three? Jesus."

"It's tight like this. You're strangling my cock, Owen. You're going to make me come so hard I'm going to shoot into parts of you I've never reached before."

"You're killing me."

He slid his hand up my spine until he reached my shoulder blades, then he shifted and pressed his arm flat against me. My chest collapsed into the mattress and his cock inched even further inside. My cock and the cage twisted in the sheets, and for as tight as the restriction was, precum still leaked out my slit, creating a sticky and painful sort of friction between my legs.

"You're a fucking dream come true," he panted, lips and tongue hot against my ear.

The pace of Archie's thrusts turned frenetic and he slammed into me over and over, thrusting me into the mattress with so much force I worried his bed would snap from the pressure of it.

"You're *my* dream come true," he said, the words catching in his throat as his body went still. Fingers and cock still inside of me, I could feel the pulsing of his shaft as he spilled into me, just like he promised.

A strangled cry ripped out of my mouth, the periphery of my own orgasm just barely out of my reach. Archie whispered something sweet and petted his hands down my back, keeping his cock inside of me until we both went soft. His release left him calm and relaxed; my lack of release had me strung tight like a high wire. Archie's cock slipped free and he moved quick and efficiently, always ten steps ahead of me.

The hard and cold plastic of a plug pushed against my tender and fucked hole and, with a deft twist of his wrist, Archie popped the substantial toy into place. The flared base rested between my ass cheeks, and the conical end stretched parts of my channel that never received as much attention as the toy was giving. I knew the hours between breakfast and lunch would be long and arduous, but they would, in the end, be worth it.

"We're going to lunch with Rob and Grayson," he said, hooking his arm around my chest and pulling me up so my back pressed against his chest. Archie licked the side of my neck, and I angled myself away from him so he had more skin to pay attention to.

"I'll die."

"Can I give you a hickey here?" he asked, ignoring my comment and pressing a kiss against the soft skin behind my ear.

"Can I come?"

He chuckled. "Later."

"Then yes."

As if I'd ever tell him no.

Archie let his hand fall down my front, fingers dancing through my happy trail and over my tattoos until he reached my cock. He worked his way backward, taking my balls into the palm of his hand. They were hard and aching from all the orgasms he'd denied me since the morning before, and the hot suction from his mouth did nothing to alleviate any of the pressure I felt in my body.

"After lunch, when I take that cage off, I want you to come in my mouth," he murmured.

"I don't even know if I'll last long enough for you to get on your knees."

"The first one's always a throwaway," he teased, giving my sac a gentle tug. "I have the blow job penciled in for number six."

"You're horrible," I rasped, knees finally giving out, taking both of our weights down to the bed and right on top of my cock. The cage bit and pulled against the tender skin of my shaft, and I cried out, partly in pain and partly in the pain that came from being denied.

Even though it wasn't really a denial at all.

It was the promise of a lifetime of pleasure, the ability to set right a lifetime of wrongs and regrets. It was the opportunity to build a better future and a life where I never had to doubt myself or the man beside me.

And just like Archie, it was mine.

ALSO BY KATE HAWTHORNE

———

Trophy Doms Social Club

Humbled

Edged

Praised

Giving Consent

Worth the Risk

Worth the Wait

Worth the Fight

Worth the Chance

All in Good Time

Necessary Space

Necessary Time

Two Truths and a Lie

A Real Good Lie

A Cold Hard Truth

A Matter of Fact

Room for Love

Reckless

Heartless

Faultless

Fearless

Limitless

A Very Messy Motel Brothers Wedding

Relentless

Secrets in Edgewood

A Taste of Sin

The Cost of Desire

A Love Made Whole

Secrets in Edgewood: The Complete Series

The Lonely Hearts Stories

His Kind of Love

The Colors Between Us

Love Comes After

Until You Say Otherwise

<u>STANDALONES</u>

Rebound

One for the Road

Daybreak - Vino & Veritas

Unfettered

Dreams

A Thousand Lifetimes

<u>COLLABORATIONS</u>

With E.M. Denning

Irreplaceable

Future Fake Husband

Future Gay Boyfriend

Future Ex Enemy

With J.R. Gray

May the Best Man Win

ABOUT KATE HAWTHORNE

Kate Hawthorne is a writer and author educator with over three dozen published romance novels spread across two successful and award winning pen names.

Known for stories that pack a figurative (and sometimes literal) punch, Kate has built a recognizable brand that consistently delivers emotionally charged and character driven happy endings for everyone.

Visit her website
http://www.katehawthornebooks.com

Sign up for Kate's newsletter
http://www.katehawthornebooks.com/extra

facebook.com/authorkatehawthorne
twitter.com/katewriteswords
instagram.com/kate.hawthorne
patreon.com/katehawthorne

Made in the USA
Columbia, SC
29 March 2024

33786098R00167